KU-478-955

RUDE BOYS

I'm being a true bitch for Don now, Hashi thought. *A true bitch for my man. Taking my man's rock-hard cock up my wet slack hole and I'm not even hard, 'cause my pleasure's his pleasure.* A rapture that oscillated across the boundary between pleasure and pain possessed Hashi's body at playing the bitch role so fully, as Don rode him as hard as he could.

'Oh use me, man!' Hashi gasped. 'Oh man, I'm in bitch heaven!'

'S'cause you *are* a bitch, Hashi man,' Don growled hoarsely.

Also available from Idol:

MORE AND HARDER
HARD TIME
CHAINS OF DECEIT
TO SERVE TWO MASTERS

RUDE BOYS

Jay Russell

This book is a work of fiction.
In real life, make sure you practise safe sex.

This edition published 2002 by
Idol
Thames Wharf Studios
Rainville Road
London W6 9HA

First published in 1998 by Headline Book Publishing

Copyright © Jay Russell 1998

The right of Jay Russell to be identified as the Author of
this Work has been asserted by him in accordance with the Copyright,
Designs and Patents Act 1988.

www.idol-books.co.uk

Typeset by SetSystems Ltd, Saffron Walden, Essex
Printed and bound by Mackays of Chatham plc, Chatham, Kent

ISBN 0 352 33723 0

*All characters in this publication are fictitious and any resemblance
to real persons, living or dead, is purely coincidental.*

This book is sold subject to the condition that it shall not, by way
of trade or otherwise, be lent, resold, hired out or otherwise
circulated without the publisher's prior written consent in any form
of binding or cover other than that in which it is published and
wthout a similar condition including this condition being imposed
on the subsequent purchaser.

To R—,
for inspiring me

One

'Suck that motherfucker, man,' Don, a shaven-headed black man in his mid-twenties, grunted as he pushed his lean, muscular hips forward, sliding the veiny rigid length of his large plain chocolate brown dick into the eager open mouth of the slim, hard-bodied Japanese boy kneeling before him, pressing its head to the back of the boy's throat, holding it there as Kam gagged and struggled to swallow it down.

'*Open* that throat, man Yesss . . .' Don sighed as he felt his cock-head press against Kam's hard palate, then slide further down and into Kam's throat. Thrills of pleasure ran up the shaft of Don's dick and spasmed through his pumped thighs and ridged six-pack stomach as he gripped the sides of the nineteen-year-old's head, the freshly buzz-cut raven hair spiky under his palms, and held it firmly in place as he pumped his cock into Kam's face, each stroke hard and deep. Kam drew snuffling gasps of breath through his nostrils as Don repeatedly plugged his mouth with his thick, stiff, uncut cock, closing off Kam's breathing passages.

'Shit, man, tilt your head back,' Don ordered Kam gruffly, wanting to get his erection further down Kam's throat, needing an angle that didn't bend it painfully in the middle as he thrust it in. 'I want to get all the way down you.'

Don ran one gold-ringed hand through the slicked-back greasy blue-black quiff that topped Kam's head, gripped a handful of the thick shiny hair and pulled Kam's head back, making the kneeling Japanese youth open his mouth even wider, stretching his throat so that the veins and sinews stood out pulsing through cinnamon skin as his neck arched back, aligning his mouth with his throat like a sword-swallower. Then Don straddled Kam's head where Kam squatted below him on the floor, and pushed his rigid cock right down Kam's throat, his totally shaven balls soft and heavy on the Japanese youth's chin; the smooth dark brown skin around his cock where Don shaved his pubic hair away pressed hard against Kam's nose, crushing it flat and closing his nostrils, making it even harder for Kam to breathe.

'Yeah, that's it, man,' Don moaned. 'Keep your head tilted back – oh, yeah . . . Further, man. Tilt it further . . . Give me more throat, man. Open all the way up . . .'

Kam slid his hands up Don's dark muscular waxed thighs to his big high butt and gripped it, pulling it down onto him, encouraging Don to fuck his face deeper and harder. Don pumped down with added vigour, excited by the sensation of the depths of Kam's throat rubbing hot and rigid and wet against the tinglingly sensitive swollen head of his stiff heavy dick.

For a second, as he gagged Kam with his dick, Don felt guilty: Kam was, after all, the boyfriend of his best friend Malcolm, even if he was a total slut. Malcolm was not only Don's best friend but also a fellow musician in the hip-hop/roots band they both belonged to, Boot Sex Massive. Don knew he shouldn't be cheating on Malcolm by fucking with Kam, however much Kam encouraged him whenever Malcolm wasn't around – hanging round Malcolm's flat in skimpy gold briefs that rode up between his neat pale pinky-brown buttocks and hugged his bulging crotch, lounging across Malcolm's sofa with his lean hairless thighs spread wide open whenever Don dropped by, arching his back as he stretched his arms up over his head, blue-black tufts in his armpits.

'When you going to let me blow you, Donald?' Kam had asked Don, about a month before this morning. Malcolm had gone to the off-licence to get them all some beers.

'Right now,' Don had said, mostly joking, and had

squeezed the bulge in his track-suit pants. But Kam hadn't been joking: he had slid onto the carpet and slunk sexily on all fours over to where Don had been lounging, and had buried his face in Don's stiffening crotch. Don, turned on but embarrassed, had stopped him.

That time.

But Don had been turned on enough to suggest they meet at his yard, the next afternoon, just before Malcolm got back from the shops and, ever since then, he and Kam had been seeing each other several times a week for hot, hard oral and anal sessions.

Don pulled his stiff shiny dick out of Kam's mouth. Kam gasped and drew in a shuddering breath, then looked up provocatively from where he was squatting before Don's bulky muscular legs, his face bloated with excitement. A thick glistening string of pre-come and saliva joined Kam's shiny pink lower lip to the slit in the smooth, spit-slicked, spade-shaped pinky-brown head of Don's pulsing erection. Don watched excitedly as Kam wiped away the clear sticky fluid from his mouth and then hungrily licked the palm he'd used to wipe with with his long pink muscular tongue.

'What you stop for?' Kam asked, his voice husky, his accent thick. He strained his head forward and ran his tongue up the underside of Don's hot rigid cock, from near the base to the pinky-brown frenum, then up and into the slit. Don gasped softly. Kam withdrew his tongue and sat back down on his heels so he wouldn't be straining his neck. Then he tilted his head and bent forward again, this time going for Don's balls, licking their smooth shaven skin, sucking on them gently with his lips; he took one into his mouth, making Don gasp, released it, then mouthed the other.

Kam was a student studying vehicle design at the Royal College of Art. He was lean, smooth and clean-shaven, and boyishly handsome, with full lips, high cheek-bones and dark almond eyes. His skin was a soft cinnamon colour. His lips were flushed red, his teeth strong and white as he tossed back his tousled quiff. There was a blue and orange carp tattooed on his shoulder. Right now, he was kneeling in front of Don wearing nothing but a pair of heavy bike-boots and skimpy leopard-skin bikini-briefs, against which his erection jutted, straining the fabric and darkening it with pre-come juices.

Don looked down at Kam kneeling before him, now with his mouth open and his thighs spread wide, his crotch angled upwards below his taut flat fat-free belly, and his dick twitched from seeing Kam so heavily turned on. *Fuck Malcolm*, Don thought. *If he can't give it to Kam the way he needs it, that's nobody's problem but his own. And if Kam ain't getting satisfaction, he's got the right to try and find it wherever he can.*

He extended a beefily muscular arm and large hand and pushed three dark fingers into Kam's eager mouth, right up to the gold on his rings. Kam sucked eagerly on Don's fingers, playing with his own nipples and working his hips in small excited jerks, while Don rubbed his bare foot rhythmically against the bulge in Kam's briefs, caressing Kam's balls. Abruptly, Don pulled his fingers out of Kam's mouth and pushed the spit through Kam's hair, slicking it back from where it had started to tousle over his face.

'You want me to fuck your face some more, man?' Don asked hoarsely.

Kam looked up at Don. The short muscular black man stood above him: shaven-headed, with gold in his ears and round his neck and on his fingers. His long heavily veined and uncircumcised cock wagged above Kam's face.

'You wanna suck it some more?' Don was teasing Kam now with his hot juicy hard-on, tormenting the eager cocksucker with it. He smiled as Kam arched his neck again and strained his tongue to lick it, flashing gold-capped and diamond-studded teeth. Don was broadly built and an amateur bodybuilder. His stomach curved towards Kam above his cock in blocks of solid muscle. A black outline tattoo on his chest was subliminally visible against his smooth dark skin. Sweat glittered on Don's forehead and gathered in diamonds on his shaven chest. He licked his full lips.

'I want to fuck your face, man,' he said hoarsely. 'I want to stick this good long dick right the way down into your stomach and pump my load into you.'

The first time Kam had been confronted by Don's totally hairless body, he had been surprised, but soon enough the extremity had started to turn Kam on; he had kissed, tongued and licked Don's shaven scalp and armpits, and now he eagerly ran his tongue around the smoothly waxed base of Don's cock and balls and slid it into Don's cleanly shaved asshole.

'Let me eat your asshole out first, please,' Kam begged. Don smiled, the gold in his mouth glinting. Kam's tongue was long and, after the time Don had first spread his immaculately depilated cheeks for Kam after a shower and told him to get down there and eat some ass, Kam had become an eager rimmer.

'Whatever gets you off, man,' Don said, and swung round so he could sit his big muscular ass down onto Kam's eager face. Kam started by kissing Don's ass with full hot lips, then began licking up between his buttocks from the sensitive spot behind Don's balls, making Don shiver with pleasure at the attention. He worked his way up Don's clean ass-crack with determined strokes to the quivering pucker of Don's asshole, then started to tongue Don's tight anal sphincter. Don moaned with pleasure as Kam worked his tongue on the star of ringed muscle.

'Oh, yeah, Kam, tongue-fuck me, oh yeah.'

Don reached back, gripped his big buttocks with both

hands and pulled them apart, spreading them wide. Kam pushed his tongue in deep, and Don enthusiastically pushed his asshole hard onto Kam's open mouth to ensure maximum penetration. Kam gasped excitedly.

'Get your tongue all the way up there, man,' Don ordered, grunting as Kam pushed his muscular tongue up through his sphincter and into Don's body. 'Oh, yeah, that's it, man,' he added, wiggling his ass from side to side so as to work Kam's eagerly exploring tongue even further up into his rectum. 'Taste those juices.'

Then Don bent over forwards and onto all fours, so he could push his asshole more firmly against Kam's face; he braced himself with both hands on the soft cream carpet of his first-floor Ladbroke Grove flat, as he ground his ass into the oriental boy's eager face. The sound of street traders from the market outside floated in through the half-open living-room window. Sweat ran down the sides of Don's shaven head as Kam ate him out. Kam's head was pressed hard against the wall behind him already, so when Don pushed his ass back onto Kam's face, Kam just had to stretch his aching jaws open wide and force his tongue as far up Don's ass as he possibly could. Sour juice ran down the groove of Kam's tongue, between his stretched open jaws, and down his open throat. This was the way Kam liked to fuck – to penetrate another man – and the only way he liked to do it; and it was Don who had introduced him to it.

Don reached back between his own legs with one hand, to where Kam was kneeling behind him, and started to fondle the stiffness in the front of Kam's skimpy briefs. With his palm, he rubbed the head of Kam's stiff cock and the bulge of his balls through the stretched fabric: gently at first, then more firmly. He could hear Kam's suppressed moans of pleasure and this made him grip Kam's ball-sack harder and start massaging it up against his pelvis vigorously.

'You work that tongue right up me, man,' Don grunted, moving his free hand on his own glistening cock in a fist. 'Yeah, that's good, man. That's good.' Pre-come slid from his cock-head and dripped in glistening clear beaded threads onto the carpet. He glanced at his watch and realised, to his annoyance, that he should have already been at the studio in Brixton for the recording session that Gregory, the lead singer of Boot Sex Massive, had booked for that morning: Don would have been on time, for once, but Kam had buzzed on his entryphone unexpectedly, just as he was drying off after showering. The youth had been on his knees, begging to suck cock, before Don could tell him there wasn't really time to do anything.

Don never had been able to avoid sticking his dick in a gift horse's mouth.

With a sigh, he pulled his ass off Kam's flushed and excited face, turned and, without pausing or saying a word, grabbed Kam's hair, pulled his head back, and pushed his stiff and dripping cock straight back down Kam's now open and accepting throat. Kam shoved his hand down the front of his briefs and started to jack off violently as Don renewed fucking his face with long deep strokes that pushed his cock-head right down into Kam's larynx. He started to build a rhythm, sliding his cock in and out, in and out. He pushed so far in that he was in danger of breaking Kam's nose with his hairless tensing stomach, and certainly made Kam's breathing difficult as his shaven crotch pressed Kam's nostrils shut, then so far out that his rigid cock would have sprung out of Kam's mouth, if Kam hadn't eagerly craned forward with every withdrawal and fastened his lips around Don's glans in time to suck the next stroke all the way in.

'Man, Malcolm was right. You're the best cock-sucker I ever had the luck to stick my dick into,' Don said roughly, his breaths coming a little shorter as his strokes became more abrupt, faster and harder. He mounted higher, standing on his toes to get a better down-thrust, his hands gripping Kam's head. Malcolm doesn't understand. Kam needs it a little rough. Don didn't pull out so far now; he kept his cock right down Kam's throat, its head rubbing against the cartilage of Kam's now-bruised larynx and sending thrills of excitement the length of Don's erection and clenching his balls and Don's gut. Kam's tongue rasped against the underside of his cock-shaft, his lips warm and wet and soft around its base. Don could feel Kam's shoulder flexing and moving against his inner thigh as Kam jerked himself off frantically while he was being gagged by thick brown cock, and hear Kam's muffled gasps of excitement as he moved his fist frenziedly inside his briefs.

'Oh, yeah, yeah,' Don groaned as he neared the point of no return, sliding his hands down from Kam's head onto his shoulders, pushing himself up on Kam's shoulders like an athlete mounting a pommel horse so he had the best possible angle to drive down into Kam's upturned mouth, with all fourteen stone of his smoothly shaven muscular ebony frame.

'Oh, Jesus, oh, Christ,' Don moaned as his rock-hard cock pressed up achingly hard against Kam's throat, its stiffness and heaviness growing as he neared his peak. Sweat fell from his nose, his lips and his stiff nipples down onto Kam's tangled black hair and glistening forehead. 'I'm gonna lose it any second now, man. I'm gonna shoot my hot load down your throat –' Don gasped, his thighs aching as he lifted himself on and off tip-toe, slamming his crotch down hard onto Kam's face and ramming his painfully-erect manhood straight down into Kam's fully-open windpipe.

'Oh, shit, I'm gonna lose it any second, man –'

At that exact moment, Don's mobile started to ring. Bobbi, the fourth member of the band, had borrowed it the day before and had left it set to an 1812 Overture ringer which Don especially hated. The stupid tune distracted him and threw him off his face-fucking stride. His aching thighs twitched and he lost his balance, slumping forward hard onto Kam's face, and banging his own face against the wall painfully, nose-first. With a gurgling gasp, Kam immediately shot his load into his leopard-skin briefs, his taut sweaty body arching and straining up and back, his thighs spreading and bucking as all fourteen stone of Don's ebony muscle shoved his cock down Kam's throat.

Irritated at having lost the moment and at hurting his head, Don clumsily pulled himself upright and pulled his now-distracted and slightly less than fully erect cock out of Kam's mouth. Kam let out a gasp of relief and slumped back heavily against the wall. His face sulky, Don stomped over to the coffee-table where the phone was sitting next to Kam's discarded denim shorts, drew a ragged breath, snatched up his phone and answered it.

'Don, man.' It was an annoyed-sounding voice with a soft Jamaican accent.

'Malcolm, man,' Don replied shortly, sounding equally annoyed.

'Where the fuck are you, Don?' Malcolm said at the other end of the line. 'Gregory just belled me and said you was supposed to been down there a hour ago.'

Don rolled his eyes and played with his semi-stiff dick idly, not even half-listening as Malcolm berated him for not even having left home for the studio yet. Don owned the van the band transported their gear in so, if he wasn't there, nothing could really get done.

'And we're *all* paying for the studio time, man, you know what I'm sayin'?' Malcolm was complaining. Don moved his fist more definitely on his cock, and it began to stiffen again.

'Yeah, yeah. Look, I'm literally out the door, man,' Don lied. 'Yeah, yeah, I know I'm late and time is money and all that shit. I'll be out of here any second, yeah. I'm hanging up now, man.'

Don terminated the call irritatedly and turned the mobile off. He palmed the sweat from his face and looked down on Kam, who was now slumped on the carpet, legs flung casually open, the front of his briefs stained. Kam pushed his glossy black hair back from where it had tumbled down over his eyes.

'Shit, man, you came,' Don grumbled, unable to stop moving his fist on his now frustratingly stiff dick.

'But you haven't, yet,' Kam said, smiling slyly. Don kissed his teeth by way of reply, assuming that, now Kam had come, he wouldn't be interested in doing anything more. But Kam kept smiling and, keeping his eyes on Don, put his slim shapely legs together, slipped his leopard-skin briefs down over his small neat butt and then carefully down his thighs, then off awkwardly over his bike-boots. He held the damp briefs up and looked into them.

'I shot a good load,' he said, still smiling up at Don.

Don watched in titillated fascination as Kam lifted the cotton briefs to his face, lifting the crotch of them to his mouth in both hands as if he were bringing water to his face from a basin. Don could see the thick pearly come he had shot lying on top of the semi-absorbent material. He started to move his fist faster as Kam opened his mouth, extended his tongue, and started to lick the come out of his own briefs. He saw the come white on Kam's long pink tongue; his cock was rock-hard and dripping again by the time Kam had licked the front of the briefs clean.

'Breakfast,' Kam said, putting his damp briefs down on the carpet. He went over to Don's king-size double-bed and lay down on it on his stomach, looking up at Don with teasing, secretive eyes. Then he rolled over onto his back, arching like a cat, lean and smooth except for black tufts under his arms and around his half-erect cock, and looked up at Don, his eyes dark, his head upside-down. Don moved his fist slowly on his dick, wondering what was going to happen next.

Kam pushed himself towards Don and the edge of the bed until his head hung over the edge of it. He opened his mouth wide. His throat was stretched, providing a straight line of access all the way down. His raven hair hung down black and glossy. His dick was already stiffening to full rigidity again as he spread his legs and toyed idly with a nipple.

'Are you sure you want this, man?' Don said as he moved into position to straddle Kam's face.

Kam nodded, his face already flushed. 'I want your cock down my throat,' he said huskily. 'All the way down. And I want your balls in my mouth all the time you fuck my throat. I want you to spray your come down my throat, over my face, my lips, my tongue –'

Before Kam had even finished the sentence, Don was pushing his stiff cock into Kam's mouth and down his throat. It felt good and hot and wet and ready in there. Don pulled his crotch back a little so he could scoop up his smooth heavy balls and feed them into Kam's mouth, one at a time.

'I want my nuts in there too, man,' Don said urgently, his voice roughened with excitement. Kam was forced to stretch his jaws even wider apart than he had before, and gasped and grunted as Don finally managed to push his whole scrotum into his mouth. Kam's lips were now stretched shiny-tight, and the feeling of constraint on his balls excited Don as they pressed against the insides of Kam's cheeks. Don looked down at his own crotch; to see the length of his cock and his entire ball-sack hidden inside Kam's mouth, filling Kam's mouth and throat to overflowing, sent excitement flushing the length of Don's body. Slowly, Don began to rotate and then pump his hips against

Kam's face; the sense of the shaft of his cock rubbing slickly over his own balls as his stiff erection moved over them, back and forth, side to side, adding to his excitement. He cupped his hands under Kam's head to take the weight and strain off Kam's neck as he poled his throat.

'Oh, yeah,' Don sighed as he began to pump more vigorously against Kam's face again, enjoying the new, more accessible angle. 'Oh, man, you have the sweetest mouth, the deepest throat . . .' Don's hard-on was hot and rigid and heavy and pulsing as it slid back and forth inside Kam's throat. Kam arched his back and masturbated excitedly, pushing his crotch up off the bed and into the air with his spread legs, his thighs tense and lean, one hand on his stiff cock, the other massaging his balls as Don pumped muscularly into his mouth and throat. Cock-juice and saliva began to run out of the corners of Kam's mouth, so much that he had to momentarily take his hand off his balls and wipe the fluid from his nose and eyes, where it was overflowing his lips and running down his upside-down face in glittering rivulets.

'Swallow that good shit, man,' Don ordered as he pumped his hips rapidly in short thrusts to avoid pulling his balls out of Kam's mouth, determined that his balls were going to be inside Kam for the whole face-fucking session. 'Don't waste any of that good love-juice, man. If it goes into your nostrils, just snort it up and swallow it down like the come-hungry cock-sucker you are. Now leave your dick and play with my tits,' he ordered.

Kam took his hands off his neat stiff cock and his tightly clenched balls and reached up for the dark sinewed domes of Don's curving chest, groping awkwardly for Don's nipples as Don continued thrusting, fucking his throat. After a moment of exploration, Kam found them, and soon he was teasing and tormenting Don as he bit into their matt dark rigidity expertly with his short nails. A new spasm of excitement passed through Don's chest at the attention his tits were receiving. He now felt totally turned on, his cock and balls firmly in Kam's mouth and down his throat, Kam's confident fingers sending electrical currents through his nipples.

'Oh, yeah. Yeah,' Don moaned. 'You swallowing that love-juice, man? You getting it all?' Below him, Kam gurgled an appreciative word that sounded like yes. 'You want me to fuck your face harder?' Don reached out and gripped Kam's, glistening cock, and started to move his fist on it fast. Kam's slim body arched and stiffened, every sinew straining as he pushed his lean hips upwards towards Don, and his muffled gasps were high and fast as Don wanked him vigorously while ramming his cock as hard as he could down Kam's throat. Juice from Don's flooding cock was running down into Kam's eyes, his snorting nostrils, his shiny raven hair as it hung down, heavy with gel and sweat and love-juice.

Between Don's legs, Kam could see the two of them reflected in a wardrobe mirror, his upside-down face framed by Don's thighs; Don's big muscular ass turned concave, convex, concave, convex with each thrust of his narrow hips. Sweat and pre-come ran visibly down into Kam's hair. Don's broad V-shaped back was dark and shining; rippled and tapered to his powerful ass from his bullet-shaped shiny skull. A perfect fucking machine; and Kam was part of that machine, the socket the power was forced down – almost too much power as Don slammed his shaven crotch against Kam's face in hard, rapid movements.

'Oh, God, oh, Jesus, oh, Christ!' Don was shouting hoarsely now, straddling and pumping into Kam's gaping mouth, leaving Kam gasping for breath between thrusts, his crotch firm against Kam's chin, trying somehow to get his rock-hard cock even further down Kam's throat.

His head held immobile, Kam bucked and reared, every

sinew in his body tensing as he pushed his groin up onto Don's hand, sliding his quivering erection back and forth in Don's fist with violent pelvic thrusts. The slippery tightness of Don's fist on his cock brought Kam to a sudden shuddering climax; his load shot from his throbbing erection with such force as he bucked his hips wildly that it spattered over Don's chest and chin. Several pearly drops even landed on Don's lips. Don licked the hot salty jism up reflexively and kept on fucking Kam's face. His balls and cock throbbed hotly and felt heavy in Kam's still-willing throat; he knew he was reaching the point of no return. He felt the weight of his cock, the small electric thrills running its length. Nothing could stop him now: he was going to shoot his load down Kam's stretched throat, pump hot man-juice straight down into Kam's stomach.

'Oh, Kam, your throat's so good, your lips are so good; oh, give me that throat, man, keep that tongue on my shaft, oh yeah, oh yeah, oh *yeah* –'

At the moment of his total loss of control, someone strong grabbed Don from behind, slid their arms under Don's armpits, then spread his arms out and back, clasping their hands behind Don's head, full-nelsoning him. Someone taller than Don, and wearing biker's leathers.

It was Malcolm.

He pulled Don back angrily from Kam's upside-down face. Don's pulsingly erect penis and swollen balls slithered out of Kam's mouth with a slurping, sucking smack. With a loud gasp, Don came as he was forced to arch back by Malcolm, his load spraying copiously over Kam's face and open mouth and neck and chest as Malcolm pinned Don's thickly muscled arms back.

'What the fuck are you doing, Malcolm, man?' Don yelped as Malcolm twisted him away from his come-spattered Japanese boyfriend, then shoved him hard so Don tripped over the coffee-table and stumbled face-down onto the floor. Don's still-pulsing dick-head brushed the pile of the carpet momentarily and a thrill shot through him from its heightened sensitivity, but he twisted round quickly and stumbled to his feet as Malcolm stepped towards him aggressively.

Behind Malcolm, Kam had quickly turned over and sat up on the bed, and was slicking his hair back into some sort of order. His face was flushed, sweaty. Come was spattered the length of his torso. It was in his dark eyelashes, his eyebrows, and in stiffening streaks in his hair. He was trying to look naïve and innocent: but all he managed to look was guilty and slutty and scared.

'What are *you* doing, man?' Malcolm snapped in return. He was a handsome mixed-race brother, tall and rangy and honey-coloured with a built-up chest and arms. His smooth buttery-brown skin was coffee-freckled and his feline eyes were a piercing green. His kinky dark-blond hair was pulled back in tight horizontal cane-rows that joined in a vertical line around the back. He was wearing his biking leathers: broad-shouldered zip jacket, tight, ass-hugging pants, and heavy steel-fronted boots.

Don always had a suspicion that Malcolm was first turned on to Kam because his surname was Kawasaki, the make of Malcolm's motorbike – his pride and joy – and that that was the nearest Malcolm could get to fucking it.

'I don't fucking believe you, man,' Malcolm snarled, his soft voice deepening with resentment, his chest filling. He unzipped the jacket to reveal a figure-hugging white T-shirt underneath. Don's eyes came level with Malcolm's nipples, which showed as raised dark discs through the soft white material.

'You're supposed to be my best fucking friend, Don,' Malcolm continued. 'What the fuck did you think you were doing, nuh man?'

Don couldn't meet Malcolm's burning eyes, so he looked

off to one side while he tried to think of a good reply. Behind Malcolm, Kam was staring at him. Don watched as Kam took his fingers and ran them through the globs of come on his chest, caressing his smooth skin as he did so. Then Kam sucked the come off his fingers, deliberately provocative, just out of Malcolm's line of sight. Don's by-now flaccid dick twitched. He wondered why Malcolm couldn't see what a total tramp Kam was. Love, he guessed. And Don was very cynical about love.

'Hey, man,' Don said finally. 'I was just using one hole. You could've plugged the other.' His tone was flippant and callous, although what he was saying was what he really felt: that he and Kam were just fuck-buddies, as far as he was concerned, and would never be anything more.

'What you doing round my yard anyway, man?' he added, going on the offensive, feeling at a disadvantage standing there butt-naked in front of Malcolm, but also feeling that to put anything on would be like admitting that what he and Kam had been doing was wrong.

'I forgot to ask you to bring the session tapes we did last year, man,' Malcolm said tonelessly. 'You'd turned off your mobile so I thought I'd come round and remind you in the flesh. Flesh,' he repeated, half to himself. He looked round at Kam then, his eyes flaring green. Kam tried to shrug lightly, and half-smiled. But he was afraid that Malcolm might lose his rag. Malcolm wasn't afraid of a fight, and drink could make him very aggressive, and he drank when he was frustrated.

'I want your shit out of my flat by the time I get home tonight,' Malcolm said to Kam coldly, after a pause. 'Anything you leave, I'll burn.' He zipped up his jacket and looked back at Don. 'I'll see you at the studio, 'cause we've got work to do. But this ain't over, man. No way is this over.' At the door he turned back. 'One day·you'll fall in love,' he said to Don, his green eyes hot on Don's brown ones. 'Then you'll know how it feels.'

Don felt the pain of his friend's betrayal then and looked down at the carpet and his own bare feet. 'Yeah, man. Well, look, I'll see you later, yeah? I mean, like, at the studio. Soon,' he added. Malcolm nodded and headed off down the stairs. The moment he was out of the flat, Kam suddenly jumped up off the bed and started to pull on his clothes – crotch-hugging denim short-shorts with the ass ripped out of them, a ribbed white vest and a small bolero-style leather jacket.

'It's too late to be in a hurry now, man,' Don said coldly. But Kam carried on struggling into his clothing fast and stumbled out of the flat seconds later, buttoning his fly as he jolted down the stairs in his bike-boots.

'You forgot these!' Don shouted after him, picking up Kam's stained bikini-briefs, which, in his haste to dress, he had left lying on the floor. Kam didn't look back. Don balled the briefs up and threw them down the stairwell after him. He found Kam's sudden discovery of loyalty irritating, and hoped Malcolm wouldn't fall for it. In a way, Don felt his having sex with Kam was something he was doing for Malcolm, proving to Malcolm that he shouldn't throw his love away on a cheap slut, however horny he made Malcolm feel.

Don heard a powerful motorbike revving outside the building as the front door of the block of flats banged open and shut beneath him. He wandered over to his studio window and looked down into the street below. Malcolm was on his motorbike, looking lean and fine in black leather, his full-head helmet on, and he and Kam were having a heated conversation, gesticulating fiercely. Don watched idly as he wiped himself down with a large towel and started to get dressed, pulling on a pair of black Calvins over his large, muscular buttocks, adjusting his cock and balls casually. The only words he heard through the open window from this distance were Kam suddenly shouting 'Fuck off!' at Malcolm.

Malcolm roared away on his motorbike, leaving Kam standing all alone in the street. After a long moment Kam turned and looked up at Don's flat, just as Don was buttoning up his figure-hugging black 501s. Then, to Don's relief, Kam turned away and started to wander down the street towards Ladbroke Grove tube station. *Thank fuck for that*, Don thought. *Never choose a fuck-buddy over a real friend.* He glanced at his watch and kissed his teeth; now he was later than ever. And even more annoyingly, even though he'd just shot his load, he still felt incredibly sexually frustrated.

He pulled on Cuban-heel boots and a tight black vest and hurried out of the flat into the bright clear summer's day, catching up the keys to the band's van as he went. *Gregory'll be seriously pissed at me*, he thought to himself, walking fast, fishing a pair of Cutler & Gross shades out of his backpocket. *Oh, well.* He put the shades on and felt cooler, better and more defiant. *Soon come.*

Two

Don was right: Gregory *was* seriously pissed off with him. Gregory was the lead singer of their band, Boot Sex Massive, and the one who had booked the studio session for this morning and put up the upfront money for it. He was a tall slim mid-brown skinned black man of around thirty. He had large feline eyes, a neatly clipped goatee and a mass of dreadlocks that tumbled down around his shoulders, when he didn't contain them in a large tiger-striped fun-fur bowler. Right now, his locks were definitely up and in the hat. He was wearing a too-small tank-top that showed off his pierced navel, silver glinting against mocha on his flat belly, above skin-tight hipster jeans that were moulded to his full crotch and neat butt. He stood listening to messages on his mobile phone, standing with his hips aslant in the small recording studio, one lanky arm hanging down, his free hand toying idly with his zipper.

Gregory wore rubber bangles round his wrists, cowries on a chain round his slender neck, and hi-top Filas on his feet. He finished listening to his messages, put down his mobile phone and put a joint to his lips. He had a large over-bite, his big white teeth filling his mouth.

'Got a light, man?' he asked the sound engineer.

'On top of the mixing desk, Gregory, yeah?' the sound engineer said, without looking round. He was bent over the studio's computer system, programming in drum and bass tracks for the band coming in to record after the Boot Sex Massive. Every so often he tapped in additional rhythm sequences on an adjoining keyboard.

Gregory watched him idly as he dragged on the joint. Thom. A handsome, even-featured and blue-eyed, brown-freckled body-builder with a tangle of dark-blond hair; he was almost Gregory's height, but much broader and beefier, and currently wearing only ripped-up denim shorts, hiking boots and a scoop-neck pale blue vest. He had earrings in both ears and, when he had first shaken Gregory's hand, Gregory had thought Thom had made the contact last longer than strictly necessary for a business greeting. But it might just have been in Gregory's imagination, Gregory knew, just wishful thinking on his part.

Thom reached over to adjust one of the levels on the soundboard and Gregory found himself admiring the smooth tanned muscularity of his extended arm, the breadth of his pinky-brown shoulders, the 'V' his back made as that broadness narrowed and tapered into blocky buttocks that extended outwards into arching thighs, dusted with golden fuzz.

In the small studio – built by Thom and pretty much run by him on his own – warm and fabric-lined and windowless, Gregory found his thoughts turning to sex. Partly, it was Thom's well-defined body in such close proximity. Partly, it was the womb-like intimacy of the sound-proofed room. The lateness of the rest of the band made him feel more generally frustrated as well.

Gregory's mind ran to the vibrator he'd treated himself to on the way to the studio – an addition to his already large and slightly obsessive collection of sex-toys. It had taken him some time to choose it from among the truly outsize traffic-cone types and the slip-up-you-and-disappear-inside-your-intestinal-tract ladies' clutch-bag portables. He wondered if he could get away with slipping upstairs with it and giving it a quick try-out in Thom's bathroom while waiting for Don, Malcolm and Bobbi to finally show up. His dick stiffened in his briefs at the thought, just as it had when he had been choosing the sex-toy in the shop in Soho. He turned away from Thom awkwardly, stuck a hand down the front of his jeans, and adjusted his semi-erect cock upwards. When he turned back, Thom was watching him, toying idly with a channel on the mixing-desk.

'Frustrating, isn't it?' Thom said to him, half-smiling, his sapphire-blue eyes twinkling a little, his accent a blur of South Londonese and Australian.

Gregory flushed. 'What, man?' he said.

'Your posse being late like this,' Thom replied, stretching back lazily in his swivel chair. Gregory stared at his nipples, his buttercream-pale shaven armpits, and then down at Thom's bulging denim-covered crotch. The material had been sand-papered to accentuate the full bulge of his cock and balls. The strong seam pulled up across the bulge, spreading Thom's hefty ball-sack out attractively on either side of it.

'Yeah, well. Them soon come,' Gregory said, trying to be cool, his eyes glued to the front of Thom's shorts. The roof of his mouth felt suddenly dry and he could feel his stiffening dick sliding upwards inside his cotton underwear as it thickened and lengthened; his cock-head pushed painfully against the zipper at the top of his fly, and the metal bit into his tingling slit. He finally managed to pull his eyes off the bulge in Thom's shorts and look up at his face again, and was disconcerted to find Thom staring at him intently.

'Maybe I can do some run-throughs and alla that,' Gregory said finally, feeling painfully self-conscious and increasingly turned on at the same time. 'Warm up me voice and shit.' He coughed, stubbed out the joint in a stolen pub-ashtray.

'Sure,' Thom said easily, gesturing for Gregory to step through into the glass-fronted recording-booth part of the studio where the singing was done. As Gregory crossed the room, Thom asked him, 'Oh, did you bring the discs with the old drum-patterns with you? It'll save us time if we can use them as a start-off point.'

'They should be in me bag, man,' Gregory replied, indicating a battered black sausage-bag that was sitting on the floor next to the mixing-desk. Thom bent over and rummaged for the discs while Gregory practised scales to warm up his voice, staring blankly at the sound-proofed wall in front of him as he did so. After a minute or so, thinking maybe Thom couldn't find the discs or that he had forgotten to pack them, Gregory looked round to see what was going on. To his embarrassment, he saw that Thom had fished out the vibrator he had brought earlier and was looking with some curiosity at the transparent plastic box. He looked up at Gregory, then back at the specs on the box.

'Multispeed,' Thom said, grinning. 'For your girlfriend?'

Gregory decided to bite the bullet. 'For me.'

'Yeah?' Thom said, looking back at the smooth cream-coloured sex-toy. 'I thought you'd go for it in red, gold and green.'

'It don't matter what colour it is when it's all the way up your ass, man,' Gregory said, shrugging. 'You know what I'm saying?'

'It's big,' Thom observed, weighing the box in his hand.

'Yeah,' Gregory said defiantly, standing with his hips slanted, angry but turned on at the same time. *Fuck his approval*, Gregory thought to himself. *Who cares what he thinks?*

'I'd like to see it all the way up you,' Thom said unexpectedly. He met Gregory's level gaze and his face flushed hotly. His slightly parted mouth was shiny and pink and moist. 'In fact, I'd like to more than see it, Greg. I'd like to slide this dildo up your ass myself. Right here and right now.' He stood up from where he'd been squatting by the bag and Gregory came over to him. They embraced tightly, kissing hotly on the mouth, Gregory's full dark lips soft against Thom's smaller, firmer ones. Their eager tongues probed each other's mouths, strong hands running over each other's shoulders, backs. Thom slid his hands down to Gregory's pert butt, gripped it firmly, and pulled Gregory's narrow snake-hips forwards so the two men could grind their bulging, aching crotches together. As they ground against each other, Gregory pulled Thom's vest up and pushed it back over his bulging chest, exposing Thom's stiff pink nipples.

'Put your arms up, man,' Gregory instructed Thom. Thom raised his arms and Gregory pulled his vest up and off in a single movement, bending his head at the same time, so that he could tease one of Thom's nipples with his lips and teeth. He threw Thom's vest down on the carpet. Then he quickly pulled his own vest up and off and they hugged and kissed again, hot mocha skin against warm buttery-pink; below their waist-lines both their cocks were now jutting painfully against the denim they were wearing.

'Let's get these pants down,' Thom said hoarsely, his face flushing with excitement as he tugged on the button at the top of Gregory's fly. Gregory's mouth was half-open now, his heavy eyelids lowered languorously as he looked down at Thom's strong eager fingers working away at the copper stud on his waist-band. It finally popped loose; the zipper started to slide down of its own accord, as the swollen crown of Gregory's long thick hard-on pressed forward stiffly inside his pure white briefs, stretching the fabric. Thom sank to his knees in front of Gregory with a sigh. But he didn't bury his face in Gregory's crotch. He didn't even touch Gregory's cock. Instead, he gripped Gregory's lean hips and started to gently swivel him around.

'Turn around, Gregory,' Thom instructed the tall black man softly. 'I want to get your ass exposed.'

Gregory turned round and leant against the mixing-desk, sticking his ass back and up, making it available for Thom. Thom gripped the waistband of Gregory's jeans and his pants inside them, and pulled them both right down to

Gregory's ankles with one decisive movement. Gregory's painfully stiff dick sprang up as his briefs were yanked down, and slapped stiffly against his belly, sending drops of precome scattering onto the surface of the desk. He gasped sharply. The close air felt suddenly cool on his cock and swinging balls and his freshly-exposed buttocks.

'You've got a beautiful brown ass,' Thom said from behind Gregory; he admired the pert muscularity of Gregory's smooth buttocks, the tense leanness of his slim, sinewy thighs as Gregory stuck his butt out for Thom's inspection and, Gregory hoped, use. 'You want to hold it open for me so I can get a look at that good-looking brown asshole?' Thom suggested, stroking his hands firmly up and down the length of Gregory's thighs. Gregory reached back obligingly with both hands, bending forward and resting his head on the mixing-deck, and pulled his ass open.

'Beautiful star,' Thom said. Then he leant forward and kissed Gregory's chocolate hole, pressing his soft pink lips against it. Gregory sighed softly, then moaned as Thom began to tongue-fuck him. At the same time, Thom reached up and began to fondle Gregory's pendulous ball-sack, massaging it and tugging at it gently. Gregory's extremely-experienced asshole dilated immediately, so Thom found that he could get his whole tongue up it and into Gregory's smooth hot bitter rectum without difficulty. Thom reached up with the hand he didn't have on Gregory's balls and began to fondle Gregory's rigid veiny pole.

He hasn't locked the door, Gregory thought as he pulled his ass even further open for Thom's eager tongue, glancing around a little anxiously at the closed studio door behind him. It had a small glass panel set into it. But no one was looking through; he knew nobody else was in the building, and anyway the good feeling of Thom's hands on his balls and cock, and Thom's tongue sliding up his asshole, made Gregory put the fear of being walked in on out of his mind.

Thom released Gregory's balls and hard-on and put his hands on Gregory's narrow hips, turning him carefully away from the desk. Thom made sure to keep his face pushed deep between Gregory's buttocks as Gregory shuffled round, the denims and pants round his ankles constraining him, hobbling his movements in a way Gregory found vaguely exciting. Thom carried on tonguing Gregory's asshole as he shuffled round.

Gregory was confused as to why Thom had turned him round until he realised that he was now bending over in front of his sausage-bag. He gasped softly as Thom gripped his cock and balls again and started to squeeze and wank him slowly again, while rhythmically pushing his tongue in and out, in and out of Gregory's by now wet and slippery asshole.

Gregory reached into the bag and fumbled about for the vibrator in its transparent plastic box, gasping again as Thom wiggled his tongue back and forth inside his hungry rectum. He fumbled the larger-than-life sex-toy out of its packet, dropping it in his haste and excitement. He snatched it up again and unscrewed its base with trembling hands while Thom rimmed him hungrily, then groped for the batteries he had bought to go in it, slotted them in and screwed the base back on again. Looking at it now, it seemed bigger than it had looked in the sex-shop – twelve inches long and almost two inches across – but his ass felt so slack and good that Gregory had no doubt Thom would soon be able to get it up him. He tested the multi-speed; the buzzing excitement against the palm of his hand made his cock buck where Thom was moving his fist on its milk chocolate brown length. He turned the vibrator off and handed it back between his legs to Thom.

The white muscleman took the dildo with the hand he had had on Gregory's hard-on. He had felt Gregory's cock quiver and didn't want the horny Rastafarian to shoot his load too soon. On impulse, Gregory took hold of his own cock and began to masturbate in slow long strokes, pulling his foreskin back and forth, just because Thom's rimming was making him feel so good.

'Take that hand off your dick, man,' Thom ordered, pulling his mouth away from Gregory's juicy, open hole with a slurping gasp. 'I want this to be all about your ass. Your asshole. In fact, give me your hands,' he continued. 'Put your hands behind you.' Excited by Thom's focus on the part of his body that gave him the most pleasure, Gregory did as he was told. Thom slid the leather belt from around the waist of his denim shorts and deftly tied Gregory's wrists together behind him. Gregory flexed his lean arms against the constraining knot. It wasn't serious. He could wriggle out of the belt if he really wanted to. But he didn't want to. The feeling of being constrained by his jeans and pants tangled around his ankles, and now having his hands bound behind his back, excited him even more.

Thom went back to licking Gregory's smooth brown ass, running his tongue up the length of it between his buttocks in long, tonguing movements that sent shivers of pleasure up through Gregory's gut and chest and made his wagging dick twitch and his nipples prickle. Thom teased Gregory's quivering asshole with his tongue for a long moment, then sat back.

'This vibrator looks too big to go up your ass,' he said doubtfully, picking up the twelve-inch length of plastic and turning it on to a low hum.

'No it ain't, man,' Gregory said urgently. 'You just got to wind it in there. Come on, man,' he pleaded. 'You said you wanted to see it up me. Up me bung-hole. You got me all wet and open for you. Just shove it up there, man. I can take it.'

Thom started to rotate the softly buzzing head against Gregory's slippery, spit-slicked asshole. He watched in excited surprise as the dark brown star opened easily to accept the smooth off-white plastic head, hungrily sucking the first inch and a half of the dildo up into Gregory's rectum. Gregory grunted as the head slipped inside him so Thom eased off on the pressure.

'Don't stop shoving it up me *now*, man,' Gregory ordered, twisting round with a desperate look on his flushed face, his lips wet, his eyes shining. 'This hot black asshole is hungry, man!'

Thom renewed pushing the vibrator up Gregory's dilating ass, flexing his tanned biceps and shifting where he crouched to get better leverage. The dark skin of Gregory's anal ring was stretched smooth and shiny around the dildo's widening stem now. Thom slid seven smooth inches smoothly and slowly up Gregory's bottom and into his rectum. Sensing a little resistance inside Gregory, Thom stopped pushing for a moment, holding the vibrator where it was so Gregory could relax inside and accommodate it. But Gregory immediately started pushing his ass down onto the smooth thick plastic length, anally swallowing another three inches; now his anal ring was stretched to its maximum circumference.

'That look good, man?' Gregory gasped, glancing round quickly and pushing down again and sucking another butthole stretching, vibrating inch up into his anal canal.

'Yeah,' Thom said throatily, unzipping the fly of his denim shorts clumsily with his left hand and groping inside them to grip his own stiff thick dick inside his jock, while keeping the dildo firmly pushed up Gregory's ass with the right one.

'Pump that big dildo in me, man,' Gregory ordered. 'Stroke me with it.' Sweat had broken out all over his smooth brown body, making it glitter. His nipples and cock were painfully stiff. Obediently, Thom began to slide the vibrator in and out of Gregory's hungry, sucking asshole with long, confident strokes. He pulled it out of Gregory's ass until he could see the bulge of its white head begin to slither out of the stretched, dilating brown hole, then pushed it right the way back in until Gregory grunted that he was full, and his thighs and calves tensed because he was trying to lift himself up off the rigid plastic length on tip-toe. With each stroke, Thom rammed the dildo a little harder up Gregory's ass, eager to make sure he was always taking the absolute maximum with each firm insertion. And, with each ram of the dildo, Gregory moaned, his dick twitched and pre-come beaded on the crown of his hard-on.

Thom began to get hypnotised by the steady motion of the shiny length of cream plastic in and out of Gregory's ebony hole. Thom had been excited to realise that the spit from the ass-tonguing he'd given Gregory had been lubrication enough for Gregory's ready hole to take the dildo. Pre-come was dripping out of Gregory's untouched cock in long threads onto the floor now. Thom twisted the base of the vibrator, turning up the speed, and it began to buzz more vigorously, and louder. The volume of the sound fascinated Thom too: loud when he pulled it out of Gregory's ass, it got muffled again as it disappeared up his dilated hole and into his anal passage.

Thom pushed the vibrator into Gregory's rectum as far as it could go and started to twist it around, wanting to stretch Gregory's insides as much as his anal opening had been stretched. Gregory arched forward as if he were trying to escape the vigorous exploration of his insides, but he also immediately started panting and gasping excitedly.

'Oh, yeah, man, oh – yeah, ram that dildo up me, man,' he groaned. 'Ram that big fucking dildo around in there; oh, oh, that's it, man, oh –'

Keeping the whole length of the vibrator up inside Gregory's ass so that only the swelling at the base stopped it from disappearing up him altogether, Thom slid round on his knees so he was now in front of the sweaty and heavily turned on Rastafarian. Every muscle of Gregory's dark, sinewy body was tensed; his hands were tied uselessly behind his back and his ankles constrained by his pulled-down trousers and pants. A large dildo was up his small, tight ass; his long stiff cock jutted out and bobbed heavily and painfully, juice running freely from his now-gaping slit.

'Oh, man, this is heaven,' Gregory gasped as Thom reached up and played with his erect tits with one hand. Now Gregory was standing upright and arching back, squatting slightly so Thom's other hand could get between his legs and keep the vibrator firmly in place, right the way up his ass.

Then, just when Gregory couldn't imagine any more pleasure, Thom bent forward and licked the pre-come out of his slit. Gregory moaned in excitement at this unexpected bonus, then groaned loudly as Thom kissed the head of his stiff swollen cock, before sliding his warm lips over it and beginning to suck Gregory off in long smooth movements; his dark blond hair tousled on his flushed forehead as he sucked Gregory's hot rigid pole. Gregory dragged in a ragged breath and tossed his head back as the feeling of heaviness vibrated in his wet, warmly-enclosed cock and balls, and the sex-toy buzzingly stretched his ass. He tossed his head back and his bowler tipped off. His dreadlocks cascaded around his shoulders like a lion's mane. Thom started to move the vibrator in and out of Gregory's bottom again, in time with his own greedy mouth.

'Oh, sweet Lord,' Gregory moaned ecstatically, the vibrator sliding in and out of his quivering, pulsing asshole, Thom's mouth sliding back and forth on his throbbing cock. 'Oh, man, oh, Jesus, I'm going to explode – oh, *yeah*!'

Thom rammed the dildo up Gregory to the very root, only just keeping a grip on the stem so it couldn't disappear up him altogether, just as Gregory, writhing and thrusting his hips and ass, shot his load into Thom's mouth in sudden gouts of hot salty spunk. Thom swallowed Gregory's whole load down before letting the shiny brown cock slip out of his mouth and the vibrator slip out of Gregory's slack open ass-hole. Then Thom gripped Gregory's cock and squeezed its shaft in his fist. A final blob of come pushed out of the slit. Thom extended his tongue and licked it up, then gave the whole cock one final suck. As he did so, he couldn't resist sliding a bunch of fingers up Gregory's open asshole. They went in easily. Gregory groaned sensually and Thom let his fingers slip out again.

Thom stood then, and kissed Gregory on the mouth, letting Gregory taste his own come on Thom's lips. Gregory kissed Thom back hungrily, surprising him.

'You glad the rest of the band was late?' Thom asked Gregory.

Gregory smiled embarassedly, and nodded. Thom saw something unexpected in Gregory's eyes. What was it? Thom wondered. It looked like – tenderness? They kissed again. Thom reached down and slid three fingers between Gregory's buttocks and bent them round and up him again. Gregory kissed him harder, then released him and pushed Thom's exploring hand back with his own bound ones, pushing Thom's fingers out of his ass.

'My hole can't take no more for now, man,' Gregory said throatily.

Thom nodded, smiling. He had brought his own cock out, long and hard and buttery-pale but purple-headed, and was slowly moving his fist on it.

Thom was still jerking off, standing in the middle of the room, and Gregory's hands were still tied behind his back with his trousers round his ankles, when the studio door banged open and Bobbi walked in on them.

'Sorry I'm late, guys,' he said blithely, totally cool, setting his bass guitar down in a corner in its case. There was a broad smile on his face and Gregory flushed as he realised that Bobbi must have arrived some time earlier and had clearly been watching a considerable chunk of his anal workout with Thom.

Bobbi was a pretty 23-year-old black boy with a cute smile, smooth aubergine-dark skin, a beefy butt and a slightly fey manner. The sides of his head were shaven, graduating in an immaculate fade to a short orangey-gold crop on top. His eyes sparkled and his full lips seemed set in a perpetual sensual pout. He was wearing white Nike hi-tops, white socks, a tight white T-shirt through which his large nipples protruded darkly, and white tennis-shorts so tight that the outline of his big – and now obviously stiff – cock and plump balls was outrageously visible. He wore a pink triangle stud in one ear and a thin gold chain round his neck and had a gold nose-stud. Of all the band, he was the most free and easy when it came to romance, and to sex. 'Trampy', Gregory called him behind his back, but he didn't really mean it unkindly. There was an innocence about Bobbi, something sweet that stopped his friends from judging him, however many men he slept with and however many romantic scrapes he got himself into.

By contrast, Bobbi had always thought that Gregory was rather repressed and even prudish about sex, especially about the indulging of spur-of-the-moment lust. So he had been especially pleased when he had arrived at the studio ahead of Don and Malcolm, letting himself in quietly, and, peeping through the small grill-glass recording-room window, had seen Gregory, trousers round his ankles, hands tied behind his back, having a large vibrator vigorously rammed in and out of his open asshole by Thom, and gasping loudly with each firm thrust. Pleased at first, and then heavily turned on, Bobbi had carried on watching the pair of them with a hand thrust down the front of his shorts, all the time wondering if Gregory would be angry if he tried to get in on the action or, much worse, get too embarrassed to shoot his load.

But now Gregory *had* shot his load. And Thom hadn't and Gregory didn't seem like he was going to do anything about Thom's throbbing purple hard-on, and Bobbi didn't see any reason why he shouldn't try for a piece of the action.

Gregory looked embarrassed, standing there with his hands still tied behind his back, his spent cock large but flaccid. 'Bobbi, man,' he said inanely, a lop-sided smile on his face. He had been going to say, 'you're early,' but actually Bobbi was late, just less late than Don and Malcolm, so his voice just trailed off inconclusively.

Thom, by contrast, didn't look one bit embarrassed. He met Bobbi's eyes levelly, and carried on moving his fist on his long thick circumcised dick, his shorts around his ankles, his mouth moving slightly as if he were chewing gum.

'What are you doing that for?' Bobbi asked, hooking his thumbs in the waist-band of his tight white shorts and smirking a little as he looked down at Thom's fist moving in leisurely strokes.

''Cause it feels so good, man,' Thom replied huskily, his blue eyes dull with lust, his face flushed pink. His tanned right pectoral dimpled with sinew as he pulled on his rigid length.

'Not as good as a pair of big hot juicy lips wrapped around it would, I bet,' Bobbi said huskily, running his tongue over his full well-defined lips.

'Are you a tease, or do you deliver?' Thom asked, now smirking too.

By way of an answer, Bobbi sank to his knees in front of Thom without another word and kissed the pulsing purple head of Thom's cock, then kissed it again. Thom grunted as Bobbi's kisses became more sucking, and as Bobbi began to tease Thom's swollen, blood-heavy glans with his teeth and explore Thom's slit with the tip of his firm pink tongue.

'That's good, Bobbi. Mmm . . .' Thom said throatily as the pretty black youth smoothly took the whole of Thom's hard-on into his mouth in a soft sucking stroke. Thom's breathing became huskier as he felt Bobbi's soft lips gripping the base of his cock, and the head of his cock pushing at the soft rigidity at the back of Bobbi's throat.

Thom glanced round at Gregory, who was looking down at Bobbi where he was kneeling. The sweat was drying on Gregory's smooth flat well-defined chest but his large long cock was starting to harden again as he watched Bobbi chowing down on Thom's hard-on, and his nipples were visibly stiffening. Gregory looked up from Bobbi's head to the face of the standing Thom. Their eyes met, brown on blue. While Bobbi kept on blowing him, Thom bent his head forward and kissed Gregory hotly on the mouth. Gregory – still tied – responded hotly, sliding his tongue into Thom's mouth, sucking eagerly when Thom pushed his tongue back into Gregory's mouth, pumping his full lips eagerly on Thom's firm tongue in time with the regular movement of Bobbi's mouth on Thom's thick rock-hard cock.

With a gasp, Gregory and Thom came up for air. Gregory was now painfully stiff again, and his asshole felt empty and in need of satisfaction. Thom kissed him again, this time softly and tenderly, then leant back against the mixing-desk and braced himself as Bobbi pumped his mouth more greedily on the blond bodybuilder's throbbing cock. After a moment, Thom started to pump his hips upwards in small motions into the face of the sexy young man kneeling with eagerly inclined head before him.

Bobbi slid his hands up Thom's thighs and cradled

Thom's hard muscular buttocks in both hands, encouraging the movement of Thom's pelvis and sucking a little harder and faster as a reward; the dark gold curls of Thom's pubic hair brushed his nose and lips as he swallowed Thom's cock-head. Thom tilted his head to one side so he could watch Bobbi's expression as he worked his mouth on Thom's swollen and now glistening hard-on. Bobbi's eyes were screwed shut in concentration at what he was doing, and in sensual appreciation of the feel and taste of the big stiff cock now filling his mouth; his cheeks were sucked in dramatically as he worked industriously on giving Thom's throbbing erection the maximum amount of stimulation. His full and fully occupied lips glistened with spit and pre-come as if he were wearing wet-look lipstick.

As he sucked Thom off, Bobbi slid a hand from one of Thom's buttocks and began to fondle his heavy balls with immaculately-manicured nails. Thom groaned again at Bobbi's expert touch. Then Bobbi let Thom's achingly stiff hard-on slip out of his mouth while keeping a firm grip on Thom's ball-sack. Thom's erection sprang up rigidly and slapped hard against his ridged stomach. Sweat glistened in the grooves between Thom's stomach-muscles, and his cockhead left a sticky slick of pre-come. Thom groaned sharply.

'Hey, guy, what did you stop for?' he asked hoarsely, looking down at Bobbi's upturned face, his own boyishly handsome features flushed with excitement, his tangle of dark-blond hair damp with sweat.

Bobbi's large brown eyes were bright as he looked up at Thom, his full lips wet and inviting, his mouth parted sensually. 'To tease you, man,' he said with a little smile. Then, before Thom could say anything in reply, Bobbi's mouth was on his cock again, pumping faster and more hungrily, this time. Thom opened his mouth in a gasp and let his head tip back. He could feel the sweat between his buttocks beginning to pool on the recording desk, but he didn't care. He closed his eyes and concentrated on the good feeling of Bobbi's hot wet mouth moving back and forth on his hard-on, the eager suction that was making the whole length of his dick tingle with excitement, the extra thrill of the slight roughness of Bobbi's grooved tongue against the underside of his heavy shaft.

'Oh, yes. Oh, suck that cock. Oh, man . . .' Thom had had a lot of blow-jobs in his time, mostly owing to his pumped, Bondi-beach physique, but sometimes because a guy wanted cheap or free recording sessions in his studio. Whatever the reason, Thom found an eager pair of lips hard to turn down. And he was extremely glad he hadn't turned down Bobbi. Bobbi was a real pro, one of the best Thom had ever had down on his knees in front of him. But more than that, Bobbi clearly enjoyed cock-sucking: his mouth was moving enthusiastically on Thom's thick, hard erection, his hands were on Thom's ass and balls. What was clearly on his mind was getting as much of Thom's good big cock into his mouth as he could, while giving as much pleasure to Thom as he could. In his cock-sucking excitement, Bobbi had completely forgotten about his own achingly-stiff erection constrained in his trampily tight white shorts, and concentrated totally on the one in his mouth. To Thom, this made him a 'true' cock-sucker, someone who got his real sexual pleasure from working another man to climax with his lips, tongue, teeth and throat on that man's cock.

Still, Thom found himself looking down at Bobbi's big beefy round ass, the white cotton of the shorts straining over its large curves, and feeling that that deserved some attention, too. He looked round at Gregory, kissing him on the mouth agam.

'Turn round, guy,' he said, his voice hoarsened by the rising excitement in his chest. Gregory turned round and Thom tugged at the belt tied round his wrists. After a moment, it came loose and Gregory's hands were free. The belt fell to the ground. Gregory turned back to face Thom, took Thom's flushed pink face in his hands, and kissed him warmly on the lips. Thom responded, and reached over and toyed with one of Gregory's small dark nipples. The Rasta's moan of pleasure was swallowed in Thom's mouth.

Thom broke off their kiss. 'Look,' he said, indicating with his head the way Bobbi was sticking his beefy butt out as he sucked hungrily on Thom's cock, moving it invitingly from side to side. 'Don't you think an ass that juicy needs some attention?' Thom slid a hand between Gregory's thighs, gripped his balls, then grasped his stiff, wagging cock, pulled back his foreskin, ran his thumb in smooth circular motions over Gregory's silky-smooth glans.

'Me no a cocksman,' Gregory said sulkily, although he was enjoying the feel of Thom's hand stroking his hard-on. 'Me *strictly* a batty man.'

'So use the vibrator, man,' Thom said, smiling, keeping his thumb moving rhythmically on Gregory's cock-head.

To his surprise, Gregory realised the idea turned him on. Partly it was voyeurism, partly a need to equalise things between him and Bobbi now Bobbi had seen him getting pleasured so explicitly, and partly Gregory felt a desire to see how capacious Bobbi's legendary well-used booty really was. He quickly struggled out of the pants that had been tangled round his black hi-tops so he would have greater freedom of movement, then went and squatted down naked behind Bobbi, where he was still kneeling in front of Thom. Gregory watched the regular movement of Bobbi's head in front of Thom's crotch from behind him and a thrill of excitement ran through him: all the sex in Gregory's life up until now had been one-on-one. He felt he was unexpectedly breaking free of something, of some dull constraint. He caressed Bobbi's buttocks through the tightly stretched material. Bobbi stuck his ass back and up invitingly and parted his thighs. Gregory rubbed his hand firmly between Bobbi's buttocks, then slid it forward between his thighs, cupping and massaging Bobbi's lumpily bulging crotch from behind. Bobbi moaned mufffledly, his mouth still firmly plugged by Thom's cock, his rhythm momentarily thrown out by the distracting and exciting attention to his ass and painfully constricted balls and cock.

'Keep sucking, Bobbi,' Thom ordered. Bobbi moved his head faster. 'Oh, yeah. That's better,' Thom said. 'You'll get that hot serving of jism soon, Bobbi. Just keep on working that pretty mouth like the good cock-sucker you are.'

Behind Bobbi, Gregory took his hand off Bobbi's crotch, and leant forward and spoke softly into his small neat ear. 'I'm gonna pull your pants down, man. Then me a go dildo-fuck you with this big dildo me did get. Me a get the whole twelve inches up you, man. And that's how you're gonna shoot your load.'

Gregory sat back down on his haunches and reached for the vibrator which was now lying nestled in his discarded T-shirt, watching the back of Bobbi's rapidly-bobbing head for reactions to what he'd said. *After all*, he thought, *Bobbi might not want to go for the full boot sex trip.* But Bobbi flexed his back decisively, sticking his ass up as high as he could, and wiggling it from side to side, demanding attention for it. *That ass is hungry, man*, Gregory said to himself as he reached round from behind Bobbi for the waistband of the randy black boy's shorts. Gregory unpopped the top button and pulled the zip down, tugging it over the thick bulge of Bobbi's hard-on and then the second bulge of his big balls. Then, with a brisk tug, he pulled Bobbi's shorts down to his knees. Bobbi now slid onto all fours, bracing himself with his hands on the carpet, keeping his mouth on Thom's cock at all times, but lifting his knees slightly so Gregory could get his shorts down to his ankles and off completely. Being on all fours, he could now thrust his big ass out more easily, and ensure it got more attention from Gregory. No longer constrained by his shorts, Bobbi could open his legs wider too, making his hole more available for whatever use Gregory wanted to put it to.

No underwear, Gregory noted as he tugged Bobbi's shorts awkwardly over his Nikes and stared at Bobbi's smooth, heavy ball-sack hanging down between his smooth curving thighs. *What a tramp*. But that trampiness didn't stop Gregory from fondling Bobbi's balls curiously and excitedly with long dark slender fingers. Bobbi moaned muffledly, but was careful this time to keep his rhythm going on Thom's thick, stiff dark-pink cock. He wasn't particularly a sex-toy enthusiast, but he enjoyed almost any attention to his ass and, anyway, he enjoyed going with the flow. He couldn't think of anything he'd ever refused to do with a guy, if the guy he was with was attractive enough.

Gregory, who was now kneeling behind Bobbi and studying his ass interestedly, pushed the mass of his dreads back off his face, then bent forward and experimentally began to tongue Bobbi's shaven, puckered brown asshole. Bobbi moaned again, more deeply and throatily this time, and pushed his ass backwards, obviously excited to be rimmed. A gout of glistening pre-come slid in a sticky strand from the head of his large stiff dick and fell to the carpet. His asshole opened receptively to the probing of Gregory's long, muscular and inquisitive tongue. Gregory pumped his tongue in Bobbi's hot hole for a while, massaging Bobbi's ball-sack as he did so. Quivers of sensual excitement ran the length of Bobbi's body; he briefly braced himself on one arm, so he could toy with his own nipples, adding to his pleasure while he continued to blow Thom.

Gregory sat up and released Bobbi's balls. For a moment, he studied Bobbi's beautiful big brown ass as if it were a work of art, admiring its smoothness, excited by the way it was being so freely and insistency offered to him, to do whatever he wanted with it. He wetted two fingers from his right hand in his mouth thoughtfully, his index finger and his middle finger. He bent forward and brushed the tip of the now shining middle finger against Bobbi's hungry brown hole, then slid its spit-slickened length up into Bobbi's ass. Bobbi grunted as Gregory pushed his finger into Bobbi right the way up to the knuckle and held it there, twisting it around a little. Bobbi, excited by the sudden insertion into his rectum, stopped playing with his nipples and braced himself solidly on all fours for some serious anal attention. At the same time, he began to pump his head on Thom's cock harder and faster, wanting both his holes filled to capacity at the same time.

Thom's breathing was starting to become constricted. His lungs felt compressed and his broad, built-up chest was heaving with excitement, both from the good feeling of Bobbi's hungry eager mouth on his throbbing cock, from which he could feel pre-come juices were now running like tap-water, and from the sexy sight of the dreadlocked Rasta – who even now turned him on more heavily than any man he'd ever been with – licking, tonguing and now finger-fucking the ass of the cute boy kneeling in front of him.

Gregory moved the fist of his left hand on his own stiff cock as he slid the middle finger of his right up Bobbi's hot slack ass. He pulled it out, then worked the index finger up alongside it. Bobbi's ass swallowed the two fingers easily. Gregory slid them out, licked the adjoining one, and pushed it along with the first two long fingers up Bobbi's asshole. This time Bobbi grunted juicily around Thom's thick rigid cock; he had to swivel his ass to loosen up enough to accommodate the width of all three digits. But once he had done that, the three fingers slid all the way up him, to the knuckle, quite easily. Gregory kept all three fingers up Bobbi while, with his other hand, he started to massage Bobbi's balls again. He avoided touching the pretty black boy's cock, afraid he might come too soon if he was too directly stimulated. He squeezed Bobbi's balls firmly, though, and started to ram his fingers in and out of Bobbi's hole vigorously and quickly. Bobbi grunted again, a little sharply, and angled his hips forward slightly, as if he wanted to pull away from Gregory's eager fingers. Gregory slowed the movement of his hand a little, looking down fascinatedly at where the pink of the palm vanished, except for his little finger, into the smooth sucking mouth between Bobbi's large buttocks.

In response to Gregory slowing the movement of his bunched fingers, Bobbi pushed his ass back and up again to show Gregory he was appreciating the attention. Gregory moved his hand a little faster, in response, in Bobbi's hot hole. Bobbi kept his ass where it was. Gregory quickly built up to the fast ramming he had been doing before and, this time, Bobbi not only kept his ass in place, but even moved his knees outwards, spreading his thighs slightly to open himself up more to Gregory's rapidly moving hand.

Heavily turned on by Bobbi's greedy ass, and thinking it was now ready for some serious action, Gregory slithered his fingers out of Bobbi. In a single quick movement, he picked up the large cream vibrator that was lying beside him, twisted its stem to activate it and, with a deft twisting movement, rotated its head into Bobbi's receptive asshole. Bobbi gasped aloud: a high, surprised, gagged and excited sound. Before Bobbi had time to think about whether his butthole could accommodate something so broad, and whether his rectum could stretch enough to contain its considerable length, Gregory had managed to work the head and a good six thick inches straight up into his asshole. The sudden fullness and the buzzing pressure inside his anus sent a violent wave of ecstasy coursing through Bobbi's gut, right the way through to his balls and up into his chest. His cock bucked and gushed pre-come onto the carpet and sweat began to pour down his arms from his armpits. Gregory turned the vibrator up to full power and Bobbi – to his embarrassment – squealed aloud in excitement.

Gregory began to move the slick cream dildo back and forth, in and out of Bobbi's ass, gratified to elicit groans and grunts with every firm stroke. Bobbi's asshole, stretched tight, glistened iridescently around the white plastic girth, curving in as Gregory pushed the plastic shaft into his anus, then curving out as Gregory withdrew it, as if Bobbi's asshole were greedily trying to hold onto the object of its satisfaction. Gregory inserted the loudly buzzing shaft deep, then paused to rotate the vibrator's length inside Bobbi, knowing it would stretch his rectum gratifyingly in every direction, giving him the maximum thrill. Gregory flushed with the excitement of the master pleasurer, the one who knows how to please – one who knows what pleasure can be given because he has received it himself. Bobbi panted around Thom's cock, his rhythm really thrown out now by the attention his ass was receiving from Gregory's butthole-stretching sex-toy.

'Concentrate on this cock in your mouth, man,' Thom ordered Bobbi, who was now tossing his head ecstatically, barely keeping Thom's dick in his mouth at all. 'Gregory, you're distracting him too much.'

Gregory nodded and returned to moving the buzzing plastic length in and out of Bobbi's back passage in long regular less-distracting strokes, wanking himself off as he did so. He was glad to see that, for all his anal eagerness, Bobbi could only take ten inches up his ass – not the full twelve that Gregory could take – however firmly Gregory pressed the bulging base of the stem up against Bobbi's widely stretched hole.

Realising that the anal attention was becoming too excit-ing for Bobbi to concentrate on active cock-sucking, Thom stopped leaning back on the mixing-desk, stood up and pushed Bobbi back a little. Then he started to pump his hips against Bobbi's open mouth, taking control of his pleasure. He gripped Bobbi's head between his large heavily-veined hands and began to fuck Bobbi's bloated shining face.

'Just take it easy, Bobbi, man,' Thom said, sliding his long thick rigid cock quickly in and out of Bobbi's mouth. 'Take it easy and take it all the way down and all the way up you. We'll do all the work, man. I'll fuck your face with this big juicy dick and Gregory'll pound your big juicy ass with his dildo. All you have to do is take it and not shoot your load till I've shot mine.'

Bobbi kept his mouth and ass receptively in place, pleased to be so totally used. With a quick glance to check what the other was doing, Thom and Gregory started to co-ordinate their rhythms so that they both thrust into Bobbi together, withdrew together, thrust in together: all the way in, all the way out. Their rhythm built in speed and intensity. They craned forward above the sweaty, help-lessly excited brown-skinned boy on all fours between them and, with Thom leaning on Bobbi's shoulders and Gregory leaning on the small of Bobbi's back, kissed hotly. When holding the angle became tiring, they broke the kiss, but some bond of affection remained between them as they went back to the business of poling Bobbi hard and fast from both ends.

Bobbi was now squealing and grunting with every inser-tion and withdrawal, in heaven at being pounded so vigor-ously from both ends: Thom's hot, juicy cock in his mouth, the pulsing veins pressing against the insides of his cheeks, the taste of it sweet and salty on his extended tongue, the exciting feeling of it moving backwards and forwards, back-wards and forwards on his tongue, Thom's soft balls bang-ing heavily against Bobbi's smooth chin, Thom's golden pubic hair tickling Bobbi's flat nose, Thom's strong fingers gripping his head, the excitement of giving up control that Bobbi so adored. And then the challenge of Gregory's dildo in his ass, the shuddering thrill of ecstasy as Gregory slammed it deep into his elastic rectum, demanding that Bobbi open all the way up, rubbing the rigid shiny plastic head against Bobbi's prostate as Gregory rotated it inside his body expertly. Bobbi's gasps were now coming sharp and fast and high; he felt that he was starting to lose control of his body so totally that he could barely manage to stay up, even just on all fours.

Above him, Thom was breathing heavily and quickly too, pumping his hips against Bobbi's face in short rapid vigorous thrusts. 'Oh, Jesus, oh, yeah, oh, fuck!' Thom moaned, his dick heavy, throbbing, flowing as he slid it in and out of Bobbi's hot mouth, his hips thrusting out of his control, his hands tight on Bobbi's head; the heaviness and the excitement were now beyond his power to stop. His balls clenched and his pulsing dick bucked suddenly as he passed the point of no return. 'Oh, you're going to get my load now, man,' he burst out throatily. 'Oh, yeah!' He pushed his cock to the back of Bobbi's throat and came explosively in shuddering waves, banging his crotch against Bobbi's face in uncontrollable pelvic spasms. 'Oh, Jesus, oh, yeah, oh, fuck!' he yelled as he exploded in Bobbi's mouth.

Bobbi kept on sucking Thom's thick hot cock while Gregory pounded his ass vigorously with the vibrator; his mouth was finally gratifyingly flooded with Thom's hot salty load. He was determined not to lose a single drop of the nourishing jism he had worked so hard to earn; his mind was on autopilot, thinking of nothing, blanked out by the ecstatic feelings he was experiencing in his stretched, filled-to-bursting asshole. Bobbi felt a weight building in his cock in response to that electrifying fullness, without him even having to touch it.

Thom's now semi-erect dick slipped slickly from Bobbi's

mouth. Bobbi dragged in a ragged, desperate, excited breath; he bowed his head for a moment, in relief to be free from the face-fucking. His neck was stiff and aching; the pounding in his ass made him want to scream for release even while wanting, needing more up in his rectum. The fullness in his swinging untouched dick was growing. His face glittering with sweat, Bobbi looked up at Thom urgently. 'Play with my tits,' he begged Thom. 'Play with them hard.'

Thom immediately slid to his knees in front of Bobbi, who was still on all fours, though every muscle in his arms and thighs was now visibly trembling with exhaustion and excitement. He reached in between Bobbi's shivering arms with both hands and pinched Bobbi's protuberant nipples between the thumb and forefinger of each, twiddling them roughly. Bobbi gasped gratefully: the electrifying thrills of pleasure sent through Bobbi's chest by Thom's fingers on his nipples, combined with the shuddering excitement turning him inside-out from the good feeling of Gregory ramming the buzzing vibrator in and out of his rectum with ever-increasing vigour and speed, overcame Bobbi. All ability to control his arms, his legs, his bowels, his cock was fucked out of him, and, without him ever touching them, his balls buzzed and his rigid throbbing cock exploded, sending convulsions the length of his body. Repeated spurts of creamy semen shot in spattering arcs over the carpet and Gregory pushed the maximum length of plastic up Bobbi's ass, as hard as he could and as far as it would go. Bobbi cried out with a sobbing gasp of violent ecstasy.

'Oh, fuck me, oh, Jesus, oh, Christ, oh, thank you, oh –' he called out hoarsely, pushing his hips forward in shuddering convulsions onto the carpet, suddenly desperate to empty his ass now as he had emptied his cock. The vibrator slid noisily out of his well-used ass with a sucking pop and Bobbi collapsed exhaustedly face-down onto the welcoming floor beneath him.

Gregory turned off the vibrator. His hard-on was painfully stiff and he realised that he was jealous of Bobbi for getting to suck Thom off, even though he hadn't offered himself. Gregory needed some relief and he didn't want to use his hand. Normally, Gregory was a hundred per cent bottom, but there was something about today; it had become a day of doing things he didn't normally do. He looked down at Bobbi's big ass, his now slightly-open butthole juicy and inviting. On impulse, he slid onto Bobbi's back, his hard-on pressing between Bobbi's buttocks. He flicked his dreadlocks over to one side and nibbled Bobbi's ear playfully. Bobbi groaned softly.

'Hey, man,' Gregory whispered softly, his voice hoarsened by desire.

'Mm?' Bobbi replied. 'What you want, man?'

'Can I fuck you, man? Just quickly? I need my sweet release, man. Please.'

'I thought you were a bottom, Gregory, man,' Bobbi grumbled mildly.

'Yeah, I am, man,' Gregory said quickly. 'But I'd just really like to fuck you.'

'So long as you don't expect me to do nothing,' Bobbi sighed, unable to turn down Gregory's sudden top-man impulse.

Gregory lifted himself up above Bobbi, who opened his legs as he lay face-down on the carpet, and braced himself in a press-up position, every sinew in his lean body standing out clearly. He moved his hips in careful thrusts, sliding his achingly stiff cock up and down between Bobbi's buttocks, before pulling back a little and aiming its smooth swollen head at Bobbi's sphincter. Gregory pressed his cock-head against Bobbi's shiny juicy asshole and pushed it inside. His foreskin slid back as he entered Bobbi, and he was surprised and excited by the tightness of the grip of Bobbi's anal ring around his shaft. Gregory began to pump his hips against

Bobbi's upturned buttocks, surprised too by how pleasant it felt to be fucking Bobbi up the ass, a position he never normally voluntarily sought out.

Thom knelt in front of Gregory and kissed him hotly and wetly on the mouth, while Gregory rammed his cock roughly in and out of Bobbi's now thoroughly open asshole.

'I'd like to see you again,' Thom said huskily after they broke their kiss, toying with Gregory's nipples as Gregory thrust his cock deep into Bobbi. Gregory could feel the excitement and heaviness building in his erection and he found himself staring into Thom's bright blue eyes as he fucked Bobbi, almost as if the excitement in his dick was being generated by Thom's eyes.

'I don't normally check for white guys,' Gregory grunted in reply, at the same time wishing that Thom would climb up behind him and fuck him while he was fucking Bobbi. 'But yeah, I'd like that a lot.' He was moving smoothly towards his climax. He looked down at Bobbi's head. Bobbi's eyes were closed and he breathed in short snuffling snorts in time with each thrust of Gregory's cock up his ass. Gregory pumped his hips harder and then he was coming in Bobbi. He gasped, shuddered as his load squirted into Bobbi's rectum, then withdrew quickly, his cock already softening. It had been pleasant, but it was attention to his own anal opening that constituted the supreme sexual gratification for Gregory. He kissed Bobbi on the shoulder.

'Thanks for letting me fuck you, man,' he said softly, running his hand along Bobbi's side.

'S'nothing, man,' Bobbi said without opening his eyes. 'The pleasure was all mine. Don't sweat it. Come up the bum is good for the complexion.'

Thom stood up beside them, yawned, and stretched his curving muscular arms up and over his head, showing off grooved marble-pale shaven armpits. Then he extended a hand to Gregory, who took it, and helped him to his feet.

The tousled blond body-builder took the slender Rastaman in his arms and kissed him softly on the mouth again.

'I guess we should get dressed,' Thom said after a while of kissing, still holding Gregory loosely in his arms. 'Lay down some killer tracks before the other guys get here. Although, under the circumstances,' he added with a boyish grin, 'I can't say I'm sorry they're late, guy.'

'But time is money, man,' Gregory said, only half-smiling, suddenly feeling whorish and possibly even used.

'I think between the two of you, you've earned a substantial discount,' Thom joked, unaware of Gregory's uneasiness.

'Is all business with you, man,' Gregory said a little sulkily. 'Sexploitation.'

'Not any more,' Thom said, suddenly serious. 'It's . . . something else. I don't know. I feel like I – I *like* you, guy. That's all. Don't sweat it about the money.'

They exchanged a shy, excited glance. After a long moment Gregory said, 'Well, anyway, we best get it together now, man. Business, I mean.' He looked down at Bobbi dozing – or pretending to doze – on the floor: naked, brown, smooth, young and well-fucked.

Together, Gregory and Thom squatted down either side of Bobbi. 'Time to get up, me bredren,' Gregory whispered softly into Bobbi's ear. 'We got music to make and stains to get scrub out of the carpet.'

Three

Horns blared as Don crashed a red light, the battered Rasta-striped Bedford van's tyres screeching noisily as he slewed around a corner onto the Uxbridge Road and headed out west to collect the sound equipment the Boot Sex Massive would need for their first-ever live gig, the following night, from a cheap but reliable hire company that Malcolm had found. Don moved his head aggressively in time with the Public Enemy rap that was pounding out of the van's speakers as he drove, cut up a bus indicating that it was pulling out, and slid through a second series of lights on the amber. A taxi pulled over sharply in front of him to pick up a fare, blocking the road, and Don gave it a lengthy blast on the horn, a payback for all the times racist cabbies had left him standing in the rain. Its passenger collected, the taxi pulled off awkwardly. Don drove too close to the back of it, harrying it until it turned off down a side-street.

He was in a really bad-mood now. Malcolm, his best friend, his spar, was seriously pissed off with him, and with good reason. He didn't want to see Kam again. And by now Gregory would be seriously pissed off with him too, again with good reason. Probably even all-smiles Bobbi was mad at him over something. He checked his Rolex and kissed his teeth: he was even later than he had thought.

A police-car, sirens wailing, shot past him. For a moment, he thought it was going to cut across and stop him for some reason (a phoney tax-disc check, a lie about the van being reported stolen) but, mercifully it didn't. One time, Don had been stopped by the pigs over some alleged report about a mugging, and he had ended up giving the policeman who stopped him a hard butt-stuffing with his own truncheon in the back of his cop-car. The beefy buzz-cut and flush-faced young constable, trousers and under-pants round his ankles, had ignored all calls for assistance while Don slammed his spit-slicked truncheon in and out of the cop's accommodating back-passage. After the con-stable had come, Don had made him suck him off as an afterthought, threatening him with harassment charges and an official complaint if he didn't. The cop had been happy enough to take up this bit of extra unscheduled voluntary community liaison work.

Don found himself getting stiff at the memory of his horny session with the cop, adding to the mounting frus-tration of the day. But, for the moment, it looked like all he was going to be humping this morning was sound equip-ment, he thought as he turned into the broad shopping street which led to the drab industrial estate where the hire company's small warehouse was located.

He pulled up outside the warehouse door, applied the hand-brake and got out of the van. There wasn't anyone in the small reception area, so he wandered round the side of it and into the warehouse proper. Shinehead's 'A Jamaican In New York' was playing tinnily over a radio somewhere out of sight, and the funny, rootsy track cheered Don up a bit. Still, there was no one to be seen.

'Anyone there?' Don called after looking around for a bit. 'Yo, shop!'

A moment later, a tekkie came out from behind a large pile of disassembled sound-stages and video-screens and Don's expression soured. Not only was the lean youth before him a skinhead with a zero crop, braces and Doc Martin boots, but he was actually wearing a Union Jack T-shirt. Don's eyes narrowed and he wondered how Malcolm – usually Mister Black Business – could possibly have recom-mended such a company. The fact that the skin had a good hard physique and nicely shaped arms, and even that the bulge in his skin-tight stone-washed jeans was substantial, just added to Don's annoyance and frustration at the whole situation.

The skinhead, who looked to be around twenty, held out his hand confidently for Don to shake, smiling. 'Hello there, mate. I'm Stevo,' he said in a strong South London accent. Don noticed that although he was wearing the figure-hugging Union Jack T-shirt, he was also wearing two red, gold and green Rasta buttons and, round his right wrist, he wore a silver Pakistani bangle. After a moment's hesitation, Don took Stevo's hand; he shook it firmly and let go of it quickly.

'Don. A mate of mine arranged for some equipment to be picked up. Malcolm.'

'Yeah, I remember him. I've got the list here,' Stevo said, glancing at a yellow receipt attached to a clipboard he was holding in his left hand. 'Speakers, mikes, mixing deck, amp . . .' he checked his way down the list, glancing over as he did so at a pile of sound equipment stacked up in the middle of the warehouse. 'Yeah, it's all there. I'll help you load it. You got a van?'

'Yeah. Thanks, man,' Don said, annoyed once again that he had been lumbered with the lumping job while the other members of the band could sit around smoking spliffs and being creative. Don was the rapper of the group, the poet, he felt. Okay, so he was no musician, but that didn't mean he had to be a beast of burden. He ran a hand over his shaven head, rubbed his tired face.

'You got a nice build, Don,' Stevo said, watching the short muscular black man as he flexed his arms and stretched, and furtively admiring the way the bulge of his crotch filled the front of his tight-fitting 501s. 'You work out a lot?'

'A couple of hours a day, most days,' Don said as Stevo handed him an arms-length of cables, leads and adaptors.

Don slipped them onto his arm up to the shoulder, then went outside and opened up the back of the Bedford van and dropped the cables inside, near the front. The lighter things they could manage separately, but the larger speakers were a two-man job. There was more equipment than Don had expected, and it took the two of them some time to load it all up. Once they'd got it all loaded into a van, they sat down sweatily for a quick fag-break – Stevo's offer. A subtle, indirect flirtation had been building between them all the time as they worked. Don cupped his hands around the match Stevo proffered to light his cigarette, pressing his fingertips against Stevo's wrist, feeling the pulsing of Stevo's blood against his skin. The lean crop-haired white youth held the match in place until he had to drop it, rather than break the small physical contact with the handsome shaven-headed black man sitting before him.

We're on, Don thought. *But do I want to get it on with this guy?* The Union Jack seemed very prominent in the cramped interior of the Bedford. Stevo was good-looking, fit, interested and looked to be well-hung, but still –

'Why you wear that flag, man?' Don asked suddenly, dropping his cigarette and treading the butt out on the ridged metal floor of the van.

''Cause I'm proud of who I am,' Stevo said, his mouth slightly parted, his grey-blue eyes clouding doubtfully. 'I don't mean it against others or nothing.'

'And what about those?' Don said, indicating the Rasta buttons.

'When I first done a stretch, a two-year stretch in Brixton,' Stevo said, dragging the last of his own cigarette, 'yeah, I admit it, I was ignorant and, you know, yeah, I guess, racist.' He looked away from Don for a moment. 'But then I ended up sharing a cell with these two guys; one of 'em was Jamaican and the other was Pakistani. And they enlightened me, man. Shit, they enlightened me so good that when my bird was up, I didn't hardly want to leave, you know what I'm saying? Two pints of piss for breakfast. Two loads of come for lunch and two cocks up the same ass at the same time after lights out and all of that shit –'

Don's dick snapped to full rigidity inside his black denims. He shifted his sitting posture to try and stop the rigid shaft of his aroused penis crushing his balls painfully.

'At first it was all what they wanted. I'd do it but I wasn't really into it. But then it was, like, I guess, I kind of got to enjoying it and they liked it more that I was enjoying it, 'cause then I'd please them more,' Stevo continued. 'And shit, man, I really *liked* those guys, you know? And the shit they got from racism, the shit *I'd* have given 'em before I learnt better, it made me feel really bad. So now, if it's a black guy or an Asian guy, I'll let 'em do whatever they want, or I'll do whatever they want: kind of to pay back, you know what I'm saying? *Anything*, man. And the Union Jack kind of gets guys stirred up, reminds them of all that prejudice. And then I let them take it out of me.'

Don could feel that his face was bloating with unexpected excitement. The lean compact skinhead's account of his time in prison had turned him on, perversely, and now the boy was begging to be used as extremely as possible. *And why not?* Don thought as his cock-head pressed painfully against the seam of his jeans, the rough fabric cutting into his slit, pulling it open.

Don rose to his feet. 'I'm gonna give you the hardest, roughest fuck you've ever had in your life, man,' he said gruffly. 'Turn round.'

Stevo turned round without another word and slid the braces off his broad shoulders in a single sinuous movement. Then he peeled off his T-shirt to reveal a butter-warm, pale, well-defined back that tapered to a narrow waist, and threw it to the ground. Don quickly stepped to the back of the van as Stevo pulled his trousers down to his ankles, sliding down the link-door to give them some privacy. Stevo was wearing Union Jack briefs too. They stretched tightly over his neat muscular ass. He hooked his thumbs in the waist-band of them and made to pull them down too.

'Don't do that, man,' Don ordered, positioning himself so he was standing behind Stevo. Stevo let his hands fall to his sides, let Don take charge. Don fumblingly unbuckled his belt and tugged at te top button of his 501s with one hand, fondling Stevo's ass through the fabric with the other, perversely excited. Then he slapped Stevo's ass with the palm of his hand – not too hard, but hard enough to feel real – and reached between Stevo's lean thighs to squeeze his ball-sack hard. Stevo grunted softly as Don applied pressure to his balls. The pale skinhead's words, *I'll do anything*, flicked into Don's mind.

Anything? Don came to a decision: that he would test Stevo a little on that, see how far 'anything' would go. He gripped his hanging belt-buckle and slid the smooth black leather length of his belt out from around his narrow waist. He doubled the belt over and snapped it sharply. Stevo flinched in excited anticipation, then pumped his butt-cheeks, flexing them, pushing them out, drawing attention to them.

'I'm gonna strap your ass, man,' Don said softly. 'Warm it up a bit before fucking it with my long hard dick.'

'Strap my ass hard,' Stevo whispered huskily.

'I'm gonna strap that Union Jack-covered ass until that flag over it is torn right off it and then I'm going to fuck the shit out of you, man. With no lube. You'll be begging me to stop, but I'll keep right on fucking you till I've finished.'

'My ass is already so open for your thick black dick, I don't need no lube,' Stevo gasped, without even glancing back at Don. 'I need to feel the friction, man. Just use my ass hard, any way you want. Just get off in my hot white ass,' he added imploringly.

Don swung his well-muscled dark brown arm and brought the belt down on Stevo's upturned buttocks with a loud crack. Stevo gasped loudly as the sharp pain lanced hotly across his ass. Juice started to drip freely from Stevo's cockhead, staining the front of his Union Jack briefs. Don brought the belt down on Stevo's buttocks again, harder this time, the smack of leather on pale, fabric-covered muscle louder; Stevo gasped again, louder too. His buttocks were already starting to feel hot all over, and he felt certain that, as he had so desperately hoped, his session with Don was going to be lengthy and hard. He closed his eyes and anticipated the next stroke of the smooth, hard leather on his eagerly-offered and rapidly reddening butt.

'Oh yeah!' he called out as the belt cracked against his ass again. Stevo had initially been afraid that Don was going to turn out to be too vanilla to give him any real punishment, but this anxiety was quickly removed by the genuine enthusiasm with which Don was strapping his warming buttocks. The pain of the repeated blows on his upturned ass was becoming exquisite to Stevo, and he wondered if he could come just from having his ass whipped, so great was the excitement that each strike of the belt sent shooting through his asshole to his tightly clenched balls.

Suddenly, Don was straddling Stevo from behind, dangling the belt in front of Stevo's face, grinding his rigid denim-covered crotch against Stevo's inflamed buttocks as he did so. He roughly caressed Stevo's pink-flushed cheek, his tip-tilted nose, his ruddy, bloated lips with the belt. 'Kiss it,' Don ordered. Stevo kissed the soft leather obediently. Don moved it away from his face and stood up again. 'I'm gonna give you the buckle end this time, man,' he said throatily.

'Give it to me, Don,' Stevo begged him, leaning forward against the wall of the van and sticking his buttocks out as far as he could. 'Work it all out on my ass.'

Don cracked the buckle hard on Stevo's upturned butt, and a tear appeared in Stevo's Union Jack briefs. Don's cock was so achingly stiff that he knew he would have to give in and fuck Stevo soon but, at the moment, he was enjoying taking out the frustrations of the day – and maybe other frustrations too – on the skinhead's eager ass too much to stop right away. Don had never had anyone beg him for serious abuse, and he was finding it unexpectedly exciting.

An idea came into Don's mind. He brought the buckle down particularly sharply onto Stevo's ass, then turned and looked round at the pile of leads and cables by the door of the van. Bending over, he rummaged quickly among the thinner leads until he found what he was looking for: crocodile clips, small but with a fierce grip. He picked them up, palming them.

'Turn around,' he ordered Stevo. Stevo did so. His face was flushed almost purple with excitement and his hard-on jutted out rigidly inside his briefs, stretching them out almost ten inches from his lean flat stomach, its swollen and circumcised head clearly outlined by the sodden fabric above the bulge of his balls. Although he was so seriously turned on, Stevo made no move to touch himself, to pleasure himself; his hands hung down by his sides as he stood in front of Don, submissive and heavily aroused, his pleasure lying in anticipating what Don would do to him next. His pink nipples were small and dark and stiff. His chest heaved. His pale skin was flushing red at its extremities. Don, his face excited, his lust-filled eyes dull and giving nothing away, reached up for Stevo's nipples with both hands, a metal clip concealed between each thumb and forefinger, and dextrously and mercilessly attached them to Stevo's protruding tits.

Stevo gasped sharply as ecstatic pain shot through his chest; his cock bucked in his briefs as he almost shot his load at the sudden extra excitement. 'Turn back around, man,' Don continued. 'I ain't finished strapping your ass yet.'

Stevo did what he was told, and Don resumed cracking the buckle-end of his belt on Stevo's eager buttocks. Don strapped the moaning, gasping skinhead for what felt like twenty minutes, until his right arm began to ache with tiredness. His hard-on was throbbing painfully and he badly needed to fuck Stevo's ass with it. Stevo's briefs were only slightly ripped by the buckle and the frustration was becoming too much for Don. Finally, he threw the belt down, wriggled a finger from each hand into one of the small rips and tore the fabric open sharply, exposing Stevo's now very red cheeks. Tearing the fabric somehow excited Don in its roughness; he gripped the waist-band of Stevo's briefs and, with a vigorous wrench and a sharp shredding sound, tore them right off him, twisting Stevo's long stiff cock painfully as he did so. Stevo gasped as his hard-on slapped up audibly against his lean belly.

'Turn round,' Don ordered the skinhead. Stevo did so. His young, boyish face was red, his mouth shiny, his lips swollen, his grey-blue eyes bright with excitement. 'Open your mouth,' Don said. Stevo did so eagerly. Then Don stuffed the torn flag briefs into Stevo's wide-open mouth, gagging the heavily aroused skinhead with them. Don then adjusted the crocodile clips on Stevo's tits so he wouldn't lose circulation – and the thrilling awareness of pain – in his nipples, gripped Stevo's hips and turned him round again so he was facing the wall. 'I'm gonna fuck you now, man. Get that asshole ready for this big hard black cock.'

Stevo pushed his legs apart and bent over a speaker so his ass was higher than his head, flexing his hard pink ass-cheeks excitedly for Don as he did so, the muscles in his lean thighs tensing in time with them in smooth lozenge shapes. Don gripped Stevo's reddened ass-cheeks with strong hands and pulled them open, exposing Stevo's trembling asshole. He inclined his head, pursed his full lips and spat onto Stevo's puckered pink anal ring. Then Don finally unzipped his own jeans and pushed them and his black cotton trunks down to his ankles. His erection sprang up stiffly, the veins along its length pulsing visibly under the dark brown skin. He licked the pink palm of his hand and stroked his long rigid pole with it, lubricating it with spittle. Then, without warning or preparation, he stepped forward, aimed his stiff cock between Stevo's reddened buttocks and rubbed the head of it up and down between them, until he felt the indentation of Stevo's puckered hole against the smooth sensitive tip. He gripped Stevo's shoulder with one hand and, keeping his cock in alignment with Stevo's anal opening with the other, shoved it right the way up Stevo's ass in one firm stroke. Stevo grunted and struggled forward, his rectum overstuffed and overstretched by Don's long thick cock, but Don held him in place, forcing Stevo to relax his insides and accommodate the entirety of Don's rigid, throbbing erection inside him.

'Oh, Don, oh, shit, you've giving it to me, man, you're giving it to me good,' Stevo groaned as Don pulled back a little and then rammed his shaven crotch even harder against Stevo's ass; the whole lean, pale and muscular length of Stevo's body, from his calves and thighs to his shoulders, tensed.

'Grip your cheeks and spread them open,' Don ordered. 'I want to get this long stiff cock even further up you.'

'Jesus, I don't think I can –' Stevo said hoarsely, his face purple and sweaty.

'*Do it*,' Don commanded. 'You said you'd take anything a black man wanted to give you. Now you're going to.'

Stevo stopped complaining and reached back obediently

to pull his ass-cheeks open. Don rammed a further quarter-inch of cock up him and their balls banged together, sending electrical thrills up through both their bodies, unifying them. Then Don rotated his hips, swivelling his ten-inch cock around inside Stevo, stretching Stevo's rectum still further with his hot stiff throbbing length. As he did this, Don felt Stevo's tensed shoulders start to relax, indicating that he was accommodating Don's hard-on comfortably now. But Don didn't want Stevo to be relaxed. He pulled his hips all the way back, evacuating all ten inches of his stiff length from Stevo's rectum abruptly, leaving Stevo's glistening pink hole gaping and dripping. Stevo gasped again, in relief at the emptiness, the lack of pressure, and in frustration at being deprived of the fullness, the thrilling pressing of hot cockhead firm against his prostate.

A moment later, and again without warning, Don rammed his cock all the way up Stevo's now-accommodating anal passage again, and Stevo drew his breath in sharp ragged gasps as Don began to fuck the skinhead's ass in long, smooth strokes. Don pounded Stevo's ass hard, gripping Stevo from behind by both shoulders so he could ram his cock up Stevo's open asshole faster, harder and rougher. Don took one hand off Stevo's shoulder and reached for the belt that was lying on a speaker beside him, never ceasing to pump his hips against Stevo's hot pink buttocks as he did so. He slid the belt around Stevo's face until it was over Stevo's mouth. The black leather length was just narrow enough to fit between Stevo's open lips like a bridle. Don gripped both ends of the belt and yanked on it so that Stevo's head was pulled up and back sharply, from behind. The veins in the sides of Stevo's neck stood out and he gasped throatily around the briefs filling his mouth and the belt gagging it, as Don kept on fucking him hard.

Don dragged on the belt like a rider breaking in a bronco; sweat running down the sides of his shaven head and waxed chest; he felt like a cowboy as he braced his weight back against the belt round Stevo's head, and pumped his hips up hard against Stevo's still-red buttocks. He pumped his rigid heavy cock in and out of Stevo's slack asshole. Pre-come was sliding in rivulets out of Stevo's open hole and trickling down the insides of his lean thighs in glistening strands. Don looked down at his thick glittering brown shaft as it slid in and out, in and out of Stevo's muscular pink ass, Stevo grunting in time with each thrust, and felt excitement beginning to throb uncontrollably along its length.

'I can't take any more,' Stevo tried to moan, unable to bear the horny vigorous ramming that Don was subjecting him to; his words were muffled to incomprehensibility by the briefs, now sodden with spit, filling his belted mouth. He felt like his asshole was going to explode with any more anal pounding. But Don only rammed his dick in and out of Stevo's butt even faster and harder. Stevo's heart began to race: what was he doing, submitting to this dominant, wild, frustrated black man who looked set to turn him inside out? He was fucking Stevo so hard, so deep, so – *good*.

Don could feel the weight in his blood-stiffened pulsing cock reaching critical mass, as he pumped it in and out of Stevo's juicy asshole. His breathing was coming in short gasps now and his chest was tight. 'Oh, fuck, oh, fuck, I'm gonna come, man; I'm gonna come –' he yelled, slamming his cock up Stevo's ass as hard and far as he could, so hard that he was shoving Stevo up onto the tips of his toes with each thrust. Don's balls clenched with painful suddenness. His big muscular buttocks clenched, too, and his cock exploded inside Stevo's ass in sudden, violent spurts. Don kept his dick slammed right the way up Stevo, sending convulsions of excitement the length of Stevo's body with each wave of hot black man's spunk that shot inside him.

After his load was fully discharged, Don slid the belt out

of Stevo's mouth and let it fall to the ground. Then he bent forward over Stevo's slumped back and kissed the lightly flushed nape of Stevo's freshly cropped neck.

'Thanks, man,' Don said, perfectly sincerely. 'That did give me some relief.'

He straightened up and, gripping Stevo's waist, withdrew his cock gently from Stevo's now-gaping asshole. A glob of creamy white come dripped from Stevo's open pink hole and fell to the floor of the van as Stevo straightened, too.

The sight of the come gave Don another idea. He pulled the briefs out of Stevo's mouth and Stevo gasped for breath; his lean chest heaved and his long circumcised cock was red and stiff and throbbing purple at its large swollen head. Then Don reached for the crocodile-clips on the skinhead's nipples, but changed his mind and left them clamped in place.

'Beat yourself off,' Don ordered Stevo. Stevo, his face flushed with excitement, his slim and hard-muscled body shiny with sweat, did as he was told, moving the fist of his right hand fast on his painfully hard hot cock. As he did this, Don ran his hand between Stevo's buttocks and slid several fingers up Stevo's slack hole. He worked them in Stevo's ass expertly and, after a few moments, slid them out and glanced at them. As Don had hoped, his fingers were sticky with the come he'd just shot up Steve's bunghole, mingled with Stevo's own ass-juices. He brought the fingers up to Stevo's face.

'Eat my come,' Don ordered Stevo. Stevo wanked himself more vigorously as he bent his cropped head forward and sucked Don's thick dark fingers clean of jism. Don kept his fingers in Stevo's mouth, mildly enjoying the warm wet suction on them, and twisted round and picked his belt up off the floor. He doubled the belt over again in one hand and began to crack it idly on Stevo's well-used buttocks.

'Oh, yeah,' Stevo groaned around Don's fingers. 'Harder,

man, harder. Strap my ass harder.' Stevo's fist was moving very fast on his cock now, and its smooth swollen head was shiny with his excitement. Don obliged him with vigorous cracks on his quivering taut reddened buttocks and, with a sudden grunt, Stevo jerked his hips forward and shot his load all over the speaker with rapid pelvic jerks. Don let the belt hang down by his side and pulled his fingers out of Stevo's mouth. Stevo immediately sank to his knees in front of Don and sucked for a few moments on Don's now less than half-erect cock, as if milking it for any more of the come that had been shot up his ass earlier. When he had sucked Don's dick clean, he finally let it slip from his mouth.

'Did I give you satisfaction?' he asked Don breathlessly, looking up from where he was kneeling in front of him, the horny young skin's facial expression ambiguous. *Christ*, Don thought, *surely he doesn't want more?*

'Lick up all that spunk you shot over the speaker and I'll be satisfied,' Don said gruffly, trying to sound domineering. Now Don had shot his load, the whole scene seemed a bizarre, mad fantasy: almost as if it hadn't happened. Stevo immediately went to work on his hands and knees, eagerly licking up his own come off the grainy matt black surface. Don glanced at his watch and kissed his teeth. The time he had gained by driving here recklessly and crashing red lights had more than been lost on his session with Stevo. Still, he now felt in a better frame of mind to make the most of the day: on the balance, things were looking up.

Now he had some idea of why Malcolm might have recommended this company. Who knew what strange fantasies Stevo had encouraged Malcolm to explore, to get off on? *This is it, Malcolm*, Don thought to himself as he buttoned his 501s, pushing his cock down into place, adjusted his balls, and slid his well-used belt into place. Free, hot sex. *That's reality. That's what masculinity is. Com-*

mitment ain't natural, man. And yet somehow, even as these thoughts filled his head, a little think of doubt opened in the corner of Don's mind. He pushed it away as he did up his belt-buckle and tucked in his tight white T-shirt, but it returned to float around his head, somewhere just out of sight. He checked his Rolex again and pursed his lips.

At that exact same moment, Gregory was checking his watch at the recording studio and cursing Don. He wasn't best pleased that Malcolm wasn't there yet either, but at least the drummer had laid down enough material at the last session for Gregory to be doing some useful work on the vocals in the meantime.

'I mean, the gig's tomorrow night, man,' he complained to Bobbi over a spliff, tossing back his mane of dreads. Thom had gone to the studio storeroom for some fresh DATs, propping the door open for ventilation and leaving them along together for a couple of minutes. 'I mean, shit, man. It like him *want* the gig to bad, you know?' He passed the spliff to Bobbi, who dragged on it then handed it back.

'I'm sure Don wants it to go well,' Bobbi said reassuringly. 'It's just he seems to be having a lot of fights with Malcolm, lately. Like an old married couple, you know?' He was struck by his observation and drew his carefully-groomed eyebrows together in sudden thoughtfulness. He shot an inquisitive look over at Gregory. 'You don't reckon him and Malcolm –?'

'What, you mean –?' Gregory said, then shook his head. 'Nah, man. Them both top-top top-man. Plug looking for socket. If one of them got to bending over for the other, though . . .' he added, shrugging, doubting it. He had first met Malcolm at a sex-party four or five years earlier – Gregory had been a regular at black sex-parties in and around Brixton and Peckham before he had foxed up – and been impressed by the honey-skinned brother's vigorous topping of five eager brothers in the course of a single evening. Gregory had even been on the receiving end of Malcolm's substantial *café-au-lait* pole at another party, and had had his own tight asshole well satisfied. When they had met again, several years later, Malcolm hadn't recognised the now-Rastafarian Gregory, and Gregory hadn't felt it would help the band's dynamic to remind him that he'd once had his cock right the way up the lead singer's shapely ass. And anyway, since then, Gregory had pretty much renounced the pleasures of cock for the exciting demands outsize sex-toys made on his anal cave. 'What man can say?' he continued speculatively. He laughed a little to himself. 'Maybe them fucking right now.'

But even as he said that, they heard the sound of Malcolm's Kawasaki roaring along the quiet, tree-lined Brixton street. The studio was stuffy in the July heat, so Gregory and Bobbi ambled out onto the pavement to see him arrive and get some air, while waiting for Thom to return from the storeroom.

Malcolm looked handsome and very sexy, Gregory had to admit, as he watched the tall light-skinned and leather-clad black man pulling up on his stream-lined, gleaming chrome and steel dream-machine, the swelling burgundy leather saddle curving up suggestively between his spread thighs as he leant back in it and drew up with a throaty rumble in front of them. He kicked out the bike-stand with one booted foot, pulled off his helmet and ran a hand over his immaculately symmetrical cane-rows, to make sure they hadn't been messed up by it.

'Sorry I'm late, me bredren,' he said as he swung off the motorbike. Gregory and Bobbi both admired his big muscular ass as he did so. It was hard to be mad at a guy who had such a great ass. Also, Malcolm looked to be in a bad mood, so it wasn't as if he was sauntering up hours after he was due, with some tale of a hot trick he hadn't been able to turn down – the sort of thing Don would do. Or Bobbi, for that matter, Gregory thought to himself. But Bobbi usually managed to wring some funny tale or another out of his sexploits, and it was hard to be mad at someone who could make you laugh. 'Don here yet?' Malcolm asked. The other two shook their heads.

Malcolm didn't look disappointed.

Behind them, Thom came out onto the stoop. He smiled when he saw Malcolm standing there. 'How's it hanging, mate?' Thom asked, stepping forward so they could touch fists.

'To me knees, man,' Malcolm said: their stock exchange.

Thom turned to Gregory. 'I only need you at the moment, man,' he said. 'Just to finish laying down the BVs we were doing earlier.' To Bobbi and Malcolm: 'You might as well get a bit of sun while we're getting this done. It shouldn't take long.'

Malcolm and Bobbi nodded, and ambled off to go and sit on a low brick wall in front of the studio that looked out over a bit of scrubby, parched parkland. Gregory went inside with Thom. The moment they were gone, Malcolm turned to Bobbi confidentially. 'I'm so mad, man,' he said quickly. 'That bitch Kam's been cheating on me with my so-called best mate.'

'Don?' Bobbi's big eyes widened. 'Shit.'

'Yeah. I passed by his yard this morning and Don had his cock *and* balls shoved down Kam's fucking throat, man. And the fucker didn't even *apologise*, you know what I'm saying? He just shot his load over the fucking place. All over my fucking boyfriend. Fucking *ex*-boyfriend.'

'How awful, man,' Bobbi said, shifting his ass slightly on the wall as he imagined the scene; his dick began to stiffen inside his tight white shorts and press uncomfortably against his ball-sack. 'It's not fair.'

'Yeah,' Malcolm agreed. Then, unsure, he asked, 'What's not fair?'

'That nobody sucked *you* off,' Bobbi said. His cock was now fully-erect inside his shorts. 'I mean, if *I'd* been Kam, I'd have felt obliged at least to blow you too.'

'Yeah, but –' Malcolm protested, feeling that Bobbi was missing the point, which was Don's betrayal of him, his spar. But then he glanced down and caught sight of the thick oblique bulge in Bobbi's shorts. And the truth was, talking about seeing Don pounding his cock in Kam's throat had got the blood pumping into his pole as well, even as anger at the memory had flushed his face. 'You would have, man?' he asked Bobbi. 'Blown me?'

Bobbi smiled boyishly. 'Sure. Don't you believe me?' His smile broadened in response to Malcolm's sceptical expression. 'There's only one way I can prove it to you, man. C'mon.' He got up off the wall and headed for the studio door, beckoning for Malcolm to follow him.

Once inside they mounted a narrow staircase, Malcolm staring at Bobbi's beefy, tightly-constrained ass as they climbed, and went through the second door on the landing, into the studio washroom. It was a largish room, white and clean with a toilet, a shower unit, a bath, a sink, and a large rectangular wicker laundry hamper in one corner. Sunlight streamed in warmly through the dimpled glass window. Malcolm locked the door behind them, unzipped his leather jacket and let it fall to the floor, exposing broad shoulders encased in tight white cotton and curving pectorals. Bobbi pulled the chest-shaped wicker hamper into the middle of the room.

'Sit down, man,' he said gently to Malcolm. Malcolm sat and Bobbi went behind him and began to massage his shoulders through the thin cotton of his T-shirt.

'You've got a lot of knots,' he said softly.

Bobbi kneaded Malcolm's muscular neck and upper back for a while, then bent forward and pulled Malcolm's T-shirt out from where it was tucked into his tight leather trousers and up from around his waist. Malcolm raised his muscular arms and let Bobbi peel the T-shirt off him and drop it in a corner. Then Bobbi worked on Malcolm's shoulders again, his hands now pressing on Malcolm's smooth bare light-brown flesh. Malcolm groaned as Bobbi worked his way expertly down his spine. His back began to soften and relax, but Bobbi's attentive touch was ensuring that his cock was stiffer than ever. Malcolm hoped that, after his flirty lead-up to this massage, Bobbi wasn't going to cop out of giving Malcolm the full relief he'd implied he was offering.

Malcolm needn't have worried; the pretty, dark-skinned lad was looking forward to sucking Malcolm's light-brown cock as much as Malcolm was looking forward to having it sucked. Perhaps even more: because Bobbi was a connoisseur of come – of jism, spunk, man-juice – and was eager to taste Malcolm's, see how it compared in thickness and flavour to the load Thom had shot in his mouth half an hour before. And Bobbi was feeling frustrated too, by the opportunity he had missed earlier: if he had only thought more sharply when Gregory had unexpectedly asked to fuck him at the end of their three-way, he could have rolled over onto his back and said, 'You can't fuck my ass, but you can fuck my face.' And then Bobbi could have lain there, and Gregory would have mounted his face, plugged Bobbi's mouth instead of his asshole with his juicy ebony-dark cock, and Bobbi could have got a mouthful of Gregory's spunk to taste, too. Annoyed at missing that opportunity, Bobbi wasn't going to let Malcolm get away without shooting his load into Bobbi's eager mouth.

Bobbi was so greedy for jism that, on the rare occasions where he didn't get a mouthful of someone else's, he would do a shoulder-stand and bend his legs over so his feet were touching the floor behind him and his cock and balls were hanging over his face, and beat off into his own mouth. But he was young and dark and pretty; not many guys turned down the offer of a free blow-job from an eager cock-sucker as cute as Bobbi. In an idle moment, Bobbi had worked out that, in an average week, he probably swallowed down near enough a pint of hot spunk, all of it shot fresh from the cock. He was even working on a song celebrating the taste of jism, entitled *Hot Load*. He doubted whether he'd be able to persuade Gregory to sing it, though, let alone record it.

As Bobbi massaged Malcolm's shoulders, he rubbed his cotton-covered hard-on against Malcolm's back in slow, rhythmic motions to keep Malcolm reminded that sex was in the offing. 'That feel good, man?' he asked, enjoying the feeling of his constrained cock-head against Malcolm's muscular shoulder-blades. Malcolm mumbled an affirmative and tilted his head to one side, closing his eyes.

'Would you suck me off now, man?' Malcolm asked eventually, his deep rich voice sexy, inviting. It was impossible for Bobbi to refuse, even if he had wanted to – even if he hadn't already tacitly made the offer.

'Sure,' Bobbi said, and moved round in front of Malcolm. Malcolm looked at the pretty young man with the orange-cropped hair standing dark and lovely in front of him, all dressed in white, shifting his hips from side to side because his turned-on cock was so heavy and thick and stiff in his shorts. *Well, he isn't Kam*, Malcolm thought, *but he sure is keen*. Malcolm began to unbutton his black leather biker's trousers.

At the pop of the first button, Bobbi sank to his knees before Malcolm, his lips parting expectantly. The pile of the carpet was soft and fluffy beneath his knees, ideal for kneeling: unlike lino, cording or earth: Bobbi was used to being on his knees. Malcolm clenched his buttocks, lifting them slightly so Bobbi could tug the soft heavy material of the leather trousers down to his knees, then fold them down over Malcolm's bike-boots. Malcolm's erection throbbed hotly inside his tightly stretched white cotton Calvin Klein's.

The contrast of the smooth *café-au-lait* brownness of Malcolm's muscular thighs and lean ridged stomach with the snowy whiteness of the briefs excited Bobbi even more. He bent forward and nuzzled the thick constrained curve of Malcolm's uncut cock through the fabric with his nose, cheek and lips, smelling the smell of clean laundry, and nuzzled Malcolm's large heavy ball-sack like a cat, rubbing his flat nose between Malcolm's testicles and eliciting a soft gasp and a sensual shudder from the handsome broad-shouldered brother sitting, thighs parted, above him.

Bobbi began to kiss the length of Malcolm's shaft, enjoying the feeling of its hot rigidity, the texture of the veins even through the cotton, the smoothness of the ridge of gristle running along its underside. He kissed the large blunt head that was now pushing up against the constraining waist-band of the briefs, and licked at the small dark stain where pre-come had oozed from the slit and dampened the fabric. Then Bobbi reached up with both hands, stroking Malcolm's smooth thighs firmly as he did so, gripped the waist-band of Malcolm's Calvins, and pulled them down to his ankles in one fast motion. Malcolm's cock sprang up and slapped his muscular light-brown belly with a sharp noise. Having his erection suddenly freed made Malcolm gasp in both excitement and relief, and the air felt cool and dry on his sweaty crotch.

Bobbi kissed the length of Malcolm's now-exposed cock, enjoying the taste of sweat and salt on his small but poutily full and sharply defined lips. He pulled Malcolm's foreskin back firmly, exposing the browny-pink smoothness of his cock-head, then began to nibble the shaft of Malcolm's quivering erection carefully with his strong, white teeth, working his way along its underside to the frenum, and finally moving up and kissing the top of Malcolm's swollen glans. A gratifying shiny clear drop of pre-come immediately beaded out of Malcolm's slit. Bobbi immediately kissed it up and then finally put his warm wet mouth over Malcolm's cock-head.

Malcolm moaned in pleasure and let his head loll back, his eyes closed, concentrating on nothing but the good feeling of Bobbi's eager attentive mouth on his throbbing hard-on. Bobbi sucked on Malcolm's head for a moment, then let the rigid cock spring out of his mouth. Malcolm gasped, excited but frustrated – but then pleased as Bobbi kissed and licked his way back down Malcolm's rigid brown shaft and began to kiss and suck on Malcolm's heavy balls.

From down in the studio below, Malcolm could hear the faint sound of Gregory's sweet high vocals as he reworked a version of Bob Marley's 'Kinky Reggae' – with rather kinkier lyrics of his own.

'Mmm,' Malcolm sighed, feeling like the song was the perfect back-drop for his session with Bobbi. 'Get those balls in your mouth, man. I wanna feel both my balls filling up your mouth.'

Bobbi angled his head obediently and pushed his face between Malcolm's tensed thighs. He sucked one ball, then the other, into his now wide open mouth, then drew his lips together at the base of Malcolm's scrotum. To have his mouth filled this way excited Bobbi. He worked his tongue around the ball-sack now almost overflowing his mouth, enjoying its weight and the smoothness of the skin of Malcolm's scrotum. Bobbi's nose was pressed firmly into the tight coils of Malcolm's neatly-clipped pubic hair and Malcolm's crotch smelt of sweat and soap and cocoa-butter. Malcolm's stiff cock throbbed angularly across Bobbi's inclined face and a drop of pre-come fell from its slit and onto Bobbi's satin-smooth cheek like a tear.

Bobbi drew his head back and let Malcolm's balls fall

gently from his mouth with a sigh and a soft sucking sound. Then he put a hand around the base of Malcolm's thick hard cock, bent it upwards, away from Malcolm's belly and, pulling back a smooth length of foreskin, put his lips around Malcolm's swollen cock-head. Then he swallowed the whole nine inches of Malcolm's throbbing, achingly stiff shaft into his mouth, gurgling and swallowing to get the head down his throat, fighting the gag reflex in order to get all of Malcolm's cock in his mouth at one go; he was excited by the feeling of Malcolm's crisp pubic hair against his lips and the rigidity of Malcolm's swollen manhood in his mouth.

'Oh, yeah,' Malcolm moaned. 'Oh, man, suck it. Oh, baby, do all the work . . . Oh, yeah . . .'

Bobbi began to pump his mouth up and down on Malcolm's pulsing erection responsively. He enjoyed being with a real man like Malcolm, who would let him suck all the cock he wanted and wouldn't spoil it for Bobbi by offering to suck *him*. Bobbi didn't generally use his own – thick and rather long – cock for anything, except as an inviting package to get another guy turned on. 'I'm a hundred per cent bitch in the sheets,' he would emphasise. 'I've got two hungry holes and I get all the gratification I need from having them filled. My cock's just a show-piece. And for beating off, if I can't get it in the mouth or up the ass. But I don't want it getting any attention in the bedroom, 'cause that means you're neglecting my holes. A real man's into getting sucked and fucking. Are you a real man?'

His brazen come-on got him a lot of offers – rising to the challenge of being true top men – and also helped him avoid awkward bottom-bottom mistakes (although he had once managed a truly memorable session with a lean, muscular Thai go-go boy who was brazenly passive too, and a double-headed dildo, Bobbi and the Thai boy ending up in frantic competition to see who could gobble the most length of rubber up his accommodating backside. But, although the Thai youth had let Bobbi eat his come while shoving the dildo up Bobbi with enthusiasm, Bobbi usually favoured the real thing). He moved his mouth more quickly on Malcolm's hot sweet stiff cock, gripping his lips firmly around its slick shiny shaft, grateful that Malcolm had needed his attention.

'Oh, yeah, suck me, man,' Malcolm ordered throatily, enjoying the good feeling of Bobbi's hot wet mouth on his stiff dick. As Bobbi eagerly pumped his mouth faster and faster on Malcolm's throbbing erection, Malcolm felt the rage of the morning melt away. All that mattered was the here and now, the pleasure running through every aching muscle of his body as Bobbi knelt in front of him and used his mouth to give Malcolm some sweet relief. Malcolm clenched his buttocks and pushed his hips up slightly, encouraging Bobbi to make sure that he took the whole length of Malcolm's cock into his mouth with each long greedy suck. Malcolm liked nothing better than having his dick sucked by a really good cocksucker; his lazy side even preferred it to fucking, because you could just lie back and let the other guy do all the work, although Malcolm wasn't quite the top-man Bobbi imagined he was. He would have enjoyed it even more if, as well as having Bobbi kneeling in front of him sucking his cock, he could have had another guy standing on the laundry-basket, pants down, in front of *him*, straddling Malcolm's face and fucking it with his big stiff pole until he served his hot load in Malcolm's mouth.

But, right now, Bobbi's unexpected and enthusiastically given free blow-job was heaven enough for Malcolm. And the way Bobbi was keeping all his clothes on, his shorts up and his fly zipped, and was using his hands to fondle Malcolm's balls and massage Malcolm's sprawled thighs – was concentrating solely on Malcolm's pleasure and not fondling his own crotch for his own – had a generosity to it that added to the pleasure and excitement for Malcolm.

Malcolm's cock was beginning to grow in weight and stiffness inside Bobbi's wet eager mouth and Bobbi could taste the increasing flow of pre-come running from Malcolm's cock-head. Bobbi's neck ached as he pumped his lips up and down on Malcolm's hot stiff erection, greedy for come but barely rested from the thorough face-fucking Thom had given him just half an hour before.

Pumping his mouth as fast as he could up and down on Malcolm's hard-on, Bobbi ran his hands up Malcolm's smooth light-brown thighs, over his ridged stomach and felt for the broad domes of his pectorals, searching for Malcolm's nipples. Bobbi found one, then the other, and began to pinch and tease them with nimble fingers. Malcolm moaned loudly in excitement and began to swivel his pelvis in uncontrollable response to the attention to his tits as well as his cock, pushing his pulsing hard-on this way and that inside Bobbi's mouth, stretching Bobbi's cheeks, sliding over Bobbi's teeth in a way that would have been painful for Malcolm if he hadn't been so heavily turned on. Malcolm felt like he was a puppet, with Bobbi's expert use of his mouth and fingers making Bobbi the puppet-master.

Electric excitement throbbed through Malcolm's chest where Bobbi tormented his nipples, and thrilled out through Malcolm's crotch and balls from where Bobbi's eager mouth was at work, each nine-inch cock-swallow he performed also pressing his clean-shaven chin thrillingly hard against Malcolm's come-filled ball-sack.

Malcolm's heart pounded heavily and noisily against his chest as he felt his whole body floating out of control with excitement. His back and thighs ached; his cock felt liquid and molten as Bobbi pumped his mouth on it in a frenzy of cock-sucking desire. Malcolm thanked God for boys like Bobbi, who understood how much a man needed to be blown and freely offered that service, as his breaths shortened and the pit in his stomach tightened. His cock was getting heavier and heavier in Bobbi's hot greedy mouth and Malcolm felt cool thrills running up the base of his balls into his shaft as it expanded into final massive stiffness.

'I'm gonna blow, man,' he gasped hoarsely. 'Get ready for that hot load I'm gonna be serving right down your throat.' Bobbi moved his mouth up and down Malcolm's stiff aching shaft even faster, and pinched both Malcolm's large protruding nipples as hard as he could.

'Oh, oh, oh, oh –' Malcolm's cries of excitement were loud, loud enough to be heard in the studio below if the door was open down there, but he couldn't control the air being forcibly expelled from his lungs, any more than he could control the clenching of his balls and the bucking of his rigid dick as he shot his load straight into Bobbi's mouth. 'Oh, Jesus, oh, fuck me, oh, fuck –!' Malcolm's hips slammed up into Bobbi's face, which Bobbi made sure to keep firmly buried in Malcolm's crotch so as not to miss a drop of Malcolm's hot creamy salty come.

Malcolm sank back down onto the laundry-basket and sprawled exhaustedly. But Bobbi wasn't finished yet. He moved his mouth slowly and firmly up Malcolm's now-spent hard-on, sucking gently to get all the come out of it. Then he let the slick brown cock slip out of his mouth and kissed its wet shaft. Malcolm moaned softly as Bobbi took Malcolm's still-rigid penis in his hands and squeezed up the length of its shaft. He looked down as Bobbi milked a further glob of come out of his dick, bent his head forward and licked it up before going on to thoroughly and enthusiastically lick out Malcolm's slit. Malcolm was glad enough to give Bobbi his satisfaction and just lay back, exhausted, a sheen of perspiration coating his smooth light-brown skin, thinking of nothing as the pretty black boy worked the tip of his tongue greedily in Malcolm's gaping hole.

Bobbi had been delighted with the quantity of spunk Malcolm had shot into his mouth although, as a lot of it had gone straight down his throat, Bobbi hadn't been able to taste it as fully as he had wanted; which was why he was being so thorough about getting the last few drops of Malcolm's jism out of his cock and onto his tongue, where Bobbi could really appreciate its strong, salty flavour.

As he knelt in front of the handsome man sprawled before him and tongued his slit, Bobbi became aware of his own stiff cock, trapped aching and juicy in his tight white shorts, and of his heavily turned-on asshole, so slack and open he felt like a marrow could fit up it. The seam of the shorts was pulled up tight between his big buttocks and teased his pulsing sphincter. Bobbi considered asking Malcolm to finger-fuck him while he beat himself off but resisted the impulse, remembering the invitation he had received to a legendarily unusual party with a notorious host that evening, in bohemian Notting Hill Gate:

Prince Fela, King Bitch
requests the pleasure of your company
Bring a Stiff Cock, an Open Asshole and an Open Mind
– the rest will be provided
R.S.V.P.

Prince Fela was the son of a wealthy Nigerian businessman, and his parties were renowned for their extravagance and debauchery. It was said that anyone who went to one was never the same afterwards, and that threat and promise made an invitation highly sought-after. Bobbi didn't want to wear himself out in the day and not be able to make the most of what was on offer at Prince Fela's that evening. He struggled to his feet, adjusting his stiff cock and smiling at Malcolm.

Malcolm watched Bobbi pulling his cock around inside his shorts and smiling, and wondered if Bobbi was now going to ask him for a blow-job. He would have been happy enough to oblige – it would be ungracious in the extreme not to – but was relieved when Bobbi just bent forward and kissed him lightly on the lips, and then surprised when Bobbi said, 'Thank you.'

'No, man,' Malcolm replied, smiling back at Bobbi. 'Thank *you*. Mm,' he added, tasting his own spunk on Bobbi's lips. 'Maybe you better brush your teeth.'

He watched Bobbi's sexy ass idly as Bobbi bent over the sink and rinsed out his mouth and imagined fucking it. The thought was pleasant, but the truth was that Malcolm was looking for more than sex, however freely given and enjoyable. He was looking for love. And Bobbi was looking for fun. Just like Kam. Malcolm's good mood began to drift away at the thought of Kam's sluttish treachery. And Don's. *What was Don looking for?*

A sharp and unexpected knock at the bathroom door made Malcolm and Bobbi jump. Malcolm sprang to his feet and awkwardly pulled up his trousers and pants.

'What is it, man?' he called out.

Gregory's voice replied, 'Have you seen Bobbi, man?'

'Uh,' Malcolm said uncertainly, looking round at Bobbi working a toothbrush briskly in his mouth. 'Yeah, he's – we were just having a bit of a chat. He's here.'

A silence from beyond the door. Then, 'Well, when you're through, Don's just pulled up and we could do with a hand unloading the gear, yeah.'

'We're through, man,' Malcolm said quickly. 'At least –' He looked round at Bobbi and whispered, 'You don't need nothing doing, do you, man?' flicking his eyes down to Bobbi's still-bulging crotch, still wondering if oral attention was going to be required. Bobbi shook his head. 'Yeah,' Malcolm repeated. 'We're through. We'll be down in a minute.'

The sound of Gregory's feet pounded off down the stairs. Malcolm wriggled into his T-shirt, his face set at the thought of coming face-to-face with Don again. Bobbi noticed Malcolm's expression and put a cool palm against his cheek.

'Keep cool, baby,' he said. 'Save your heat for the bedroom.'

Four

'No, fuck *you*, man!' Malcolm yelled angrily into Don's face, jabbing a finger at the shorter man's swelling chest. Don surged forward to grapple with Malcolm, his eyes bugging, his face contorted in anger, but Gregory stepped in between the two men sharply, pushing his chest against Don's, bouncing Don back, while Bobbi tugged at Malcolm's upper arm to prevent him from shoving forward into the fight.

The atmosphere during the recording session had been heavy and tense from the moment Don and Malcolm ended up in the same room together. The small studio was airless and hot on the baking July day, which would have frayed anyone's temper, but Don and Malcolm were already spoiling for a fight. Gregory and Bobbi had tried to act as peacemakers, but Gregory was in a bad mood himself because the late start to the session meant they were going to run out of time to finish recording tracks for the tape they had been hoping to sell at their live gig the following night. And if Gregory was annoyed with Don, he soon became annoyed with Malcolm, too, for relentlessly needling Don until an explosion was bound to happen.

The catalyst was Thom's computer crashing, which left everyone standing around with nothing to do to keep them busy for the best part of an hour, while Thom got on the premium-rate telephone helpline for technical support. And Malcolm had goaded Don until a fight had broken out.

'Get a new drummer!' Don yelled into Malcolm's face, addressing Gregory obliquely. 'Get some motherfucker in with a ounce of motherfucking talent! Or, better yet, a fucking drum-machine.'

'Yeah, well, I ain't being in no band with no fucking rip-off-merchant-thinks-he's-street asshole anyway, no way, man,' Malcolm snarled in reply. He wrestled free of Bobbi's grip and stomped out of the room.

'Yeah, that's right, man,' Don shouted at Malcolm's broad, retreating back. 'Run away from a bit of honest conflict!'

At that, Malcolm turned abruptly and stormed back in. He pushed his face to within an inch of Don's. 'The honest unconflicted truth is, man,' he hissed, 'that you are a treacherous piece of shit.'

'Well, at least I know how to fuck,' Don snapped in reply. 'You don't see no one get up off my bed and go looking for more dick.'

They stared into each other's eyes, faces set, chests rising and falling in unison. Then Malcolm said, quite calmly, keeping his eyes on Don, 'I'm sorry, Gregory, man. I can't play no gig with this – *brother*.'

'Suits me, man,' Don said coldly, pulling the corners of his full mouth down disdainfully.

Malcolm turned on his heel and walked out, snatching up his motorcycle helmet on the way. Don looked round at Gregory. 'I'm sorry, man,' he said. But Don didn't sound sorry, he sounded spiteful. 'I need a piss,' he added, and stomped out of the room and up the stairs to the toilet. Bobbi looked round at Gregory uncertainly, then decided to hurry off after Malcolm.

Gregory turned to Thom, who had watched the whole scene in tense, awkward silence, the phone cradled under his chin, ready to jump forward if any damage to the studio equipment looked like it was going to happen. 'Man, *now* what the fuck me a go do?' Gregory asked, sighing.

'Well, maybe it ain't the place or time to say it,' the blond body-builder replied tentatively, hanging up the phone, then looking down at his hands. 'But they need time to cool off, maybe work it out together. And you're stressed, too, man. You could do with a bit of R&R.'

'Rest and relaxation?' the tall, lean Rastafarian said, raising an eyebrow questioningly.

Thom's handsome face flushed pink and he nodded, then shrugged. 'I'm just trying to ask you out, man,' he said softly. 'I'd just like to try and get to know you better. Inside and out. I mean, maybe this evening, if you ain't too busy –'

It was Gregory's turn to blush. He felt his cock stiffen in his pants and his asshole open receptively at Thom's offer. 'I ain't too busy,' he said quickly. Thom smiled at the swiftness of Gregory's reply, and shifted in his swivel chair: his dick was stiffening in anticipation, too, and pressing awkwardly against the seam of his tight denim shorts.

Out on the street, Bobbi ran to catch up with Malcolm, who was striding away from the recording studio towards his Kawasaki. Bobbi caught at Malcolm's arm. Malcolm shook him off roughly, irritated, sending Bobbi stumbling into the gutter. Then, realising he was out of order, Malcolm took a breath and forced himself to stop.

'I'm sorry, Bobbi, man,' he said, his tone genuinely apologetic, turning back and touching Bobbi gently on the shoulder. 'I didn't mean to take it out on you.'

'S'alright,' Bobbi said, shrugging. 'But look, Malcolm, I think you need to put this whole big fight with Don behind you.'

Malcolm glowered, looking unwilling to make any concessions on that score.

'Well, what I was thinking was, you really need to put Kam behind you,' Bobbi continued. 'And the best way to do that is to get out, have a wild time and meet some fresh prospects.' Malcolm shrugged. Bobbi carried on, 'I'm going to a party tonight; I can give you my invitation, 'cause I'll be on the guest list. And you can come and get really out of it and really get off on it. Please say you'll come. 'Cause if you do, you will.'

'Maybe,' Malcolm said, as Bobbi pressed the gold-scripted invite into his hand. 'Look, I'll think about it, man. But I ain't promising. I just feel too –' He shrugged.

'You won't be sorry,' Bobbi said, smiling shyly and eliciting a sulky smile from Malcolm in return. 'Oh, can you give me a lift into town?' he went on. 'I'll just have to go and quickly say goodbye to the others.'

Malcolm nodded and Bobbi hurried back inside.

By that time, another bunch of musicians had arrived to lay down a track, a dodgy-looking grunge band, and the Boot Sex Massive's recording session was curtailed. Bobbi made his goodbyes, then jumped on the back of Malcolm's motor-bike, eager for the feel of vibrating leather between his legs. Thom fixed up a time for his date with Gregory and then started attending to his new clients. Bobbi and Gregory headed off their separate ways, leaving a bad-tempered Don to load up the instruments, including Malcolm's drum-kit, into the van for the gig tomorrow night, in the vague hope that somehow everything would be patched up enough by then for it to actually happen. *More donkey work*, Don grumbled to himself. The two fights with Malcolm, and now the possibility of the whole band breaking up, had put Don in a bad mood; frustration coursed through him. All he could think was that he needed some rough sex to relieve it, fast. *Studwork*, much more his bag.

Meanwhile Kam, all his possessions shoved carelessly into a bulging duffle-bag, was sitting in a bar in Soho, getting drunk. He was angry and resentful – at both Don and Malcolm – and badly wanted some attention to flow his way to compensate him for his ill-treatment by them. He had

changed into the most trampy outfit he could dig up: a pair
of flimsy silverised rubber short-short hot-pants that hugged
his ass and left nothing to the imagination, bike-boots and
– in the heat of the afternoon – nothing else. With his
petite, well-defined physique and immaculately gelled-back
hair, Kam looked like a go-go dancer on a break.

Out of the corner of his eye, Kam became aware that a
couple of guys were eyeing him up. He slid his ass out on
the bar-stool to give them a better look at its tasty curves
and, when he took a swig from the bottle of import lager he
was drinking, he made sure to push his lips out and move
his mouth down suggestively on the neck of it.

The two guys glanced at each other, then sauntered up
to Kam, one taking a stool on either side of him. One was
black and one was white, and they both had close-cropped
hair, were clean-shaven and looked to be in their mid-
twenties. They both wore faded blue jeans stretched tightly
over their bulging thighs and asses, and both of them had
sandpapered their crotches to emphasise their considerable
baskets. On their feet, they wore army boots, and their
pumped-up chests were covered by tight white T-shirts.
Both of them had tattoos on their upper arms and, as they
turned to look at Kam from either side, they each put a
hand on one of Kam's thighs.

'I'm Bertil,' the black guy said, flashing a white smile.
His accent was Cockney, his skin was very dark and smooth,
his face round, his features boyish, his chest swelling. 'And
this is Joe,' he added, introducing his friend. Joe smiled,
too. He was handsome in a more rugged way, pale and
Celtic-looking although, if anything, his chest was even
more pumped than Bertil's. Kam immediately imagined
nuzzling on their tits and his cock stirred against the silver
latex hugging his crotch.

'We're paras on leave, Bertil and me,' Joe said, his accent
Glaswegian and strong. 'And we've come to Soho looking

for a good time. You look like you might be up for a good time too,' he said suggestively. 'We've rented a swank hotel room,' he added. 'Four stars in the Michelin guide.'

Kam nodded, excitement rising in his chest in anticipation of hot sex with two macho soldiers. 'I do like a good time,' he said. 'But which one of you wants me?' he asked, feigning innocence. 'I'm a nice boy.'

Joe and Bertil flashed a look at each other. 'Both of us,' Bertil said, still smiling, flicking a glance down at Kam's silver-clad ass. 'At the same time. In every way. And we both think you're a nice boy. Nice mouth. Nice ass . . .'

'Nice and easy,' Joe added. Kam smiled. 'What's your name?' Joe asked him.

'Kamitaki,' Kam replied, slipping off his bar-stool and picking up his duffle-bag. 'Horny Japanese boy. Lots of good times. Come on, let's go.'

'You sure?' Bertil asked.

'You want to treat me like a piece of meat?' Kam asked in reply, his face flushing in anticipation.

'Whatever gets you off, boy,' Bertil replied, smiling a wide wicked smile that Kam returned with mock-modesty.

Outside the bar, Joe hailed a cab and the three of them piled inside: Joe first, then Kam, then Bertil. Joe gave the driver the name of the hotel he and Bertil were staying at and the cab pulled out. Sitting between the two burly paras, Kam opened his legs, spreading his thighs to give their hands access as they uninhibitedly felt him up, squeezing his balls, his cock, pushing their fingers under and up to squeeze his ass and then, as he moaned softly, going on to push aside the shoulder-straps of his silver hot-pants and toy with his small brown nipples.

With one accord, Bertil and Joe unbuttoned Kam's shoulder-straps and folded down the front of the hot-pants. Then they began to tug them down over Kam's hips and buttocks. The brazenness of the two men excited Kam, and he wanted to let them strip him off in the cab in the middle of a bustling city street and fuck the consequences, but he was worried that the cabbie might take offence.

Kam needn't have worried: the cabbie, a handsome older African guy with large gold studs in his ears and cropped silver hair, looked round with a wicked golden smile and said, 'So long as you don't light up afterwards, boys. Smoking bad for the health, you know.' The two soldiers stopped for a moment to nod that they wouldn't smoke. 'Just let me know if you need another stiff dick in there,' the cabbie added with a laugh, before turning back to concentrate on his driving. 'I won't put it on the clock.'

Throwing all inhibitions to the wind, Bertil and Joe gripped Kam's hotpants by the waist-band and tugged them straight down to his ankles. Kam's small thick erection sprang up and he gasped as it slapped his belly. Bertil and Joe roughly wrestled the hotpants over Kam's bike-boots and off, and threw the crumpled silver fabric down on the floor of the cab. Then the two beefy men pulled the naked Kam's legs open and started to firmly massage his balls and finger his ass. Kam swivelled his hips and butt to give them maximum access to his private parts. Then he reached out for Bertil's crotch with one hand, Joe's with the other, squeezing their stiff bulges through the soft warm denim of their figure-hugging jeans.

Joe and Bertil took it in turns to kiss Kam hotly on the mouth. Joe preferred to suck on Kam's tongue, Bertil to thrust his tongue deep into Kam's mouth. Their hands played over Kam's bare, hairless chest, toying dextrously with his nipples as they kissed and tongued him, forcing Kam to gasp for breath. Every so often Kam would toss his raven hair back and glance with almond eyes at the cabbie's wing-mirror, and every time he would see the cabbie's wide brown eyes watching him being pleasured by the two holidaying paras.

Now Bertil was wanking Kam's cock roughly and vigorously while Joe chewed on his nipples, moving quickly from one to the other, Kam moaning softly.

Now Joe was squeezing Kam's ball-sack while Bertil pushed a hand palm-upwards under Kam's ass and shoved a long index finger up Kam's asshole, making Kam squeal with pleasure.

The cab eventually pulled up outside a grand but dilapidated hotel in Bayswater. 'We're here now,' the cabbie said. 'That'll be ah . . . twelve quid.'

Joe and Bertil went through the pockets of their tight denims awkwardly, the search made more difficult by the fact that their large erect cocks strained the fabric even tighter around the hips and crotch. They only managed to drag out four pounds in coins between them, and looked to Kam, who shrugged that he didn't have any money either. (As it happened, Kam *did* have some money; £176 rolled up in his duffle-bag, but he was fucked if he was going to pay cab-fare for two squaddies on salary. Anyway, it was for the tops to pay, he reckoned.)

'We've only got four, mate,' Bertil said, offering the coins with a shamed face.

'Don't "mate" me, man,' the cabbie said. 'I want me money. I got a wife and kids to feed. I want me money or I drive straight to the police station.'

'There must be something we can do,' Bertil said, fondling Kam's smooth lean cinnamon-yellow thigh, keeping his eyes on the cabbie's. 'Look at Kam here. He's all turned on, man. He's a real slut, man. He's begging for it.' Bertil turned to Kam and squeezed his balls hard. 'You'd get your legs up in the air for him, wouldn't you, Kam?'

Kam nodded with a soft gasp, tossed his hair and licked his lips provocatively, running his muscular pink tongue over small white teeth. Without another word, the cabbie turned off the engine and opened his door and stepped out onto the pavement. Despite his silver hair, his skin was smooth and his physique – in Bermuda shorts and a vest that showed curving thighs and a lean chest and arms – was good. His exceptionally large hard-on stuck out through his shorts like a pole.

Leaving his own door open, the cabbie opened the passenger door. Joe stepped out onto the pavement and stood close by him. 'Shield me, man,' the cabbie instructed him. Joe glanced up and down the street. Cars were passing by but there was no one walking, and the open doors of the cab shielded the cabbie from view from below the waist.

'Get on all fours and stick your ass out for me,' the lean African ordered Kam. The slim Japanese boy struggled onto his hands and knees on the leather passenger seat and stuck his booted feet and his bare ass out of the doorway for the cabbie's free use. The cabbie finger-fucked him briskly, working one, then two fingers up Kam's accommodating asshole, with a dexterity surprising for a family man. Then he leant forward and spat onto Kam's asshole, again with an inappropriately practised accuracy, glanced up and down the street to make sure no one was walking their way, then pulled his Bermuda shorts down to his ankles to reveal an impressively long thick cock that rose up slowly, it was so large and so heavy with blood.

'Wow, mate,' Joe said, impressed by the cabbie's massive cock. 'That's some weapon. A real footer.'

The cabbie turned his head towards Joe and smiled his gold-capped smile. 'What's your name?' he asked Joe.

'Joe,' the pale muscular soldier replied. Meanwhile, inside the cab, Bertil was encouraging Kam to nuzzle his bulging denim-covered crotch while waiting to be fucked by the cabbie, pushing Kam's face down onto his lap.

'I'm Oba,' the cabbie said. 'What I want you to do, Joe,

is –' He flicked another quick glance up and down the street: still empty. 'What I want is for you to fuck me up the ass while I fuck this boy up his ass. Could you do that?'

Joe nodded, stepping up behind Oba and fumblingly unbuttoning his fly, then pushing his own jeans and Calvins down to his mid-thighs. His stiff thick purple dick sprang out and he pressed it between Oba's high round dark brown buttocks. Now it was his turn to glance down the street. 'We're gonna have to be quick, Oba.'

Oba nodded and guided his very large cock-head between Kam's buttocks and pressed it against Kam's glittering pinkish-brown sphincter. Then he put his hands firmly on Kam's slim waist, braced his hips and pushed his cock-head up into Kam's asshole. Kam gasped out loud as he was forcibly opened up by Oba's big cock; the sudden dilation, the sudden fullness was agonising – but then, as he began to stretch and accommodate it, exciting. Oba slapped Kam's ass, a sharp crack as the pink palm of his dark brown hand came down on Kam's smooth cinnamon-coloured skin. 'Take it, bitch,' Oba grunted, ramming his whole length, a literal foot of rigid meat, up into Kam's rectum. Kam moaned and groaned as Oba began to fuck him in quick, rough strokes, the pain melting into pure pleasure as Kam's asshole relaxed into its naturally open and receptive state.

Joe was running his hands over Oba's muscular hairy ass as Oba slid his large, thick cock in and out of Kam's open, juicy asshole. Oba's breath already seemed to be quickening. Oba turned his head towards Joe. 'Fuck me, man,' he grunted, his hips moving rapidly backwards and forwards against Kam's butt. He was now gripping the door-frame of the cab to brace himself, relying on Kam to enjoy being poled up the ass enough to voluntarily keep his butt in place. Which Kam did, his cock throbbing, his nipples tingling, his asshole aching, his thighs and arms tense and stiff, unable to resist the good feeling of being ass-fucked by Oba.

Joe moved his thick cock up and down between Oba's buttocks until he felt the dimpled softness of Oba's anal opening against his circumcised head. He gripped Oba's hips for a moment, so he could position his cock against Oba's asshole, and then pushed his cockhead up into Oba's rectum. For a family man, Oba certainly had a very slack and accommodating asshole; Joe was able to slide his thick, stiff cock all the way up Oba in one thrust, and Oba barely grunted as he took Joe's whole length up his back passage, without lubricant or preparation.

Joe started to fuck Oba in short rapid strokes, as Oba fucked Kam's ass where it was stuck out of the cab doorway. Joe kept grinding his hips against Oba's muscly ass, eager to make sure his cock didn't slip out of Oba's hot hungry brown hole, which in turn encouraged Oba to keep his mammoth cock as far as possible up Kam's ass. Kam was now actively pushing his ass out of the car door to enable it to swallow as much of Oba's cock up into his body as possible, even though it felt to Kam like Oba's cockhead was already pushing up into the bottom of his stomach, it was so long and thick and hard.

Oba pumped his hips faster and harder, Joe keeping time with him and keeping his cock jammed up Oba's backside. With a grunt and a sudden loud gasp, Oba came, spurting his load up Kam's asshole in excited jerks. Kam inhaled sharply in excitement at the extra pressure against the walls of his ass when Oba's load spurted out, and then exhaled in relief as Oba stopped pumping his hips and, a moment later, pulled his slick and already drooping cock out of Kam's now slack and dripping hole.

'Stop fucking me, man,' Oba ordered Joe. Joe obediently pulled his stiff cock out of the African's slack butthole. Oba bent down and briskly pulled his Bermuda shorts back up. Sweat was running down his armpits and the sides of his face. He patted Kam on the ass. 'You give it up good, boy.' Then he bent forward and looked into the cab's interior. He met Bertil's eyes. 'Well,' Oba said. 'They've worked off their share of the fare. What are you going to do?'

Bertil looked at Oba blankly, unable to think of a reply.

'I sure would get off on seeing you felch this boy,' Oba said, grinning another wicked golden grin. 'I sure would like to see you eating my come out of the boy's asshole. But I would guess you aren't broad-minded enough to earn your fare that way are you, soldier boy?'

Bertil shrugged. 'For a queen who's a cunt,' he said. 'Yeah, I'll do it.' He met Kam's eyes. 'Turn around and give me your asshole, man,' he said to Kam. Kam turned around obediently, turned on by the idea of being eaten out anyway, and rolled over onto his back. Oba slid into the front of the cab, closing the driver's door behind him. Joe slid in next to Kam, pulling Kam's head onto his lap, and closed his door, too. Kam stared up at the curving ceiling of the cab as Bertil lifted his thighs, pushing his long slim legs up and back until Kam was doubled over on the back seat, his bike-booted heels pressing against the roof above him, his ass up in the air and accessible; Bertil's strong hands supported Kam's lower back, holding him up and open.

Oba was watching from the driver's seat, with one hand down the front of his shorts, and started to beat off vigorously as the black soldier bent his close-cropped head and pressed his lips against Kam's slack and well-fucked asshole. Then Bertil began to slide his long, muscular tongue deep into Kam's dilated anus and take increasingly eager plunges into the Japanese boy's anal cavity. Kam moaned as Bertil felched him, his hands straying to his stiff cock and tingling balls. Oba was wanking, gasping noisily as he watched eagerly, working towards his second climax in five minutes. Even Joe was turned on by watching his buddy's tongue in action in Kam's butthole.

And the truth of it was that Bertil was turned on too: he'd always enjoyed rimming, feeling that that was what God had given him his long tongue for, but the taste of Oba's spunk, hot and fresh in Kam's rectum, had given it a new level of pleasure for him. Bertil's cock was achingly stiff in his jeans but he ignored it, concentrating on tongue-fucking Kam. He was surprised by what a big load Oba had shot up Kam's bum, how much there was for him to lick out – and pleased, too, as it allowed him to keep on exploring the inside of Kam's ass with his tongue.

Oba was getting off on seeing the muscular young black man sliding his long pink tongue in and out of the Japanese boy's asshole: he hadn't expected Bertil to agree to do it, and so he was making the most of the unexpected voyeuristic treat and beating off his aching meat as hard and fast inside his shorts as he possibly could. Finally, with a loud exhalation, sweat bathing his body, Oba came inside his shorts. He stopped moving his hand on his cock and reached for some tissues to clean up his crotch, which he then dropped out of his open window.

Now that he had come, Oba was all business again. 'Okay,' he said, turning and settling back down in his driver's seat. 'You've paid your fare. You can go now.' Bertil stopped felching for a moment and looked up at Oba. 'You can go now,' Oba repeated. 'C'mon, c'mon,' he hurried them. 'Time is money. Be quick, please.'

Bertil kissed Kam's glistening asshole then carefully lowered Kam's butt back onto the seat. Kam struggled upright, picked up his silver latex hot-pants from where they lay tangled on the floor of the cab, and wriggled quickly back into them, while Joe buttoned his fly, straining to pull the denim across his thick stiff prick.

A moment later, Joe, Bertil and Kam bundled out of the

cab and onto the street in front of their hotel. Oba waved out of the driver's window as he pulled off without looking back and then sped off, ignoring a couple of yuppies with a pile of suitcases who were signalling for a cab a little way down the road.

'Shit, man,' Joe said as Oba disappeared off round a corner. 'He came twice and we're all standing here, stiff as sergeants on parade and twice as horny.'

'So let's do something about it,' Bertil said. 'I don't know about you two, but I'm ready to fuck ass and get my dick sucked all weekend.'

Kam nodded eagerly and they hurried up the steps into the soldiers' hotel. The dowdy woman on the desk didn't bat an eyelid as the two squaddies escorted the scantily-clad Japanese boy up to their fourth-floor room, despite the painfully obvious hard-on jutting out from his crotch through the clingfilm-thin latex and the way their hands explored his ass, in full view of the entire lobby, as they waited for the lift.

Once inside the lift, Joe got grinding his crotch against Kam's ass while Bertil fondled Kam's tits and tongued his moist open mouth. Kam could taste just the faintest residue of Oba's come on Bertil's tongue. He sucked it eagerly and was just about to beg Joe to pull his pants down and fuck him right there in the lift, when it arrived with a clunk and a whirr at their floor.

The doors slid open and the three of them stumbled out of the lift, arms around each others' shoulders, horny and delirious, pushing past a group of dowdy straight tourists on their way out to see an Andrew Lloyd Webber musical up in the West End, intent on staging their own unforget-table spectacular in the privacy of their hotel room.

'Oh, God, I need cocks up my ass!' Kam shouted, striding into the middle of the large blue-and-gold room and throwing his arms up and his head back. 'I need big cocks rammed up my ass now!'

His dick aching in his jeans, Joe slipped a 'Do Not Disturb' sign onto the outer door-handle of their room, closed the door, and locked it. Bertil was already peeling off his T-shirt, his dark nipples protruding engorged from his pumped-up chest.

Kam started to grind his hips provocatively for the horny soldiers. 'Fuck me!' he said loudly. 'Fuck me now!' Fumbling with excitement, he unbuttoned his hotpants and wriggled them down to his ankles and tugged them off, turning as he did so to give Bertil and Joe a good view of his shapely ass. Then Kam bent over, spreading his legs, sticking his ass up in the air and waving it about invitingly; he looked upside-down between his legs at Bertil and Joe, who had also stripped off his T-shirt to display a big built-up chest. 'Come and fuck this ass!' Kam begged the two heavily turned-on squaddies. 'Free ass! I need to be fucked right now!'

Exchanging a grin, Bertil and Joe unbuttoned their jeans and pushed them down, unlacing their boots to get their jeans and their white Calvin Klein briefs off over their feet, revealing strong thighs and calves as they did so. They then stepped back into their army boots, lacing them back up – after all, a fondness for uniforms was one of the main reasons they had both joined up – and stood naked, except for their heavy leather foot-wear, behind Kam, moving their fists slowly on their large, stiff cocks. They then changed hands so that Bertil's dark brown fist was moving slowly on Joe's stiff purple cock while Joe moved his pale hand on Bertil's long dark rigid shaft. But they eyed Kam's ass all the time they wanked each other off: they were buddies, not lovers, and buddies in fucking, not fuck-buddies. They just appreciated each other's bodies, too.

Bertil stepped forward and slapped Kam's ass. Kam gasped and wiggled it some more. Bertil ran his fingers up and down Kam's crack, then reached between Kam's legs and squeezed his balls, pressing them up firmly against his groin. Kam grunted, then gasped a second time as Bertil reached further up between Kam's legs and masturbated his stiff penis briefly.

'Let's fuck him on the coffee-table,' Joe suggested. Bertil nodded, and gestured for Kam to assume an all-fours position on the low hardwood table in the middle of the spacious room. The surface of the table was thick mirrored glass, which briefly felt cold against his knees and the palms of his hands as Kam obediently climbed up onto it and assumed the position. He looked down at the reflection of his pale, lithe body, his ball-sack hanging down, his circumcised hard-on jutting out from his crotch, the black tuft at its base, his taut, defined belly. He had meant to spend the afternoon working on a design for a new sports car but right now nothing seemed more streamlined than his own body, no shape more beautiful than the muscular curve of Joe and Bertil's erect cocks, no combination more meaningful than the insertion of those big stiff poles into Kam's greedy rectum and eager mouth.

As Kam had hoped, Bertil and Joe were so randy by that point that they fucked him like a piece of meat. Bertil grabbed Kam's hair, pulled his head up sharply and shoved his long brown cock straight down Kam's open throat, making Kam gag, while Joe positioned his rigid dick against Kam's pouting sphincter, then held Kam's buttocks open and slammed the whole thick length of it right the way up Kam's ass to the root, making Kam grunt and buck as Joe's cock filled his asshole to bursting.

Bertil and Joe slammed Kam rough and fast from both ends, transporting the horny Japanese youth to sexual heaven. *If Malcolm had only understood him better!* Kam thought. *If Malcolm had only had the sense to know that Don had been right when Don had told him to put his possessiveness aside and get busy fucking Kam's free hole . . .* But now Kam was with Bertil and Joe, and the two hard-bodied squaddies understood exactly what Kam needed and were determined to give it to him until he begged them to stop – and then carry on giving it to him until they were satisfied.

Drops of glittering pre-come dripped from Kam's erect cock onto the mirrored surface below him in sticky threads, soon joined by saliva and pre-come beading from Kam's stretched lips and running out of his open asshole. Kam's body glistened with sweat as Bertil and Joe poled him vigorously from both ends. He grunted and shuddered as they pumped their hips against his mouth and his asshole in unison, ecstatic at being used so fully, at being stuffed so completely.

At a signal from Bertil, both men suddenly pulled their cocks out of Kam. Kam let out an anguished gasp, sucking in breath but wiggling his ass for more anal attention and keeping his mouth wide open. Bertil and Joe quickly walked around the coffee-table and, a second later, the cock that had just been all the way up Kam's ass was shoved into his mouth, and the cock he had slicked with his own spit was being rammed up Kam's open bunghole. Now Kam was sucking Joe, and Joe's thick cock filled his mouth more completely than Bertil's had done. It had a sour taste from having been up Kam's ass, but Joe wasn't giving Kam any choice but to swallow it. At the same time, Bertil's longer cock was stretching Kam's rectum further than Joe's had done, and that was exciting for Kam, too.

Bertil started to spank Kam as he fucked him: not seriously hard, just hard enough for Kam to appreciate that his ass was getting some extra attention. The sharp smacking sound added to the grunting and regular rhythmic slapping of beefy muscular thighs against ass and face.

'You want us both to fuck you?' Bertil asked suddenly, continuing to smack Kam's butt. 'Both of us at once? A double-fuck?' Kam seemed to gurgle an affirmative from around Joe's thick stiff dick as it slid in and out of his mouth. Bertil met Joe's eyes, looking to see if he was up for it.

'Let's do it,' Joe said, his voice throaty with excitement. He and Bertil couldn't often persuade guys to take two cocks up the ass at the same time – their speciality – and it wasn't often a boy as slim and lean as Kam had enough of an anal cave to accommodate two big stiff pricks up him, even if he was prepared to try.

They pulled out of Kam's asshole and mouth, leaving Kam naked and on all fours on the coffee table, sweaty and trembling with excitement, then lay down on the plush carpet on their backs, facing away from each other. Kam watched curiously as the two squaddies then opened their legs, pushed their thighs down and undulated their bodies together until their crotches and balls were squeezed together and their two cocks – one mid-brown, one buttery-pink – appeared to arch up from a single source. Bertil reached down and closed his fist around the two cocks and pressed their shafts together. Then he turned his head and smiled at Kam.

'Come and sit on these two dicks, Kam,' Bertil invited. 'I bet you'd like that, yeah? Having two big dicks up you at the same time.'

Kam felt thrills of excitement run through his chest as he toyed with his own stiff prick. He went and stood looking down at the entwined and heavily aroused soldiers. He *did* like the idea, it had been a fantasy he'd had for years, one of many extreme anal dreams. But he wasn't sure if his ass could take it. He hesitated for a moment.

But it only took a moment for the urge to fulfil the fantasy to win out. Kam stepped over the soldiers, straddling their fused crotches, and slowly sat down on the two throbbing erections, facing Bertil. Joe held Kam's ass-cheeks open wide and guided him as he lowered his pouting hole onto the crowns of the two cocks, while Bertil held the two cocks together and started to work first one head, then the second, into Kam's dilating anal opening. Kam moaned and tossed his head, screwing his eyes shut as he tried to relax his asshole enough to accommodate the two thick blunt heads, both bloated with blood and large, though at least smooth.

'Sit down on it, boy,' Bertil encouraged. 'Yeah, yeah, that's it. You can do it. Slowly, now. Oh, that feels so *good*, boy,' he groaned as he felt Kam relax and start to open wide enough to take in both heads. 'Oh, *yeah*,' he gasped, as the smooth head of his cock slithered inside Kam's anal ring, which slipped shut, gripping it behind the hood and pressing it against Joe's adjacent cock-head firmly. 'You in there properly too?' Bertil called to Joe, checking that Joe's cock wasn't going to pop out of Kam's tight hole when he thrust up into the Japanese youth's rectum.

'Yeah, man,' Joe gasped throatily in reply. 'My cockhead's way up this horny bunghole.'

'Play with your tits, bitch,' Bertil ordered Kam, who had squatted facing him. 'And, while you're doing that, slide that slack juicy bunghole all the way down on these two big stiff dicks and start giving your men some real pleasure.'

Kam slowly lowered himself on the two rigid poles of muscle, playing with his nipples as Bertil had told him to. He felt his rectum stretch to near bursting-point as the two thick shafts filled him up inside. Cock-juice ran freely from Kam's slit, so intense was the pressure on his prostate, and he felt as if he was losing entire control of every muscle of his body, inside and out. The feeling was so extreme that his thighs and calves began to tremble and he realised that he couldn't control his legs enough to lift himself up off the two cocks, let alone pump his tightly-stretched ring on them.

Feeling Kam tremble, Bertil and Joe reached out to help him. First they gripped Kam round the waist and pulled him down, forcing him to take both their cocks up his bottom to the root, but giving him a chance to rest his aching and widely-spread legs once he was sat all the way down on their crotches. Then, once Kam had squirmed about so that his rectum could swallow the two soldiers' rigid hard-one comfortably, Bertil and Joe put their hands on Kam's waist again, this time lifting him up and supporting some of his bodyweight, enabling him to start to pump his asshole up and down on their sticky, rigid and muscularly conjoined dicks.

Although he had at first felt he had been dilated too far, Kam gradually began to enjoy working his fully-stretched anal ring up and down the stiff cocks of the soldiers lying face-up in opposite directions beneath him. The great fullness of his asshole satisfied him more than any anal experience had ever done before, and he had had many. As he squatted down heavily on Bertil and Joe's hard-one, he started playing with his own tits again, pinching them eagerly and gasping as he did so. Then he pulled his asshole up the length of the two squaddies' cocks, gratified to drag groans of pleasure from both of them as he did so. Then down again. Then up. Now he was getting into the rhythm, Kam didn't need Bertil or Joe's supporting hands on his waist; he just braced his spread thighs with his elbows and concentrated on lifting his bunghole up and down on the two soldiers' thick rigid poles in a disciplined squatting motion.

Joe and Bertil arched back, stretching their heavily muscled arms up and back behind their heads, and concentrated on pushing their joined crotches rhythmically upwards into Kam's rectum as he pushed downwards. Up and down Kam moved, up and down, sweat pouring the length of his lean compact body, his glossy black hair tumbling slickly over his face, his ruddy lips parted to show small white teeth, his cock thrust out and dripping man-juice constantly, his fingers moving on his erect nipples. He felt as if Joe's and Bertil's throbbing erections were filling his entire bowels with their pulsing stiffness and that each long juicy pump of his ass turned him inside-out, outside-in, in ecstasy.

Kam kept his small muscular rump moving up and down on the twin poles until he was panting shrilly with excitement, almost hysterical with sexual arousal. Beneath him, Joe's and Bertil's hoarse groans were coming with greater and greater volume and rapidity.

'Oh, yeah, oh, fuck –' Bertil yelled abruptly. 'Oh, shit, man, I'm losing it – Oh!' He came violently inside Kam's bottom in shuddering waves, his muscular back arching convulsively as his buttocks clenched reflexively. At the same moment, with a loud cry, Joe shoved his hips upwards, arching his back also and spraying his load up Kam's stretched asshole and into his bruised rectum; the two men's cocks slickly joined together in a flood of hot semen.

As if propelled by the momentum of their explosions, Kam staggered awkwardly up from his squatting position to his feet, his thighs aching, his asshole aching, and his stiff juicy dick aching most of all. Joe's and Bertil's cocks slipped out of his asshole and flopped, spent and heavy, onto their muscular bellies. Kam could feel that his well-fucked back passage was still gaping open. He felt insane with sexual excitement.

'Felch me,' Kam ordered Bertil, and he turned and sat down on the black soldier's handsome face without waiting for a reply. 'Stick that tongue up my slack ass. Eat that come while I beat off.'

Kam half-expected Bertil to angrily shove him off, now

he had come. But, to his gratification, Bertil gripped the slim thighs of the Oriental youth sitting on his face and pulled them back, encouraging Kam to press his butt and asshole down onto Bertil's mouth as hard as he could. Kam began to frig himself as he felt the whole length of Bertil's tongue slither up his open backside and start to lick the come out of Kam's rectum.

Even though he had only just come himself, Bertil started to masturbate his own cock vigorously, pulling his foreskin back and forth over his sensitised cock-head, using the come that coated it as a lubricant for extra sensual pleasure, but primarily gaining his orgasm orally; he licked the come out of Kam's gaping bottom as Kam pushed down slightly to encourage the thick creamy jism to trickle down into Bertil's eagerly awaiting mouth. Kam's hand was now moving so fast on his cock, it was a blur. With a sobbing cry of ecstasy, Kam lost control; his hips jerked forward and he shot his load in a spattering arc across Joe's and Bertil's crotches. Drops of Kam's spunk even landed on Joe's belly, so explosive was his eventual orgasm.

Then Kam sat back down on Bertil's face, while Bertil jerked himself off with his tongue up Kam's back passage. At one point, Kam even reached back and pulled his buttocks open to ensure Bertil had full access to the depths of his rectum.

Bertil beat off rapidly with Kam sitting on his face and came with a muffled groan, shooting a surprisingly large load, given that it was the second orgasm he'd had in five minutes.

After a minute or so of keeping his ass in place, to make sure the eager black soldier had done all the eating out he wanted to, Kam got up. Bertil gasped and passed a hand over his mouth to wipe away glittering saliva, ass-juice and jism. Then Bertil looked round at Joe and Kam with a wide self-satisfied grin. 'Man,' he said. 'Who'd have thought I'd get a taste for felching? Fuck 'em, then eat 'em out. That's gonna be my motto from now on.'

The three exhausted men lay there on the soft plush carpet for a while, muscles aching, sodden with sweat and utterly spent. Then Joe went and ran a shower. The others followed him in and they all soaped and rinsed each other down. They dried each other off gently and then went and lounged in the bedroom, on the king-size double-bed they hadn't yet tried out. Bertil ordered some room service. After it had been delivered – fancy beers and smoked salmon sandwiches – and they had refreshed themselves, Kam asked what Bertil and Joe planned to do with the rest of their weekend's leave.

'Just a ton of fucking. Why?' Joe asked him, running a hand over Kam's bare thigh. 'Do you have something in mind?'

Kam shrugged. 'There's a party on tonight I've got an invitation to. It's supposed to be a wild all-boy, all-fucking kind of event, with live sex shows, everything. The host's called Prince Fela. He's supposed to really be one. A prince, I mean,' he added.

'Sounds like our kind of party,' Joe said.

'Yes. All the ass you could want to fuck,' Kam said to Joe. 'And as much spunk to lick out of assholes as you could want,' Kam added, looking over at Bertil with a cheeky smile, bending over to kiss the blushing black man on the lips.

Bobbi and Gregory were speaking on the phone around the time that Kam first managed to slide his well-stretched asshole down on two cocks at the same time, talking about tomorrow night's gig and how Don and Malcolm would have to patch things up or it just wouldn't happen. They were also worried because neither Gregory nor Bobbi wanted the band to split up, and that looked all too possible, given the way Don and Malcolm had been going for each other. Bobbi, ever the peacemaker of the group, said to Gregory that he'd give Don a ring and try and sort things out, then call Gregory back to let him know what had happened. But Don was out when Bobbi called, and his mobile was switched off. Bobbi rang Gregory back anyway.

'So now what can we do, man?' Gregory asked wearily: the Malcolm-Don rivalry had been going on too long for him to feel anything other than tired of it.

'Well, look,' Bobbi said. 'This has to be sorted out, right? And tonight?'

'Yes,' Gregory replied. 'Yeah, it does, really.'

'Well,' Bobbi said. 'I don't have any plans for this evening till late. So what I can do is go and trawl through all Don's favourite night-spots and hope I manage to dig him up and have a chat with him.'

'Yeah, I suppose so,' Gregory said doubtfully. 'But what about Malcolm? He was the one who stomped off mad.'

'I know he'll be happy enough if Don apologises for getting it on with Kam,' Bobbi said. 'I mean, Malcolm knows it takes two to sixty-nine, you know? Kam has to take at least half the blame.'

'Okay, man,' Gregory said eventually. 'Thanks for offering to drag your ass all over town. You're on the side of the angels, man, you know that?'

'I try to be,' Bobbi said brightly. He checked his watch, cradling the phone under his chin. 'Anyway, it's time you got dressed up for your date, man. So I'm gonna hang up now. Speak to you later.'

'Later, man,' Gregory said, hanging up too.

After loading up the Boot Sex Massive's gear, Don had driven up to Hampstead Heath, parking his van on a quiet side-street between a jeep and a black cab and padlocking it carefully. He was now sprawling back against the trunk of a vast old beech tree in a small clearing, luxuriating in the warm sun on his face and arms and chest, and the texture of the bark against his back; he struck a butch pose, with arms folded, and stood with one leg straight, the other crooked at the knee, his heavily booted heel pressed against the bark. He had changed in the back of the van, into a black lycra one-piece that showed every contour of his smooth muscular body, including the clear and substantial outline of his thick cock and big balls. Apart from showing off his well-honed physique to best advantage, the leotard also had the advantage that it could be hooked off his shoulders and pulled down to his ankles at any moment for fast, hard fucking action.

The look on Don's smooth darkly handsome face as he arched back and pushed his bulky tackle forward proclaimed, 'I'm waiting for trade, but I pick you, you don't pick me.' His expression was glowering, his full lips were drawn downwards at the corners in sensual disdain, and his eyes were hazy with free-floating lust as he looked out across the greenery-filled bowl of the Heath. The sun was bright and hot, the sky was blue and the air was still and silent. The figures of men looking for action drifted along dirt paths among the greeny-brown tangles of undergrowth in the cruisy part of the Heath where Don was hanging out; men with hips constrained by tight denim or crotches revealed by flimsy running-shorts, men with asses that needed to be fucked or cocks that needed to be sucked, men with hungry eyes . . .

Don had already had several interested looks from the passing trade, but none of the guys who'd met his eyes had really appealed to him: they had been too tall, too short, too mad, or just too ordinary . . . Nothing that made his dick stir more than marginally. He was just beginning to think that his visit to the Heath was going to be a total bust, and that he should have gone home and jacked off to a Joe

Simmons video instead, when he heard the juicy clicking of an approaching bicycle-chain, and a striking-looking pony-tailed Pakistani cycle-courier came strolling past him invitingly, pushing a mountain-bike as he went.

The courier was wearing black lycra shorts and a lycra vest with fluorescent green strips up the sides; it hugged his slim, clearly well-defined body like a synthetic skin. The shorts showed a large cock sprawled down one thigh and heavy balls unconstrained by underwear spread out below it down the other, it was a provocative and porno-graphically-explicit display of his assets to anyone who glanced below his waist. The courier's body was lean as well as slim; every muscle and sinew showed beneath his *café-au-lait* skin, and his large ass looked tight and rock-hard from months or years of pumping round the city on his bike. His face was handsome, with strong cheek-bones and large lips, and his eyes were large and dark and feminine. His hands were large and strong. He wore a neatly-clipped goatee and had long dark hair that hung halfway down his back and was tied in a ponytail. But best of all, as far as Don was concerned, as he ran his eyes up and down the young Pakistani man's well-made body, was the perfect smoothness of his bare legs and forearms, the sort of silky smoothness that only shaving or waxing could produce on a man's skin. Hopefully, Don thought, the youth shaved his ass and pubic hair off, too, for a completely clean and hairless look.

Don could see that the Asian man was checking him out from the corners of his dark, inviting eyes as he idled past the tree Don was leaning against, so he raised his dark and sinewy arms above his head in a faked yawn, and stretched so that the guy could see that Don shaved his armpits, too. Don's move had the desired effect: the long-haired Pakistani youth came to a stop and turned and looked Don full in the face. His dark eyes glittered in the sunlight. His generous lips were shiny as he ran his tongue over them nervously.

'You got the time, mate?' he asked Don blandly, gesturing nominally at his bare wrist, his accent pure South London.

'I got the time right now,' Don replied, not even bothering to look down at the Rolex on his own wrist, keeping his eyes on the Asian guy's eyes, excitement thrilling through his chest as he felt his cock beginning to swell in his black lycra one-piece.

The Pakistani youth came over to where Don was leaning under the shade of the tree, guiding his bike with one hand. Don could see the guy's cock thickening in his skin-tight shorts, the sheer fabric allowing Don to see every detail of its expanding outline: the smooth mushroom-shape of its large swelling head, the curve shifting into straightness as the shaft grew into a rigid and muscular full stiffness. The youth's full lips were parted slightly in sensual anticipation, and his chest was rising and falling excitedly as his manhood hardened in his shorts.

'I like to rim,' he said nervously and abruptly, his voice catching in his throat at his admission, looking around quickly as if they were likely to be overheard. No one was nearby, and the several drifting men Don could see weren't looking their way.

'I like to fuck,' Don said, reaching out and stroking the Asian youth's bare light-brown arm. The young man shivered in pleasure at being touched, and in anticipation of much more, and tossed his long ponytail. 'How old are you?' Don asked him, imagining taking hold of that glossy ebony ponytail and pulling the youth's head back sharply as he fucked him from behind.

'Twenty. My name's Hashi.'

'I'm Don,' Don said. 'I want to fuck you.'

'Suck me, then you can fuck me,' Hashi replied breathlessly, although the quickness with which he offered the trade suggested he would have given his well-muscled ass up to Don even if Don had refused him oral satisfaction.

'Do you want to go somewhere?' Don asked the turned-on Pakistani, his own cock now heavy and stiff in his lycra one-piece.

Hashi shook his head. 'I like doing it here,' he said, struggling to gain proper control of his breathing. 'Outside. It's more natural out in the open – and exciting. Shit might – I dunno – something might happen. You know? Like getting seen. Or getting caught. It just makes it more –'

Nodding, Don reached down between Hashi's legs and squeezed the bulge of Hashi's crotch, massaging it with the palm of his hand: he could feel the hardness of Hashi's cock straining against the lycra of his shorts, the plumpness of Hashi's balls against his palm. Hashi extended his hand to squeeze Don's large ball-sack in the front of his one-piece. Don gasped softly. They both suddenly looked round to make sure that no one was watching them, now they were beginning to get down to business. There seemed to be no one about, but they decided wordlessly to move away from the path anyway, and slip into the more concealing under-growth a little way back, where there was less chance of being interrupted.

Soon they found a sunny grassy spot in amongst thick briars, and beech trees, where the danger of being stumbled across – except perhaps by other dedicated cruisers looking for a trysting-place of their own – seemed fairly minimal. Hashi lay his bike down carefully on the grass, making sure he gave Don a good chance to look at his large muscular ass as he did so. Don pushed his one-piece off his shoulders and began to toy with his own small but stiff nipples as he watched Hashi bending over. Nothing turned Don on more than a guy offering him his asshole so freely.

Without turning round, Hashi straightened up and

peeled off his top, dropping it by the bike. Don noted the hairless grooves of Hashi's shaven armpits with approval. Hashi's shoulders were capped with muscle, and his smooth brown back tapered to his lycra-covered and narrow hips and waist. His long raven-black hair hung down his back, and the shaven-headed Don found it unexpectedly exotic and provocative. Hashi turned round to face Don, his eyes dull with lust, his mouth open as if to speak, and slid his tight black shorts down to his ankles. Hashi's large circumcised cock sprang up heavily from his completely shaven crotch and his big hairless balls hung down loosely between his legs. His light-brown skin was totally smooth. He stepped out of his shorts and stood before Don, naked except for a thin gold chain around his waist; his face was bloated with desire and his cock was stiff and tattooed with thick, throbbing veins.

His full lips parted and shiny with desire, Don sunk to his knees in front of Hashi, mesmerised by the aerodynamic lines of Hashi's immaculately waxed cock and the silky grey-brown skin around its base. To Don, a shaven male body brought out masculine muscularity in its fullest, cleanest, most sharply-defined: body-hair was just dirt and clutter, inessential, something to be got rid of in order to get closer to the real male body. He twisted Hashi's stiff arching dick to one side, so he could kiss and lick the smooth area around its root. As he did so, Don ran his other hand up between Hashi's legs and slid his fingers between Hashi's buttocks, making sure that Hashi had completely waxed his crack and asshole, too. The skin was totally smooth against Don's fingertips; the thought of the Asian youth's hairless butthole gripping his cock-shaft added to Don's building need to give Hashi a deep and thorough ass-fucking.

Don began to lick his way up the length of Hashi's rigid shaft with strong strokes of his muscular tongue, tasting the slight bitterness of the aftershave Hashi splashed around his crotch each time he shaved down there. Hashi gasped in excitement as Don then put his mouth over Hashi's smooth cock-head and swallowed it down. Hashi's long thick cock was heavily veined and ridged, and Don felt every throbbing vein and ridge against his sensitive lips as he slid his mouth down the length of the shaft, until they were pressed against Hashi's waxed-smooth groin. Then Don started to pump his mouth up and down rapidly on Hashi's rigid brown pole.

'Fondle my balls,' Hashi ordered throatily, looking down at the shaven-headed muscular black man kneeling in front of him, and enjoying the feeling of Don's hot wet mouth pumping up and down on his throbbing cock. Hashi moaned as Don obeyed his order, his shoulders flexing as he did so, his dark skin starting to glow with sweat. The Asian youth arched back, placing one hand on Don's shaven head to keep it in place, and started pumping his hips upwards against Don's face. He tossed his long raven hair again, and felt it swing against his clenched buttocks as Don sucked his aching brown pole.

The rustle of the wind in the leaves and the singing of the birds in the trees was only broken by the soft wet sounds of Don slurping enthusiastically on Hashi's, hot and pulsing dick, and Hashi's throaty moans of pleasure as his saliva-slickened manhood slid in and out of Don's greedily swallowing mouth. Don moved his lips quickly on Hashi's throbbing pole and sucked as hard as he could; Hashi could feel an exciting heaviness building rapidly inside the length of his shaft as Don blew him. He looked down at the kneeling Don's blocky lycra-sheathed ass pushed out invitingly below him on top of smooth dark curving thighs: Hashi certainly wasn't going to shoot his load without getting himself a taste of Don's shaven asshole. He pulled his hips back before Don could suck him to the point of no return, and his cock popped out of Don's mouth with a loud juicy smack.

'Let me rim you,' Hashi begged Don hoarsely, his spit-slicked dick tingling as he sank onto his knees, so he was now facing the muscular young black man. 'Please let me eat out your asshole, Don. You'll never be rimmed so good, man, I guarantee, 'cause my tongue's long and it was made to go up other guys' assholes.'

With a shrug of indifference – though secretly pleased – Don turned around and pushed his one-piece down to his knees, exposing his hairless crotch and butt. The warm air felt pleasant around his cock and balls and asshole and a thrill of pleasure ran through Don's groin at exposing himself that way. The grass and twigs yielded stiffly under his knees and hands. There was the rich smell of loam and the sweet smell of bracken. Don leant his head on his forearms and stuck his big ass up in the air in Hashi's face, then closed his eyes, drifting in sensation. He wasn't disappointed. Soon he felt soft lips kissing his sensitive, puckered and clean-shaven hole, and then a rough wet tongue licking up and down between his buttocks. He groaned softly, enjoying the attention Hashi was paying to his shapely ass. Hashi started to probe Don's butthole with his long, muscular tongue. It was tight, a brown star, and to relax it Hashi reached between Don's legs, gripped Don's stiff cock, and began to move his hand slowly but firmly up and down on it. The veins on Don's shaft pulsed against the palm of Hashi's hand. Don gasped in excitement, his anal ring clenched reflexively, then relaxed and opened for Hashi's tongue to push its way greedily into Don's rarely-penetrated rectum.

As Hashi tongue-fucked Don's now open asshole, and with the hot sun on his naked body, Don found his mind wandering to fantasies of asking Hashi to fuck *him*, instead of the other way around: although Don was a top-man, every so often he found himself being extremely turned on by the idea of getting fucked, of receiving anally the pleasure he gave to so many other guys with his long thick ten-inch dick. But then he thought of Hashi's shaven hole, and the thought of his erect cock sliding in and out of its spit-lubricated tightness made Don's dick stiffen and swell even further in Hashi's grip. Don let the anticipation of the hard fucking he was going to give Hashi float in his mind, while Hashi moved between licking his ass and probing his sphincter hungrily.

'Mm, that's good, man,' Don said eventually, his breathing a little heavy at the pleasure Hashi's eager rimming was giving him. 'You really know how to work your tongue in a guy's asshole, don't you, ass-licker? But now I want to fuck you, man. I want to push my chocolate pole up your ass, right the way in. You want that, man? You want those ten good inches you've been wrapping your fist around?'

Hashi kept on tonguing Don's muscular bung-hole without answering. Eventually, he managed to get out a muffled 'yes', before finally pulling his face back from where he had buried it between Don's buttocks. Don sat up and swivelled round, his rigid dick swinging heavily above his swollen ball-sack as he did so, and kissed Hashi on his wet shining lips. There was a bitter taste to them, the horny sour taste of Don's asshole. Hashi's cock was stiff too, and their electrically charged cock-heads brushed together, making both of them gasp in hyper sensitised excitement.

'Do you want to fuck me face-up or face-down?' Hashi asked Don breathlessly, tossing his long black hair back over his shoulders. At some point during his enthusiastic rimming, Hashi's ponytail had come untied, and now the hair hung shining and free.

Don stroked Hashi's handsome expectant face. 'Face-down man,' he said. 'You're pretty and shit. Don't get me wrong. But I save face-up for romances, and this is just horny fucking.' In fact, Don didn't 'do' romance, ever: but he liked the line, the defiance of sentimentality.

Turned on by Don's rough tone, Hashi went straight down onto his hands and knees, spreading his thighs and moving his ass and hips back so that, without moving, Don was kneeling between his legs. Hashi glanced back at Don. 'Horny fucking is what I'm looking for,' he said breathlessly, his shiny and dripping cock curving up almost to his lean belly, his balls swinging as he moved his ass invitingly backwards and forwards. The gold chain around Hashi's waist glinted in the bright sunlight, contrasting with his warm brown skin.

Don looked down at Hashi's totally waxed brown ass. Suddenly, he realised he needed to do a bit of ass-eating too. Partly because Hashi's butt looked so tasty he just had to get a mouthful, and partly because it would also get Hashi's tight-looking asshole ready for a good bum-fucking session. Don held Hashi's hard muscular buttocks open, bent his head down and began to lick Hashi's waxed asshole.

At that moment there was a clearly-audible crackling sound, as of someone treading accidentally on a fallen branch. Don looked up sharply and ran his eyes around the glade, trying to make out if anyone was watching from the furze. He couldn't see anyone. *Well, the pigs would have got in on the act by now, so it ain't the pigs. And whoever it is, if they want to watch, fuck 'em,* Don thought to himself, once he had made as sure as he could that whatever watcher was there was just a voyeur, not the filth out for some pointless arrests to boost their statistics. *Fuck 'em. I'll just make sure they get a good show of red-hot male-on-male action to jack off to before running back to the wife and shit.* He moved his mouth back down towards Hashi's shaven and quivering upturned asshole. The Asian boy didn't seem to have noticed the noise and was keeping his butt available and up in the air. *So long as anyone who's watching keeps quiet and don't try to muscle in on the act,* Don thought, *who gives a fuck, anyway?* But he didn't give Hashi any sign that he thought they were being watched, in case the Asian lad got scared and didn't want to go bottom-up for an audience.

A shiver of pleasure and excitement ran the length of Hashi's sinewy body as Don pressed his full lips against Hashi's anal sphincter and began to muscularly tongue-fuck him.

'Oh, man, yeah,' Hashi moaned as Don tongued him. 'Oh, shit, I'm a whore for your tongue, man. Oh, yeah! Get that tongue all the way up into my asshole, Don!' Hashi was finding being firmly rimmed by Don so exciting that he felt an almost hysterical excitement running in electrical currents between his asshole and the base of his balls. Don's hot wet tongue made him feel slippery and freaky and out of control. He reached for his own cock to give himself some relief as Don worked in his now-juicy butthole, but Don slapped Hashi's hand away from his painfully stiff and dripping hard-on.

'I want you to feel it all up the ass today,' Don told Hashi in a loud voice that any lurking voyeur could hear clearly, pulling his mouth away from Hashi's butthole momentarily and with a loud slurp to tell him this. 'Forget your cock, man; your cock's just where the come comes out. Today you're a bitch with a greedy boycunt. You're a hungry asshole. Just concentrate on your ass and what's going up it. 'Cause today you're a hot bottom and you're going to love it, man.'

'I'm your hot bottom, Don,' Hashi replied hoarsely, swallowing with difficulty. 'I'm your bitch. Your total bitch. Please fuck me so hard I won't be able to walk straight for days,' he begged Don. 'Fuck your bitch so good, the next time I sit on my saddle, my asshole's so open the saddle goes right up in me and I need to have it surgically removed.' There was a pleading in Hashi's voice, a desperate need for anal action that sent thrills of excitement through Don's chest and throbbing dick.

'I'm your dream top-man, Hashi,' Don said huskily, straightening up and aiming his thick dark stiff cock between Hashi's firm muscular buttocks. Hashi's asshole was now shiny with Don's saliva, and pouting invitingly. The twigs pressed hard against Don's knees and the sun was hot on his back and thick muscular neck. 'I'm gonna ram you without mercy, man,' he told Hashi. 'You can beg me to stop but I'll go right on fucking you, 'cause I know that's the only way you're going to be truly satisfied.'

Don put his cock-head against Hashi's trembling sphincter and started to push firmly against the shiny brown star of Hashi's anal opening. Rather than go for a full-length ram, as he had with the skinhead Stevo, this time Don was going for a slow entry: one thick hard centimetre at a time. Hashi put his head down, his long raven hair cascading around his shoulders. 'Oh, man, it's too big,' he moaned: the smooth dome of Don's crown, the foreskin pushed back, began to dilate Hashi's saliva-slickened hole as it started to enter the Asian youth's body. 'Oh, shit, man, I can't take it, it's too thick.'

'Course you can take it, man,' Don said, slapping one of Hashi's buttocks sharply, making Hashi gasp. 'Your bitch's ass is hungry for a big stiff dick.' But he relaxed the pressure on Hashi's asshole; Don wanted Hashi to enjoy being fucked, to get off on Don's cock going up his ass, not suffer it in discomfort. 'You ready to try again?' Don asked after a moment's pause, encouraged by the fact that Hashi had kept his ass in place, plainly waiting to take Don's next push up him.

Hashi's head bobbed up and down in assent. Then, to Don's pleasure, Hashi began to actually push his hips backwards onto Don's shaven crotch, gradually swallowing Don's thick stiff dark-brown dick up into his accommodating rectum. Don looked down at his jutting cock as Hashi's bottom moved slowly down on it, turned on by the sight of

Hashi's hungry and clean-shaven hole taking his stiff and throbbing manhood up into it, inch by inch. All Don had to do was keep his hips firmly in place, until Hashi's smoothly waxed buttocks were pressed hard into his crotch and his entire erection had been swallowed by Hashi's capacious butt. Their smooth ball-sacks were pressed together, hot and heavy and tingling, as Hashi took Don all the way up to the root.

'I'm open now,' Hashi said, tossing his long raven hair, his flatly-muscled chest full of excitement, his ass full of Don's thick hard-on. 'Open for business. For all the ramming you want to give me.'

Don moved his hands up to Hashi's square muscle-capped shoulders, gripped them, and began to pump his stiff cock in and out of Hashi's hot slippery asshole in long, easy strokes. The tightness of Hashi's anal ring around the thick shaft of his prick, and the smooth warmth of the lining of Hashi's rectum against his thrusting cockhead, thrilled Don and encouraged him to ram his achingly stiff manhood as far up Hashi's backside as he could.

Hashi gasped sharply with each firm thrust of Don's hips, feeling Don's cock-head slam hard against the sphincter at the top of the inside of his rectum that opened into his intestines, and each insertion made Hashi's rigid dick kick and its piss-slit bead with pre-come as Don's crown massaged his prostate.

Suddenly, Hashi had the feeling they were being watched. It was hard to focus his attention as Don's hard-on slithered rapidly in and out of his now-open bunghole. He tried to look around him as he knelt on all fours, stripped, his crotch shaved, his asshole open, being fucked by another man for anyone who passed to see. Maybe at an earlier stage fear would have made Hashi stop what he was doing, but right now there was nothing more important than the length of rigid dick being slammed up his asshole, and nothing mattered more than shooting his load with Don's throbbing hard-on up his back passage. All had to do was shoot his load, and everything would be fine.

And anyway, Hashi thought as his whole body pulsed and trembled from the hard poling Don was giving his ass, *if they want to – uh – watch, if they're getting off on it, if they're – oh, fuck – envious – and if I was them I fucking would be – oh, fuck me, yeah, why should I give a shit that I'm being watched doing what they wish – oh, God, oh, fuck – they wish they could be doing right now? Oh, Jesus, I got to relax, open up inside –'*

Hashi stopped squinting into the surrounding bushes and concentrated on the movement of Don's rigid pole inside his stretched rectum, the hypnotic, compelling back-and-forth of Don's pulsing erection inside his willing anal cavity; the dizzying pleasure from the pumping motion inside his back-passage spreading through Hashi's entire body as he stayed there, on all fours, being butt-fucked.

Not wanting to come in Hashi's excitingly tight asshole too soon, Don pulled his cock right the way out of Hashi's ass for a second, making Hashi exhale with a loud groan of relief and loss, then plugged it all the way back in, filling Hashi's rectum to capacity with stiff pulsing cock and making him cry out with a high gasp.

'You like that?' Don asked thickly, pulling out and reinserting his hard-on into Hashi's quivering hole a second time, but Hashi was too overcome with excitement to do more than moan ecstatically in response. Don now resumed fucking Hashi without withdrawing, slamming his hips against the Pakistani youth's upturned willing ass as hard as he could; each thrust was accompanied by a grunt of exertion and the noisy slap of smooth muscular thighs against firm shaven buttocks.

Hashi's back was a sinuous map of glistening tensed muscles and his ebony hair was flicked back loosely along the elegant curve of his spine. Don took his hands off Hashi's shoulders and gathered the mass of the Asian boy's hair into one long ebony ponytail. Then he pulled Hashi's head back, fucking Hashi even harder as he did so, making Hashi arch his back in a sinewy curve and spread his lean thighs even wider, and open his buttocks even wider as he did so.

So watch this, Don thought, sure they were still being observed by some guy hiding in the undergrowth. *Watch this and stick a branch up your ass and get yourself off on it, 'cause you ain't never seen nothing this hot, fucker.*

'Oh, yeah, man,' Hashi yelled hoarsely. 'Ride me like a fucking pony, man. Ride me and fuck me like a stallion!' His neck ached, his back ached and his stretched and battered rectum ached most of all as Don kept Hashi's head pulled back with his reins and bridle of raven hair, totally controlling the ecstatic Asian youth; he pounded Hashi's open ass-hole with rapid movements of his narrow muscular hips that kept his thick and rigid pole slamming back and forth inside Hashi's tense and trembling body. The violent thrustings of Don's rock-hard manhood in his rectum was now sending electrical thrills of pleasure through Hashi's gut and down into his own cock and balls: the regular back-and-forth of Don's rigid pole of muscle in and out of Hashi's slack asshole was making Hashi's untouched cock start to tingle and gain in pre-orgasmic heaviness. Hashi felt as if water was dripping from his cock-head, and he realised that, any second, he was going to come just from being fucked up the ass. His whole body seemed like it was entirely out of his control: not just his cock and balls but his chest, his nipples, the aching thighs and arms he was trying to brace himself up with. If Don hadn't been holding him up by his long hair, as if Hashi's lean body was a bow and Don the archer, he would have collapsed forward, unable to support himself, all muscles turned to water.

Hashi's gasps came sharp and fast as Don's long thick erection slithered in and out of his asshole more and more rapidly: then, suddenly, Hashi was aware that come was spurting out of his involuntarily bucking cock.

'Oh, my God, oh, Jesus, oh, fuck, I'm coming, I'm coming,' Hashi cried out hoarsely: his load spattered out over the grass in convulsive spurts and his hips and his whole body bucked. He wanted to slump forward immediately, to slide his asshole off Don's massive, throbbing cock, to regain control of his body, to relinquish the bitch role he had been so keenly playing until his cock had exploded. But Don kept Hashi held firmly in place, his head still pulled back in a painful arch by his hair, and carried on rhythmically fucking him with deep, rectum-filling strokes. Hashi's ass felt in turmoil as Don kept on pounding into it with his big stiff dick, his own soft cock flapping backwards and forwards with each vigorous thrust of Don's hips; Don clearly wasn't going to stop fucking him until he bust his nut.

Normally, once he had come, Hashi would have wriggled his asshole off the other guy's cock, however insistent the guy was about getting his own, and told him to jerk himself off; or maybe Hashi would jerk him off, if he was feeling generous. But there was something about the way Don had fucked him – was fucking him – that stopped Hashi from denying Don all the butt-stuffing he wanted to do as Don carried on vigorously poling him. To be so totally used by another man was profoundly exciting to Hashi.

I'm being a true bitch for Don now, Hashi thought breathlessly. *A true bitch for my man. Taking my man's rock-hard cock up my wet slack hole and I'm not even hard, 'cause my pleasure's his pleasure.* A rapture that oscillated across the boundary between pleasure and pain possessed Hashi's body at playing the bitch role so fully, as Don bum-fucked him as hard as he could.

'Oh, use me, man!' Hashi gasped loudly as Don carried on ramming his thick heavy pole in and out of Hashi's open asshole, the veins on his stretched neck and throat standing out with throbbing sharpness. 'Oh, man, I'm in bitch heaven!'

'S'cause you are a bitch, Hashi, man,' Don growled hoarsely. He kept on pumping his hips against Hashi's submissive butt. Don had been worried that, once Hashi had come, he wouldn't have wanted to carry on pleasuring Don with his anal canal, and Don wouldn't have been able to enjoy fucking a guy who wasn't loving having Don's rigid cock slammed up his asshole. But Hashi was a true bitch who got the thrill of being used like a whore, and that encouraged Don to fuck him even harder, with deep, rapid strokes that filled the Asian youth's backside.

'Take this cock, bitch,' Don ordered in a loud voice. 'Take it right the way up you, bitch. I'm satisfying you up your horny hole –' Don knew the voyeur's fist would be moving fast on his cock in the bushes now, and the thought of making someone he couldn't even see come, of drawing that pleasure out of some unseen man by the vigour with which he was fucking the youth on all fours in front of him, inspired Don to pound Hashi's ass even harder.

As Don poled him hard, Hashi became aware that all the excitement in his ass was making his own dick unexpectedly firm up as it swung between his legs, and rapidly stiffen to full throbbing erectness again, from the continued attention to his well-stretched rectum. As his pleasure mounted, in a body over which he had totally surrendered control, Hashi became excitedly aware that Don was offering him the nearest a man can get to multiple orgasm. On top of that, Hashi now felt his asshole was so wide open, a whole arm could disappear up it, so thoroughly was Don fucking him; and the feeling was good.

Don's breathing was coming faster and hoarser and every

muscle in his powerfully pumped body ached as he slammed his hips against Hashi's buttocks and thrust his rigid, throbbing cock as deep into Hashi's rectum as he could manage; his shaven crotch was shiny with sweat, and dark against Hashi's smooth brown butt. Don's cock felt heavier and heavier as he slid it in and out of Hashi's receptive bunghole and his balls clenched.

'Oh, oh, oh, I'm coming, bitch!' he gasped throatily as he lost control of the thrilling weight of his slithering cock. 'I'm shooting that load up your horny bitch-ass, Hashi, man! Oh, Jesus! Oh, God! Oh, fuck me, yeah –' He pumped his hips against Hashi's ass with liquid rapidity, jerking them in sudden spasming ecstasy and, while keeping his hands in Hashi's hair, forced Hashi forward, so his face was suddenly pushed into the crisp warm grass as Don shot his load up into Hashi's back-passage. Excitement lanced through Hashi's balls and cock as Don came inside him but he didn't, couldn't, come this time; instead, he was left with a brand-new throbbing hard-on that needed some serious attention if Hashi was to leave his encounter with Don feeling truly satisfied.

Concealed in the bushes, from which he had been watching the entire encounter with his trousers round his ankles, Oba, the horny African taxi-driver, thrust his narrow hips forward, his fist by now a blur on his twelve-inch cock, his chest pounding painfully as he held his breath and shot his thick creamy load onto the fallen leaves and twigs and loam beneath him in spasms and spurts of thick white spunk.

Don kept his cock all the way up Hashi's ass for a long moment, then carefully withdrew it from Hashi's body. It flopped heavily and semi-erect out of Hashi's asshole with a soft pop. Hashi immediately rolled over onto his back and threw his legs up in the air as wide as he could. His large brown cock jutted stiffly over his lean belly and his shiny ass-hole gaped succulently open between his shapely buttocks.

'Get some fingers up me while I frig myself off,' he begged Don. 'I really need some fingers up me.' Don, unable to refuse such a direct request, slid three fingers up Hashi's juicy asshole while Hashi masturbated himself, working his fist on his long thick cock in smooth fast strokes. The muscles in Hashi's chest and right arm tensed with sinewy tightness as he moved his hand rapidly up and down on his throbbing and aching hard-on.

Don worked his fingers back and forth in the Pakistani youth's spunk-lubricated asshole while Hashi cupped a hand around his heavy balls and wanked his aching pole to climax, breathing more and more heavily as the throbbing excitement started to course the length of his rigid dick. He came with a loud cry, his whole body arching and straining upwards, with three of Don's fingers shoved right the way up his bottom to the knuckles, and come spattered across his belly and chest.

Hashi slumped back onto the ground. Don withdrew his fingers carefully from Hashi's butthole, leaving it gaping. The still air was now tinted with the sharp smell of come as well as the musky scent of the dark, loamy soil.

Don bent over the sweaty and totally exhausted Hashi, who now lay supine in the sunshine, and kissed him on the mouth. 'You've got the sweetest ass, man,' Don said quietly, smiling softly, worn out himself.

'Hey,' the Asian youth said, returning Don's smile. 'Any time you want it, guy.' He reached over for his courier bag, fumbled in it and handed Don the card of his cycle-courier company. 'Call this number. Taking rear-entry deliveries is our speciality. Any time of the day or night, yeah?'

Don smiled again as he took Hashi's card. But as he looked down at the handsome youth, he felt an unexpected twinge of dissatisfaction. Could it be that Malcolm was right? That he needed more in his life than just fucking, however horny, however exciting? That he needed love? Suddenly needing to move on, he rolled over and went to pull on his lycra one-piece.

Unseen and forgotten by both Don and Hashi in the undergrowth, Oba shook the last drops of spunk from the head of his softening weapon, pulled up his jeans, zipped his fly, and stole away quietly. Oba's sex-drive was so high that, even as he made his way back to his black cab, he was thinking about the next possible male-on-male sexual encounter.

Five

Gregory stood in front of his bathroom mirror, a large white towel wrapped around his slender waist, getting ready for his date that evening with Thom. He had bathed and shampooed his shoulder-length dreadlocks, and was now trimming his goatee with electric clippers so that the hair was little more than a sharply-defined cheekbone-enhancing outline of stubble. Since he already had the clippers out, Gregory loosened the towel around his waist, letting it fall to the floor, and quickly gave his pubic hair a close shave, too, leaving a neatly-clipped 'V' of hair rising up from his groin towards his belly-button. The vibration of the clippers against the skin around his cock and balls was vaguely arousing. Then he rubbed cocoa butter all over his body, giving himself a fairly full hard-on as he did so.

He resisted the urge to masturbate in anticipation of the evening ahead, instead going through to his bedroom to pull on a pair of skimpy black hipster briefs that hugged his basket and rode up between his taut buttocks. Gregory checked himself in the mirror: just wearing such provocative underwear made him feel a little kinky, a little like he might just have to do anything Thom asked him to tonight. His heart began to pound in his chest. His cock stayed hard, pushing out against the soft black material of the briefs, making him feel up for passionate sex at the earliest possible opportunity.

Gregory pulled on a tight red, gold and green horizontally striped T-shirt that rode up over his lean belly, exposing his ridged stomach muscles and the flat disc of his gold-pierced navel, and went over to his wardrobe to get out a pair of Timberland boots. Various pairs of boots and shoes sat in a neat row on a low shelf at the bottom of the wardrobe. On the shelf above them, and arranged similarly neatly, sat Gregory's considerable collection of sex-toys: in many different sizes, colours, shapes, textures and types. His cock stiffened further in his briefs at the sight of them all sitting there, ready for action. Maybe he could just have a quick session before Thom arrived to pick him up? Gregory resisted it. Instead he went through to the living-room of his spacious, shrewdly-scammed council flat, unzipped his sausage-bag, and pulled out the vibrator he had treated himself to that morning, and had then had so enthusiastically used on him at the studio. He took it, wiped it down with a damp cloth, and went back through to the bedroom to put it with the others. Then he quickly closed the cupboard door before he could get too tempted by the sight of them all standing there, upright in a row, waiting to be sat all the way down on.

Gregory wriggled his lean, slender legs into the tightest, narrowest-fitting pair of white jeans he owned, adjusting his basket in front of the bedroom mirror to show his tackle off to its full advantage. His eyes were shining and his lips were full. He wanted it bad, this evening, he realised. He clipped his mobile onto the waist of his jeans in the small of his back and went into the hall of his fifteenth-story tower-block flat to pick a jacket from the peg. He tried on several, then decided against wearing one at all; the temperature during the day had been hot and the evening would most likely be warm enough for him not to have to bother. Anyway – and more importantly – he didn't want to cover up his shapely sinewy arms. He checked his watch nervously. Thom was due in less than five minutes. Abruptly, the fear of being stood up coursed through Gregory. He tried to put the idea out of his mind, challenging himself. *Why would Thom stand up a gorgeous guy like you, anyway? He'd have to be crazy.*

Because he's already sampled your horny body once today, came the unreassuring answer. *Maybe he thinks your butthole's too slack and he's going to want a tighter ride tonight. Or maybe he want a guy who's not a total bottom, and he could tell your studio session ass-fucking Bobbi had about as much feeling as a bitch with a strap-on.*

But then he recalled the warm soft feeling of Thom's lips on his, after they had come, the muscular closeness of Thom's arms around him. And after all, it was Thom who had suggested going for a date.

Suddenly, Gregory remembered that he had been going to give himself an enema before Thom arrived, to make sure that his asshole was totally cleaned out for the evening's activities. He looked at his watch again: Four minutes until Thom was due. If he was quick, he would just about have time for a session.

Gregory hurried through to the bathroom and ran warm water into the sink. Then he opened the bathroom cabinet and rummaged about for the douche-bulb he kept there for regular use. Three minutes until Thom was due. Gregory fumblingly unbuttoned his jeans and shoved them down to his knees, then pulled his underpants down too. He dangled the smooth blunt-ended nozzle of the enema kit's hose into the sinkfill of warm water and pumped the soft black rubber bulb with a squeezing, massaging motion, expelling air and drawing in water. Gregory's breath was coming more rapidly as he rhythmically sucked the water up into the bulb, and his dick was stiffening at the thought of pushing the rubber hose up his own ass.

Once the soft rubber bulb was full and heavy with warm water, Gregory lifted the hose-end out of the sink, twisted round awkwardly and plugged it into his asshole, letting out a small gasp as the smooth and slightly swollen wet end slid into his rectum. He bent forward, sticking his ass back and up so that the hose couldn't pop out too easily;

although, until he had emptied the black rubber bulb, now wet and shining, he would hold the tube in place with one hand anyway. With his other hand he squeezed the bulb, sending warm water coursing into his back passage. As Gregory's anus began to fill up his cock stiffened to full rigidity again. He squeezed the bulb firmly until all its contents had been pumped up his ass, getting more and more excited as the liquid started to stretch his rectum, then let the hose slip out of his hole. He clenched hard, enjoying the feeling of fullness, and looked at his watch. Two minutes to go – and that was only if Thom was actually on time, which Gregory, a Londoner born and bred, wasn't really expecting him to be.

Bzzzzzzzzzzzzzz!

The sudden loud sound of the door-buzzer being pressed in the tower-block's lobby far below startled Gregory and made him jump – Thom was *early*, for fuck's sake!

'Oh, fuck!' Gregory cursed. Emptying out always took a bit of time, and he couldn't risk Thom thinking he'd got the wrong address and giving up, or that Gregory had stood *him* up, and leaving before Gregory could get to the entry-phone to buzz him in. He'd just have to let Thom in and tell him to fix himself a drink while he used the toilet. Nothing odd about that, Gregory reassured himself.

Tightening his anal ring with a professional's efficiency, Gregory quickly pulled up his trousers and briefs, buttoning his fly hastily as he hurried over to the phone to let Thom know he'd got the right flat and let him into the building. Hearing Thom's deep rough-smooth voice reminded Gregory how much he fancied Thom. Gregory felt turned on by the thought of seeing Thom again, and also by the pint or so of warm water he had pumped up his ass, and the two types of excitement blurred together and made him feel strange and giddy.

When Gregory opened his front door to let Thom into his flat a few minutes later, shy and awkward and excited and smiling, he wondered why the first thing Thom did was glance down curiously at what Gregory was holding in his right hand. To his shock and embarrassment, Gregory realised that he'd been so flustered when the buzzer went that he had answered the door still holding the now-empty black rubber enema bulb.

Thom's broad handsome face broke into a questioning smile, making his slightly tip-tilted nose crinkle between his wide cornflower-blue eyes. Gregory could feel his face burning. He let Thom come in and closed the door behind him.

'I was just . . .' Gregory began, trying to think of a suitable euphemism for giving oneself an enema in the expectation of being anally fucked senseless. He couldn't, and at that moment he felt a tiny trickle of water begin to escape from his clenched anal star and wet his underpants. 'I just need to use the toilet,' he said eventually, moving awkwardly from one foot to the other, keeping his buttocks clenched together as hard as he possibly could.

'Did you just give yourself a full tank, mate?' Tom asked, making it sound completely normal and as if they were standing in the middle of a garage forecourt together. Gregory nodded wordlessly. 'Cool,' Thom said, still smiling. Then he pushed his head forward and kissed Gregory hotly on the mouth, his firm coral-pink lips against Gregory's larger brown ones. Gregory's dick stiffened at an uncomfortable angle in his pants as they explored each other's mouths, and cramps lanced through his water-distended intestines with a sharp thrill.

'Can I watch you empty out?' Thom asked Gregory abruptly, breaking off the kiss, his smile a little wider now, a little shyer, his face flushing hotly.

Gregory blushed again, about to refuse. But then he

thought, *Well, why not, if he wants to? It's what me do. And if it get me off, why it shouldn't get him off too?* Gregory took a deep breath. 'Sure, man,' he said to Thom. 'You can watch. Close up as you like. But it got to be right now, 'cause me bursting.'

Thom nodded and Gregory – asshole straining to remain closed for just a few seconds more, against what felt like a dam about to explode out of his ass and flood down his legs – led the tanned freckle-faced and eager body-builder quickly into his clean white bathroom, to watch him pump out.

Thom had chosen to wear new white cross-trainers, a loose and skimpy chest-revealing white vest, and very short soft grey trunks for their date, and was looking even more handsome than Gregory remembered. It felt weird to Gregory not to be closing the bathroom door behind him as he prepared to open his bowels, and weirder still to have Thom standing there, watching him keenly as he shoved down his trousers and pants with desperate urgency. He glanced at Thom's bulging crotch as he turned sideways on to the muscular Australian, and was pleased to see Thom's cock was visibly lengthening and hardening inside the soft elastic dove-grey fabric as Thom watched Gregory get ready to empty out his ass.

Gregory's asshole was already glittering with the small trickle of water that had slid out of it as he pulled his briefs down. His dark-brown cock sprang up, long and pulsing and heavy with blood. Thom watched in mounting excitement as Gregory bent over and took hold of the towel-rail on the wall opposite the toilet with both hands, pushing his shapely ass out, moving it slightly from side to side as if taking aim at the porcelain bowl, some four feet away behind him. Gregory's balls hung down heavily between his legs and his stiff cock arched up in a rigid curve, its head bumping against his well-defined belly. Thom moved his position slightly to get an intimate view of Gregory's shining sphincter.

'You getting a good look, man?' Gregory gasped. ''Cause me must relieve myself now or me a go burst all over the place.'

Thom nodded excitedly, and began to move his fingers back and forth on the blood-hard shaft of his cock through the grey cotton lycra of his skimpy shorts, his bright eyes fixed on Gregory's pouting chocolate star. As Thom watched, a small spurt of clear liquid shot out of Gregory's hole, splashing on the clean white lino of the floor and scattering in diamond drops. Then the water erupted from Gregory's ass in a steady clear hose-like stream as Gregory pushed his diaphragm down to expel the liquid from his bottom, arcing it perfectly into the toilet-bowl behind him. Gregory gasped repeatedly and panted in relief as the water ran for about twenty seconds at high pressure out of his asshole. Then the stream slowly started to slacken. As it did so, Gregory lowered his ass gradually onto the toilet-seat so that not another drop of water missed the bowl. Gregory expelled the last few squirts and gave a shuddering gasp of relief as he sank down onto the toilet-seat.

Thom reached over and toyed with Gregory's nipples through the fabric of his T-shirt as Gregory sat there on the toilet, with his thick brown prick sticking upright between his legs, his chest heaving.

'Where did you learn to aim like that?' Thom asked with a smile, surprised and impressed and highly turned-on by Gregory's display.

'There was this guy I used to see back before I foxed up,' Gregory said, the pleasure Thom was giving his nipples with his deft thumb and forefinger making Gregory more confidential than he might otherwise have been. 'Shit, man, I was hot for him. And I loved him too. I'd do *anything* for him, you know what I'm saying? And one of the things he'd get me to do was dance for him, like, you know, strip. And I'd fill up before starting my little act 'cause that was what he really liked most of all, and the end of my performance would be my pants coming down and me pushing my ass in his face and squirting my contents into his mouth. The better my aim was, the more of a mouthwash he got and the more he liked me. I saw him for a couple of months, so I got pretty good. I was always clean, though,' Gregory added insistently. 'I'd wash out first before putting his pint of ass-champagne up me. It weren't a scat scene or nothing dirty like that, it was just – just excess, I guess. Not wrong but – me na do that stuff nowadays, you know?'

After this confession, Gregory tried to struggle to his feet, but found it hard to brace himself; his legs felt wobbly from the sudden gushing out of the enema. He sat back down heavily, his thigh muscles twitching.

Looking down on the slender, vulnerable, emptied-out Rastaman sitting beneath him, Thom felt a rush of genuine warmth. He bent forward and slid his hands under Gregory's armpits, and then gently helped him to get to his feet. With Thom's firm and muscular support, Gregory did then manage to stand somewhat shakily, although every muscle in his body was still weak and trembling from the relief of emptying out. Still being held up by Thom, Gregory bent over and fumblingly pulled up his skimpy briefs and tightly-fitting jeans, buttoning his fly awkwardly over a stiffly protruding dick that the elastic cotton and unyielding denim could barely contain, and that didn't look like it was going away.

A moment later, blood began to flow freely through Gregory's limbs again, and within a minute the trembling had passed from him, and he felt strong once more, and more than that: pure and glowing. Thom released him and he stood freely.

'I'm hungry now, man,' he said to Thom, feeling suddenly confident and assertive. 'Let's go grab something to eat and you can tell me about some of your *dark* secrets,' he continued. 'Confession not a one-way street you know, man. It must be give and take.'

'Sounds good to me,' Thom said. 'What d'you fancy? Thai, Indian, Chinese, Jamaican, vegetarian . . .?'

'Just something with plenty of meat in it,' Gregory said, stroking his forefinger along the groove in Thom's tanned muscular bicep and giving him an inviting look.

'My chariot awaits,' Thom said, grinning, holding up the keys to his two-seater Suzuki jeep with one hand, and gripping Gregory's muscular ass with the other. Then, his expression serious, Thom pulled Gregory's crotch towards him so that Gregory was straddling one of his firm bulging thighs. Thom pivoted his knee so his bare thigh rubbed hard against Gregory's bulging crotch. Gregory grunted softly at the contact, his balls getting squeezed – painfully, thrillingly – in his tight denims. Thom met Gregory's glowing obsidian eyes with his bright blue ones. 'You certainly look like you need something hot inside you, man,' he said playfully, a small teasing smile on his well-shaped lips.

'Yeah,' Gregory agreed throatily. 'So let's get going, man.'

Malcolm put down his adjustable spanner wearily and struggled to his feet so he could stretch his aching body. He had hoped that stripping down and fine-tuning his motorbike would put the day's arguments out of his mind and help him forget about the disaster of his romance with Kam, but it hadn't worked. Even the name of the bike made Malcolm think of his cheating ex-boyfriend. The work had made Malcolm sweat, so he had stripped down to a pair of tight black leather shorts that he wore around the flat, a little fetish that had grown out of the way his biking leathers had made him feel so sexy and masculine. He now had a black leather vest and a blaxploitation-style leather cap in his wardrobe too, although he only wore these items in the privacy of his own home.

Malcolm wiped a greasy hand across his brow as he strolled through to the kitchen and reached in the fridge for an ice-cold beer. Sweat ran in rivulets down his chest as he tipped his head back for a long swallow of Red Stripe. He drained the can, crushed it, and threw it into the swing-bin in the corner of the kitchen. Then he wandered through to the bedroom, leaving the bike sitting on a tarpaulin in the lounge, thinking of losing the bad thoughts of the day in a short nap.

The drawers of the dressing-table gaped open where Kam had hastily torn around the bedroom packing up his belongings earlier that morning. The sheets on the king-size double-bed were lying where they had been casually thrown aside – after he and Kam had made passionate love on them only the night before, Malcolm realised, him holding Kam face-down on the bed and poling Kam's hot asshole with his thick rigid dick until he had shot his load up Kam's hungry ass, and then kept it shoved all the way up there while Kam had quickly jerked himself off, splattering a large load of come over the clean white cotton beneath him.

Malcolm lay down on the bed at full stretch, resting his face on one of the pillows, and pushed his crotch down onto the mattress. He took in the faint smell of Kam's hair-gel, vaseline and sweat. Malcolm felt melancholy and slightly turned on as he lay there, and closed his eyes in the hope of drifting off to sleep. Then he found himself remembering the load that Kam had shot over the sheets that night. Malcolm didn't think Kam had bothered to wipe up the results of their passionate fuck. Almost without thinking about it, Malcolm slid round on the bed to where he had been butt-fucking Kam, to where Kam's crotch had been when the horny oriental youth had climaxed, looking for the semen-stains on the sheets, suddenly desperate for a taste of Kam's man-juice.

It only took Malcolm a little time to find the spunk-stiffened place where Kam had ejaculated. Malcolm pressed his nose flat against it, inhaling the faint scent of Kam's jism, at the same time grinding his leather-covered hips hard against the mattress and flexing his ass, enjoying the sensation of pressure against the stiffness in the front of his shorts. Malcolm began to lick the semen-stiffened sheet. His saliva reactivated the smell and taste of the come. He inhaled deeply and began to lick more enthusiastically, feeling slightly perverted but extremely excited as his tongue moved over the now damp and salty-tasting material. Malcolm contemplated pulling down his shorts and jerking off with the handle of the adjustable spanner up his ass while he licked up Kam's cock-juice, but decided not to: too elaborate.

And if I'm that horny, Malcolm thought, keeping his hips still for a moment, *I really should go to that goddamn party Bobbi was pressuring me to go to.*

He got up off the bed, cock still painfully stiff in his tight leather shorts, and went through to the lounge to look for the invitation, which read: *Prince Fela, King Bitch.* King Bitch? It all sounded kind of wild to Malcolm, but maybe he could do with something wild, he reflected. *And I could wear my leather*, he thought. The idea excited Malcolm as he imagined himself striking body-builder poses in his skimpy leather shorts and skin-tight leather vest and cap, in front of a roomful of cute, admiring and fuckable pretty-boys.

Now eager for night to fall, he went into the bedroom to try on his leather vest, Kam finally – if maybe only temporarily – pushed out of the forefront of his mind.

*

Bobbi brushed his neatly-plucked eyebrows outwards with a toothbrush until they looked smooth and exactly symmetrical, then rubbed just a hint of foundation over his face so it looked completely flawless. He had stopped off at a local barber's on the way back to his flat and had his fade redone, so it was now immaculate. Bobbi liked to look immaculate. Gregory had once accused Bobbi of going for a 'featureless, plastic, sex-doll kind of look' and Bobbi had laughed with him and agreed. He shaved his armpits regularly, trimmed his pubic hair once a week and waxed his bikini-line. He also attended saunas regularly, to flush any impurities out of his skin, so that it looked as even and blemish-free as possible – in addition to being a good way of keeping up his daily quota of cock-sucking, a keenly felt extra plus for the come-hungry young man.

Bobbi slipped on a pair of bright yellow bikini briefs and stood admiring his smooth shapely body in his full-length bedroom mirror. Really, he thought, looking himself up and down, it was a shame he had to wear anything else (except for a pair of boots) at all. At heart he was a go-go dancer, and he believed in letting it all hang out as much as possible and in as many places as possible. After all, why not make sure it was all on offer to whoever might be interested, as much of the time as you could? Bobbi felt he had a lot of loving to spread around.

He went through his wardrobe, looking for his most trampy outfit; the choice was slightly constrained by it having to fit in sufficiently well in a lot of different venues when he went hunting for Don. Eventually, he settled for faded bluejean short-shorts, so brief that the seam practically cut his balls in half, it was so constraining; it was also pulled up impossibly high between his buttocks, making the tight denim material ride halfway up Bobbi's big beefy ass, exposing the large smooth domes of his ass-muscles above his smooth curving thighs. Bobbi then pulled on a tight white bra-top that hugged his slightly pumped chest but left his firm stomach fully exposed.

All that was left for him to put on was a pair of chunky red bike-boots for his feet and silver bangles for his wrists. An afro-comb for his hair thrust into a back-pocket, and Bobbi was ready for action. He checked himself out in the full-length mirror in his hall, and was pleased by the trashy look he had managed to achieve. He adjusted his cock and balls in his shorts to make his bulge as impressive and inviting as possible to any casual eye.

Now all Bobbi had to do was try and figure out which bar or club Don was most likely to spend the evening hanging out in. He had more than a few ideas, but the search threatened to be quite time-consuming, and was made more difficult by the fact that Don wouldn't just stay put in any one place, but would probably bar-hop himself. *Well, if I've got to drag my ass round every gay bar and club in Zone One for the sake of the band*, Bobbi thought to himself, pouting at the mirror and running a hand down over his chest to his bare stomach and squeezing his denim-covered crotch in a provocative way, *the least I can do is make sure I have as much fun as I possibly can on the way.*

Bobbi grabbed a small bill-fold from the mantelpiece and stuffed it into his shorts' pocket – he wouldn't need much cash, he reckoned, as he was on the guest-list of most of the hot gay clubs and, being a good-time boy, he rarely had to buy his own drinks – and he was ready to go. Sex, business and pleasure: there was nothing Bobbi liked better than combining the three. He clattered down the steps outside his house in his heavy boots and went to hail a cab. Unusually, one pulled over immediately. Dusk was falling, and the street-lights were flickering into life, yellow against the blue of the deepening sky. Bobbi got into the cab.

'Where to, man?' Oba said, looking round casually at the

trampy young black man sitting casually on the passenger seat, with his smooth bare legs spread wide and his crotch bulging.

'Soho,' Bobbi instructed him. 'Compton Street.' The handsome and silver-haired African cabbie nodded and pulled out into the falling dusk.

Let's hope this one can't make the cab-fare, Oba thought to himself, eyeing Bobbi up in the rear-view mirror. He could just do with taking another cute young guy up the ass before heading home to his wife and kids for his evening meal, and Bobbi certainly looked like the type who would cheerfully trade a ride for a ride. And who knew? He might even give it up for Oba just for the pleasure of a fast, hard fuck . . . Oba's outsize cock stiffened in his shorts as his mind ran ahead of itself. He reached over and flicked the single person excess on his meter.

Night had fallen by the time Gregory and Thom found themselves strolling hand-in-hand along the South Bank of the Thames, past post-classical concert yuppies and skateboarding street-kids, talking easily as they walked. The air was warm and still, at body-heat, and sex and romance seemed to saturate the humid atmosphere. The two men had eaten at a classy Nigerian restaurant in Covent Garden, Thom insisting on picking up the tab. Gregory, with a fey toss of his dreadlocks, had let him, enjoying Thom's proprietorial attitude towards him. Normally Gregory would have been uncomfortable about playing the bottom role so fully with a white guy, but there was something about Thom that made him feel comfortable enough to push the feeling aside and go with the flow of the evening.

'Isn't it a problem for you, being a Rastafarian and going with guys?' Thom asked Gregory, his beefy peach-coloured arm rubbing against Gregory's lean plain chocolate brown one as they walked along.

'Nah, man,' Gregory said. 'Cos Jah is love, seen. And is Jah give me me appetites. Him wouldn't have given them to I if he ain't want I&I to act pon them, you know what I'm saying? Him wouldn't have put thoughts into I mind about how I&I might use I&I body; me cock, me asshole. Me heart,' he added, surprising himself. 'If others them give me shit, them is just small-minded, you know? And you?' Gregory went on to ask Thom, after falling silent thoughtfully for a moment. 'Is it a problem being Australian and – ah – going with guys?'

Thom smiled. 'No problem at all, sport,' he said easily.

They strolled past the National Film Theatre and through the South Bank complex to where Thom had parked his jeep. Thom unlocked it and they got in.

'D'you fancy coming back to my place?' Thom asked Gregory, reaching over and rubbing his hand firmly along the inside of Gregory's thigh. Gregory nodded yes, and the two men turned to face each other and stare into each other's eyes, then kissed hotly on the mouth as Thom turned over the motor of the jeep, making it roar throatily into life.

They drove down to Brixton fast, speeding through the city's less busy night-time streets with carefree ease, and made their way to Thom's flat, which was on the second floor above the recording studio. Thom parked the jeep in a space directly in front of the studio and the two men got out and hurried inside, their hearts pounding, their cocks stiff in their pants. The vibrations of the car's engine, and the anticipation of the sex to come, had kept them both fully turned on ever since they had left the restaurant. They mounted the stairs quickly, Thom leading the way in the dark. He fumbled with the keys to his flat on the unlit landing, but eventually he got the door open, and gestured for Gregory to go in ahead of him.

The decent-sized front room was lit by the rosy glow of

two small lamps. A large leather sofa faced a wide-screen TV with large speakers either side of it. A stack system sat in one corner, next to five towers of CDs. There were several potted plants with gleaming healthy leaves positioned around the room. Against one wall was a small book-case. Against another, a high table served as a drinks cabinet; bottles of scotch and whisky sat on top of it, next to inverted tumblers. Doors opened off to a kitchen and two bedrooms and the thick green floor-length curtains were closed tightly against the night.

But the thing that had really caught Gregory's eye the moment he glanced round the room was the long smoked-glass coffee-table that was positioned in front of the sofa: on its freshly polished and reflective surface sat two rows of dildoes of every conceivable type, size and shape. Gregory found himself struggling for breath and became aware that his asshole was opening up in anticipation of the filling it was going to get from Thom, in every way, in a very short time from now.

Thom seemed to have every sort of sex-toy, from slim silver 'lady's purse' vibrators that could slip up a guy's bottom in a second to donkey dildoes over eighteen inches long, to black rubber 'traffic cones' that spread out to almost twelve inches across at their broad bases. A jar of Elbow Grease sat by the upright rubber and plastic toys, its glass sides glinting enticingly in the lamplight.

'You like what you're looking at?' Thom asked Gregory hoarsely, closing the front door of the flat behind him.

Gregory nodded speechlessly. 'Yes, man,' he eventually managed to stutter. 'Yeah, I do. A lot. But where you get them from? I mean, they're yours, yeah?'

'Well, they were kind of left to me,' Thom said, crossing the room to pour out a couple of whiskys. 'See, I sublet the flat's other bedroom to this guy. And he sold all sex stuff, videos, leather and rubber gear, magazines and sex-toys.

Anyway, he apparently wasn't too good at selling, because he couldn't pay the rent. And one day he just did a bunk, leaving all this stuff behind and leaving his unpaid bills, too. The company he worked for used to phone me and hassle me to give them back the gear, because he was only meant to be selling it and getting a commission, so it wasn't really his. But I was real pissed off with him at the time, so I told them he'd taken it all with him when he'd cleared out. Well, he did owe me money, so I thought I ought to get something out of it, you know? I gave away the other stuff to friends as presents. But for some reason, I kept all these –' Thom indicated the dildoes as he handed Gregory a tumbler of whisky. 'I dunno why, mate. They just did something for me, I guess. And I feel like I might have finally met somebody who would appreciate them. Like, the person they've been waiting for. Maybe.' Thom looked at Gregory with please-be-pleased eyes.

Gregory ran his fingertips over the smooth rubber head of one of the traffic cones and felt an electric thrill run up his arm to his chest. It was too big to contemplate actually using, but as a vision of excess it excited him.

'It's a good collection,' Gregory said finally. 'The best I ever seen. Better'n mine.'

Thom came and stood behind Gregory and wrapped his tanned muscular arms around Gregory's flat chest and narrow waist and kissed him on the side of his neck. Gregory closed his eyes at the warm touch of Thom's lips and sighed. 'Yeah,' he moaned softly as Thom held him tight. Then Gregory moaned again as Thom fondled his chest, finding and squeezing his nipples through his tight-fitting T-shirt, and started to grind his ass back against Thom's crotch.

Gregory could feel Thom's stiff cock pressing hard against the soft, rough denim that was stretched over his buttocks, and he liked the feeling of it being there. He tossed his dreadlocks back and opened his mouth in a silent gasp as Thom's other hand began to explore his bulging aching crotch. Gregory was so excited that he realised his asshole was already fully dilated and he hadn't even got his pants down yet. He kept on grinding his butt against Thom's thrusting hard-on. Thom swivelled his hips rhythmically in response, keeping his cock firmly in place between Gregory's buttocks.

Eventually Thom said in a husky voice, 'Let's move to some music, man.' He released Gregory and slid a tape into his stack system, picked up the remote and pressed a button. Dennis Brown's sweet reggae vocals filled the room. Gregory smiled. He'd always loved Dennis Brown. 'I've got one more surprise,' Thom said unexpectedly. 'Wait there.'

Thom disappeared into one of the bedrooms. 'I've never used this before,' he called from the darkness as he started to drag something out from the unlit room. It was some sort of frame with a couple of blankets thrown over it. 'I've been keeping it in the spare room, up till now, 'cause I didn't really know what to do with it.'

Thom dragged the frame into the middle of the living-room, pushing the sofa aside to make space for it. Gregory watched, intrigued.

'What is it, man?' he asked as Thom pulled the object into position.

'Look,' Thom said, pulling the blankets off the frame with a theatrical flourish. Gregory looked and was immediately intrigued. From somewhere Thom had managed to get hold of a pair of stirrups, like those gynaecologists use for intimate examinations. Gregory immediately pictured himself sitting on the inclined seat, his hips tilted back for ease of access to his asshole, his legs spread wide open, his feet hooked up in the stirrups high above the level of his head and held apart, all attention flowing towards his insatiable brown star. It was to him a vision of pure ecstasy.

'I won't even ask where you got this from, man,' Gregory said, running a hand over the cold metal rods that made up the frame. He could already feel the curved aluminium supports cool under his bare heels as he slid into examination position. 'I just want to sit in it, real bad.'

'Cool,' Thom said, his blue eyes bright with excitement. 'I thought you might like it, man.'

Thom peeled off his vest in one easy motion, his large pectorals flexing as he did so. Gregory watched him strip excitedly, admiring the solid slabs of shaven chest-muscle and the chunky six-pack of Thom's stomach, and glanced down hungrily at the large thick bulge of Thom's cock in his soft grey cotton lycra trunks, his eye caught by the dark spot where pre-come had dripped from Thom's slit and stained the pale fabric.

'Well, what are you waiting for, mate?' Thom said throatily, seeing that Gregory was just standing there dumbly, hands hanging by his sides, paralysed by excitement and anticipation. Without waiting for an answer from Gregory, Thom took hold of Gregory's T-shirt at the waist and pulled it up. Gregory raised his arms to let Thom slide it up and off him and bare his chest, too. As he did so, Thom bent his head and teased Gregory's erect nipples playfully with his teeth. Gregory gasped. Thom got Gregory's T-shirt off, and tossed it onto the sofa.

Gregory, now naked to the waist, sank straight to his knees in front of Thom, whose impressive physique was covered only by a pair of figure-hugging grey trunks, stretched tightly over his firmly constrained cock and balls. Gregory ran his hands over Thom's thick sinewy thighs and buried his face in Thom's bulging crotch, nuzzling the rigid curve of Thom's long stiff member through soft cotton that smelt of fresh laundry, and rubbed his needy bearded chin against Thom's full fabric-covered ball-sack. Thom moaned above him and reached a hand down to toy with Gregory's mane of dreadlocks as the horny Rastaman knelt in front of him and kissed the shaft of Thom's cock through the fabric of his trunks.

'You want to suck it?' Thom asked urgently, his voice breathless.

'Yes, man, I want to suck it,' Gregory replied hoarsely. 'I want to get my lips around your hot stiff meat and suck the spunk up out of your balls.'

At Gregory's reply, Thom hooked his thumbs into the waistband of his trunks, and pushed them down to mid-thigh, revealing a band of smooth buttery-pale flesh. Thom's thick cock sprang up rigidly, bouncing off Gregory's full brown lips as it did so, making both men gasp excitedly. Gregory gazed at Thom's pulsing manhood for a moment, admiring its hard, curving, muscular beauty. Then he reached up and gripped Thom's heavy balls firmly, eliciting a noisy groan from Thom, and pressed his pouting lips against Thom's hot smooth crown, kissing it hotly. 'Oh, *yeah*,' Thom exclaimed throatily as Gregory began to tongue his slit. 'Oh Gregory, that feels so *good*. Oh, *tease* me, man.'

Gregory slowly moved his lips down over Thom's pole, enjoying the feeling of having a hot sweet cock in his mouth for the second time that day. This time, it tasted even better because Gregory knew that, here in Thom's flat, there was no fear of interruption. He had all night long to enjoy every inch of Thom's body. He moved his wet hungry mouth slowly and firmly up and down on the tousled blond muscleman's hot and throbbing shaft, determined to get Thom as hard as he possibly could without shooting his load. Gregory didn't want that to happen until much, much later.

It was in kneeling in front of Thom that Gregory took most complete control of him, and it was a form of control

Gregory particularly enjoyed exerting on another man: the giving – or withholding – of pleasure through the worship of the cock.

Thom was enjoying the good feeling of Gregory's mouth on his achingly stiff manhood, glad that his dick was getting some thorough attention from at least one of Gregory's holes that evening; the other one, Thom now pretty much knew, required considerably more demanding filling than Thom could provide, even though his cock was generously proportioned and he was a passionate and unrestrained butt-fucker.

Gregory took his mouth off Thom's hard-on and started to nibble the underside of his shaft with large white teeth, starting by teasing Thom's frenum. Thom grunted in pleasure as Gregory worked his way down the throbbing muscular pole to the Australian body-builder's hanging ball-sack. Gregory then twisted around so that he could push his head between Thom's smooth arching thighs and licked and nibbled at the sensitive area behind Thom's balls. Thom gasped and opened his legs, squatting slightly to give Gregory's eager mouth easier access. Gregory wrapped his dark sinewy arms around Thom's tanned bulging thighs and slipped his head right the way between Thom's legs, so that he could start licking Thom's asshole, too.

'Oh yeah,' Thom grunted as he felt Gregory's tongue working its way up between his hairless buttocks. 'Oh, God, oh, lick that ass,' he ordered Gregory. 'Rim that ass, oh, yeah. Get your greedy tongue up that hole.'

Gregory obeyed, turned on by Thom's assertive manner, teasing Thom's tightly clenched and sensitive sphincter with the tip of his tongue. Shivers of pleasure ran through Thom's body as Gregory worked on him attentively. Thom could feel the slight roughness of Gregory's tongue as Gregory rimmed his hole, the smoothness of Gregory's nose wedged firmly between his buttocks and the roughness of Gregory's goatee against his dangling balls, even the occasional brushing of Gregory's swinging dreadlocks against the backs of his thighs. Thom became so excited at the thorough anal attention he was receiving from Gregory that he had to quickly move his hand on his cock for some momentary relief or he thought he would have to scream.

Gregory, aware of Thom's hand moving fast on his thick cock because it was sending Thom's swinging ball-sack bouncing off Gregory's chin, reached up between Thom's legs, gripped his wrist, and pushed Thom's fist off his cock. *No way you coming now, man*, Gregory decided mentally. *Not without my say-so.* Thom grunted in frustration, but then sighed as Gregory closed his own slim cool fingers around Thom's throbbing cock and began to move them slowly up and down its stiff length. Being pleasured this way was intensely gratifying to Thom, his flirtation with being a bottom, and he stretched his heavily muscled arms up and folded them behind his head, giving himself up to the simultaneous movement of Gregory's tongue in his wet asshole and the firm regular back-and-forth of Gregory's fingers on his aching cock.

Gregory plunged his tongue deeper and deeper into Thom's increasingly receptive anus. Thom reached back and pulled his buttocks open so that Gregory could get right in there and press his full lips tightly against Thom's hot wet hole. Gregory rimmed Thom with a passion, knowing that the better he made Thom feel, the more pleasure he gave Thom and the more he turned him on, the more pleasure Thom would be willing to give him in return. Also, Gregory enjoyed penetrating the butch Australian body-builder's body, even if it was only with his tongue. It was his one flirtation with being a top-man (bar the completely out-of-character session with Bobbi that morning, where he had had the chance to act out an unexpected impulse to use his cock for penetration). For some reason, having his cock up another guy's ass had never really excited Gregory. He *could* fuck, certainly; but for him it was nothing beside the total and absolute pleasure of being fucked. Occasionally he would wonder how straight men coped with such restrictive roles in the bedroom. *Loads of straight men must be dying to have their girlfriends strap something on and fuck them up the ass*, he reckoned, *but never have the chance to do anything about it.* He thrust his tongue even further up Thom's ass, until the root of it was aching and straining and he could fully taste the sourness of Thom's rectum and its bitter juices, as they ran out of Thom's asshole and into Gregory's eagerly waiting mouth.

As Gregory rimmed Thom for all he was worth, Thom bent forward, reached back between his own legs and began to massage the front of Gregory's tight white jeans. Gregory's moan of pleasure was muffled by Thom's ass, but he pushed his thighs open and angled his crotch upwards, to allow Thom's hand full access in exploring his denim-covered rock-hard cock and heavy tingling balls. Thom explored Gregory's constrained bulge fully, rubbing his hand firmly over where Gregory's ball-sack pressed against the thick, strong material. Gregory responded to the attention to his crotch by rimming Thom as fast and deep as he could. Thom gasped and, continuing to fondle Gregory's crotch with one hand, reached back behind him with the other hand and gripped a bunch of Gregory's dreads to take some of the weight of Gregory's head, and so ease the strain on Gregory's neck – which Thom knew must be aching by now – hoping this would encourage Gregory to keep on rimming.

It worked. Gregory tongued Thom harder, stretching his jaws wider than a snake's and getting what felt like the entirety of his tongue into Thom's ass to the root. Gregory's pleasure in rimming Thom was increased by the way Thom was pressing the lean Rastafarian's face in between his large muscular buttocks as hard as he could, while at the same time squeezing the shaft of Gregory's stiff aching cock through the rough fabric of his painfully tight jeans.

Cramp finally lanced through the thickly muscled arm Thom was using to hold Gregory's head in place behind him and, regretfully, he released the black man from his rimming position. The moment Thom's hand was removed from his head Gregory slumped back with a loud gasp, sucking in air; his mouth gaped, his full lips shone and his dark eyes were wild. He wiped his wet mouth with the back of his hand and, still breathing so heavily he was almost hyperventilating, stumbled eagerly to his feet. He stared at Thom with an intensity of desire that was almost frightening as he tore at the buttons of his jeans, desperate to get them and his skimpy briefs down round his ankles; he was desperate to get his feet up in those stirrups. Now it was *his* turn for some hard-core attention.

Thom reached out and gripped Gregory's nipples between the thumb and forefinger of each hand as Gregory frantically yanked at the buttons of his jeans, making the lean black man gasp in excitement. Gregory finally got the fly of his jeans open and shoved them and his underpants down to his knees. His throbbing cock sprang up, long and thick and dark and painfully stiff, slapping his flat belly. Gregory ignored its bobbing heaviness, bending over and struggling to push his trousers and briefs down to his ankles and then tug them off over his feet so he could get his legs spread and up in the air. All the while Thom kept his hands firmly on Gregory's nipples, teasing and twisting them, keeping Gregory panting with excitement as he stripped.

At last, with a grunt and a shake, Gregory got his jeans and briefs off, kicking them aggressively out of the way into a corner. Thom slid his hands down to Gregory's lean waist, held him there and, lifting him bodily, carried him backwards and placed him in the tilted seat of the examination chair. Gregory gasped aloud as he felt the cool padded plastic against the hot skin of his sinewy back and buttocks, and a shudder of anticipation ran the length of his body, making his dick buck and his balls clench with a painful suddenness. He gazed deeply into Thom's eyes, sliding down in the seat as he did so, so that his hips were tilted upwards and his buttocks were pushed up for easy access. Thom kept his eyes on Gregory's as he took hold of Gregory's ankles and gently opened his legs wide. Gregory put up no resistance, letting Thom take total control of his body. Thom peeled off Gregory's socks before setting Gregory's feet in the stirrups. Now Gregory was totally naked, and totally available.

His legs now up and spread and his asshole fully exposed, Gregory arched back in the chair, stretched his arms up over his head and exhaled heavily. Now it was all up to Thom, he thought excitedly. All Gregory had to do was accept whatever pleasure Thom chose to give him. Gregory tilted his head and looked over towards the coffee-table where all the dildoes were sitting. Which ones would Thom use on him? How much length would he be able to take? How much width? Electric thrills of anticipation ran through Gregory's chest.

Thom reached for the jar of lubricant as he sunk to his knees between Gregory's spread legs. He kissed Gregory's chocolate star and tongued it briefly. It opened up to the full length of his tongue on Thom's first push. The slackness of Gregory's hole excited Thom, but he realised that it would take much more than his tongue to open Gregory up any further, to get him ready for a really intense dildo session. Thom licked his way up to Gregory's heavy ball-sack and sucked on Gregory's balls for a while. Gregory moaned as Thom got both Gregory's balls into his hot wet mouth and tugged on them gently.

'Oh, yeah, pull on those balls, man. Your mouth so good and hot and wet,' Gregory sighed hoarsely.

At the same time as he got himself a mouthful of Gregory's smooth bulging balls, Thom unscrewed the lid of the jar of lubricant. He stuck a finger into the cool greasy jelly and then stuck the same finger up Gregory's ass. Gregory's asshole swallowed Thom's finger to the knuckle without the slightest resistance. Thom slipped it out and stuck all four fingers into the lubricant, making his whole hand shine with grease, this time. He then ran the greasy palm of his hand between Gregory's upturned and open buttocks. Gregory shivered and his hole puckered as Thom's palm passed over it, slick with lube. Thom then pushed two well-lubricated fingers into Gregory's anus. Again, they were swallowed to the knuckle without resistance.

'Oh, *man*, you know what I like,' Gregory exhaled, keeping his open butt in place. 'Mmm . . .'

Thom let Gregory's balls slip out of his mouth and began to work his way up the curve of Gregory's achingly stiff hard-on, kissing and teasing its underside with his lips and teeth, sliding the two fingers out of Gregory's hole as he did so. Gregory's erection pressed its head against the lean Rastafarian's flat belly, and Thom had to take it in his hand and pull the rigid shaft to an angle of forty-five degrees in order to get his mouth over the head of it. Gregory's foreskin slid back smoothly as Thom took Gregory's crown into his mouth and swallowed it down.

As Thom went down on Gregory he slid three fingers up Gregory's backside. This time, he elicited a loud low growl from Gregory, as if he were now finally being genuinely stretched a little. Gregory still took the three fingers straight up his hot brown ass to the knuckle, though. Thom moved his three fingers in and out of Gregory's asshole rhythmically as he pumped his mouth up and down on Gregory's rigid veiny manhood, the heavily turned on black man's clear love-juice starting to fill the white body-builder's mouth instantly. After a minute, Thom folded his fourth finger in next to the other three and worked all four fingers in Gregory's hungry asshole. Gregory groaned again, and this time squirmed his butt slightly. Taking four fingers up to the knuckle *was* an effort for him. But it was an effort Gregory was willing to make, to please Thom.

'Man, *now* you're stretching me,' Gregory moaned. 'Oh, yeah . . . Give me them fingers, man. Don't stop . . .'

Thom let his mouth slip off Gregory's cock, which sprang up against Gregory's belly with a loud wet slap that made Gregory gasp sharply. Thom looked down at his pale fingers sliding in and out of Gregory's beautiful brown asshole, which was now stretched smooth and was wet and shiny with lube. Thom couldn't resist trying to slip his thumb into Gregory as well, just to see how far Gregory could open up. Gregory groaned again, but didn't complain or resist in any way; in fact, he actually pushed his hips down slightly onto Thom's hand.

'Oh, shit, man,' Gregory groaned. 'You've giving me the whole lot up me battyhole, now.'

'Believe it, man,' Thom said hoarsely. 'I'm giving it and you're taking it.'

Thom watched Gregory's asshole slide open as he pushed all four fingers and his thumb up into Gregory's rectum. Thom could feel the pressure of Gregory's taut anal ring around his knuckles, squeezing them tightly, so tightly that it was almost painful.

'Oh, Jesus, man,' Gregory moaned hoarsely, barely able to believe that he was letting Thom do this to him but enjoying it too much to be able to resist. 'Man, your hand's so *big*.'

Feeling that he had reached Gregory's point of maximum dilation, Thom was about to withdraw when he felt Gregory soften, slacken and spread a little further. Then, to Thom's surprise – and delight – his hand was sucked smoothly into Gregory's rectum. Gregory's asshole sucked closed around Thom's wrist and Gregory cried out ecstatically, 'Oh, *Jesus Christ*, fuck me, man!' as Thom's hand suddenly and unexpectedly filled his asshole to beyond what Gregory had previously believed it could possibly take.

'Are you all right, Greg?' Thom asked, worried the presence of his hand was too much for the Rastaman's accommodating asshole. After all, Thom had only meant to loosen Gregory up with his fingers, not fist-fuck him; and he only wanted to give Gregory pleasure, not hurt him or damage him in any way. Although Thom had to admit that the feeling of his hand inside Gregory's tight hot yielding ass was very pleasant, and turned him on more than he could have possibly imagined it would.

'Yeah, I'm all right, man,' Gregory replied, his voice hoarse and breathless, his chest heaving. 'Better than all right, you know what I'm saying? I'm fucking- stretched to fucking *capacity*, man. Shit –' He tossed his head wildly from side to side, flashing his dreads wildly. 'Oh, fucking shit!'

'Shall I pull out, man?' Thom asked in alarm, rotating his wrist in Gregory's asshole carefully to try and give him some relief.

'No way, man,' Gregory gasped as Thom's hand moved inside his totally-filled rectum, stretching it one way and then another as Thom twisted his wrist inside the horny black man's bottom. 'Now you're in, I want you to give I&I some action, yeah. A bit of manual back-and-forth, yeah. An anal workout – oh, yeah, man! That's it, man! Yeah!' Gregory shouted out breathlessly as Thom obediently began to move his fist back and forth inside Gregory's gratifyingly elastic rectum, first in short movements, then with longer, more vigorous thrusts into Gregory's ass.

Gregory grunted sharply, tensing his whole body with each thrust upwards of Thom's fist, then slumping down in the stirrups and relaxing with each pull back towards withdrawal from his body cavity that Thom made, his heart jack-hammering as he was thoroughly fisted. Thom began to move his bunched hand more quickly inside Gregory, then more quickly still, until he was pumping his arm backwards and forwards as fast as he would pump his fist on his own stiff cock if he was beating himself off. Gregory was moaning loudly now, his moans juddering into gasps with the rapid motion of Thom's fist in his anus. Finally, Gregory got his breath enough to say, 'Don't forget the dildoes, man; I need that hard rubber right the way up me, too!'

Thom slowed the motion of his hand inside Gregory's pulsing body gradually, and stopped. Then he closed his left hand around his right wrist – the one embedded in Gregory's bottom – and, rubbing lube around it as he did so, very slowly and carefully withdrew his right hand from Gregory's body. Gregory tensed. His asshole dilated and spread open as Thom's hand re-emerged from his anus, bulging out to the knuckles, then slipped shut with a soft sucking sound as Thom's fingers slid slowly out of Gregory's butt-hole. Thom gazed at the gaping anal orifice, now so open that he could see right up inside Gregory's brown-framed pulsing rectum.

'Man, you're so *open*,' Thom said softly, excited by the sight. He moved his greasy right hand on his own stiff cock as he watched glistening lube slide out of Gregory's asshole and drip down onto the seat beneath his angled hips.

'Is slackness,' Gregory replied. 'Make the most of it, man.'

Thom looked round at the dildoes lined up on the table. The fisting session had made most of them redundant: too short, too slim, or just too small. But there were still a few that had either the requisite length or thickness – or both – to satisfy Gregory's hungry anal hole, Thom reckoned. First of all, he opted for the donkey dildo. It was black, thick but not massively so, and eighteen inches long. Thom wondered how much of it he could get up Gregory. *Only one way to find out*, he thought to himself, reaching for the rigid length of matt-black rubber.

Thom had used the collection of sex-toys on lovers before, but mostly the guys he had dated hadn't really been turned on by them, and had just allowed Thom to dildo-fuck them a bit to humour him. Even the few who had found the idea of anal penetration by rubber or plastic genuinely sexy hadn't been able to take much up their backsides, when push had come to shove. Gregory was the first guy Thom had ever met who found sex-toys as much of a turn-on as he did, and had the anal capacity to go on a genuine journey of discovery with Thom. He was also the first man that Thom had ever had the chance to try the donkey dildo out on. He held it up in front of Gregory's face.

'This is what I'm going to put up you, man,' Thom said, holding the cricket ball sized matt black head near Gregory's face. Gregory's lips were parted and wet with anticipation. 'Kiss it,' Thom ordered. Gregory craned his head forward and kissed the cool static rubber dome. 'Lick it,' Thom said hoarsely. Gregory extended his long pink tongue and ran it over the matt rubber, turning it patent with his saliva. The taste was strong and clean.

'I'm going to slide this all the way up you to the base, man,' Thom said breathlessly. 'If you want me to,' he added, his eyes on Gregory's.

'I want you to,' Gregory replied thickly. 'I want that dildo up my ass.'

'Beg me,' Thom ordered.

'Man, I'm begging you,' Gregory replied urgency. 'Stick

that motherfucker up my ass! Bum-fuck me with it! I don't just want it up me butthole, I *need* it, man!'

Thom took the thick rubber length away from Gregory's mouth and knelt down between Gregory's spread and elevated legs. Thom's cock was painfully stiff and his heart was racing in his chest as he started to rotate the thick black rubber head of the outrageously over-sized sex-toy against Gregory's juicy brown asshole. Gregory moaned as the smooth rubber crown began to dilate him.

'Oh, yeah, man, you're opening me up! Oh, oh, oh, yeah –'

His moans became louder as the head slipped suddenly inside Gregory's asshole and Thom began to push the dildo's heavy length up into his well-lubricated rectum. Two inches disappeared inside Gregory's asshole, then three inches, four inches, five inches . . .

'Oh, man, oh, Christ, it's too fucking much, man –' Gregory groaned as the greasy rubber cylinder slithered up inside him to a full six wide inches. 'Oh, fuck me, it's too big, man.' He arched up in the chair, bracing his leanly-muscled arms and trying to lift his butt off the excessive length and width being introduced into his back passage.

Thom eased the pressure, allowing the dildo to slide an inch or two back out of Gregory's asshole, relieving him a little; but he didn't remove it, keeping Gregory stretched wide. Gregory blew like a weight-lifter struggling to take on the next barbell in a contest, took a deep breath, held it in, braced himself, then slowly pushed his ass down onto the thick shaft of the dildo, exhaling as he did so. Thom watched excitedly as Gregory managed to swallow another three inches of solid black rubber in his ass.

'You okay, man?' Thom asked him hoarsely.

Gregory nodded wordlessly. Then Thom started to actively push the dildo further up into Gregory's anal passage again. Gregory dragged in another breath, exhaled, and the slow progress of the donkey dildo up his distended asshole continued.

'You're swallowing that dildo up your ass, Gregory, man,' Thom said admiringly. 'You're taking it right up your hungry butthole.'

'Shit, man,' Gregory replied, struggling for breath. 'I'm being stretched so fucking good in there –'

Ten inches of black rubber had slid up Gregory's butt when he gasped again for Thom to stop forcing it up him. He could feel the dildo's smooth blunt head deep inside him, pressing firmly against the top of his fully stuffed rectum. He was afraid of being damaged by any further penetration for a moment, but then he became overpowered by the desire to feel the dildo going further up him, to feel it sliding right the way up into him, opening him totally as it went.

'Push it up me some more, man,' Gregory ordered Thom in a rough whisper. 'But go nice and easy, 'cause it going into unexplored territory. Virgin anal territory.'

'Whatever you say, man,' Thom said, putting his palm to the base of the heavy long donkey dildo, in readiness for further penetration.

Gregory struggled to relax his internal sphincter in response to the insistent pressure that Thom applied to it as he started to press the dildo up Gregory's stretched and dilated asshole again. At first, Gregory thought he wasn't going to be able to accommodate any more of the thick rubber shaft, but gradually he felt himself starting to open up deep inside. Suddenly Gregory was fully open, and the black rubber length abruptly slid another three inches up into Gregory's splayed body. Gregory's cock throbbed achingly as the penetration into his anal passage deepened, and pre-come started to run from his gaping slit and slide down his tense pulsing belly, in response to the thrilling pressure of the dildo inside his rectum and lower intestine, its heaviness and solidity against Gregory's prostate. The feeling of ecstasy coursing through his body was more intense than anything Gregory had ever experienced before. Thom stopped pushing, and held the dildo in place for a moment.

'How much is up me now, man?' Gregory asked breathlessly, looking down the length of his lean, sweaty body at the flushed-faced blond body-builder, his tousled, honey-dark hair slick with sweat, kneeling between Gregory's spread legs. Surely he must have taken the whole length up him by now, Gregory thought. He couldn't imagine any more length being forced up his ass, however good what was up there now was making him feel.

'Twelve inches, man,' Thom said hoarsely. 'Only six to go and you'll have taken the whole of it, mate.'

'What, man?' Gregory gasped in disbelief. 'No way can I get it up me battyhole, man.'

'Course you can, man,' Thom said encouragingly. He now felt a burning need to see all of the donkey dildo disappear up into Gregory's lean brown body. 'You just need a pause, that's all. But I know you've got the capacity.'

Gregory didn't answer as Thom held the pole of rubber pressed up into his butthole. The handsome blond man's desire to stretch his dilated asshole and distended rectum well beyond the limits of what he had imagined was their full capacity frightened Gregory – but it excited him too. To be taken beyond the limits of anal ecstasy was Gregory's ultimate fantasy, and here he was being offered the chance to make his fantasy flesh. *And how often does that happen, man?* He asked himself.

Looking for a reaction, Thom let eight inches slip quickly out of Gregory's slack stretched anal opening, making Gregory gasp loudly at the sudden feeling of emptiness inside him.

'Oh, man, no,' Gregory moaned loudly. 'I need it up me, I need it all the way up me, man. Please, man, please. I'm begging you, push it right the way up my ass. I'll take the whole of it, man, I swear. Just take me easy, yeah. But get it up me, I'm begging you.'

'Whatever you say, Greg,' Thom said, sliding the eight inches back up Gregory's well-lubricated and now gaping asshole, and pushing a further two inches up into Gregory's anal canal for good measure. Now ten inches were inserted up Gregory and he was gasping excitedly and pushing his hips down onto the thick black rubber length. Thom reached up to grip Gregory's stiff throbbing cock and give him some relief, but Gregory batted his hand away.

'Don't, man,' Gregory said hoarsely.' I'll come if you touch me dick and I don't wanna come yet.'

Thom gripped his own aching hard-on with one hand and moved his fist on it slowly to relieve his own excitement a little, while with his other hand he pushed the giant dildo further up Gregory's unexpectedly and unbelievably capacious ass. Thom worked the dildo up Gregory by pressing it up him firmly, then withdrawing the heavy rubber length a little way, then sliding it back up Gregory's anal passage just a little further than it had gone before, slipping it up into him a fraction of an inch at a time. Gregory moaned loudly with each insertion.

'Oh, God, man, oh, Jesus, oh fuck –' But he didn't move his ass, just kept it where it was, available for Thom's total use. Sweat ran down Thom's brow as he worked the giant rubber length in Gregory's stretched elastic butthole, and Gregory's whole body was bathed in it, making his skin look like it had been oiled. Lubricant was running out of Gregory's ass around the dildo like water from a tap, and the head of his erection was shiny and dripping with pre-come.

'How much up me now, man?' Gregory called down between his legs, groaning thickly, the entirety of his insides now feeling as if they were wrapped tremblingly around the massive rubber length inserted up his ass, as if any second now it would push up through his stomach into his throat and cut off his air-supply.

'Most of it, man,' Thom replied. 'You'll soon be full.' His tone made what he was saying sound matter-of-fact, but the truth was that Thom was absolutely astounded that Gregory had been able to take even this much of the thick black rubber sex-toy up his ass. Seeing the black rubber balls at the base of the dildo only inches away from Gregory's spectacularly dilated, gleamingly lubricated and totally smooth asshole, Thom found it impossible to believe that fourteen inches of thick rubber had already vanished into Gregory's body, and would come slithering out of him if Thom took the pressure off the dildo's base. He swivelled the shaft of the dildo inside Gregory, and began to try and squirm the remaining inches up Gregory's back passage while Gregory shuddered and moaned ecstatically above him.

'Oh, oh, oh, oh, oh, Jesus, oh, Jesus,' Gregory gasped as another two inches slipped up inside him, between his spread buttocks and thighs.

'Yeah, that's it, man,' Thom said, wanking himself fast as he kept the pressure up on the thick rubber dildo where it extruded from Gregory's butthole. 'Suck that dildo up into your ass. Suck it up there. Yeah. Yeah, you're doing it, Greg, it's going up you, mate, all the way up you. Oh, my God –'

After what felt like an eternity of throbbing, pulsating, disorientating excitement inside his stretched anal passage, Gregory became confusedly aware of a soft cool fleshy touch below his hole and between his buttocks. It was the balls at the base of the massive donkey dildo, finally all the way up him at last. 'Oh, man, it's up me,' Gregory shouted hoarsely, triumphantly. 'Move it in me now, man. Fuck me with it.'

The body-builder obliged eagerly, allowing most of the dildo to slide heavily out of Gregory's rectum, then shoving it all the way back up the asshole of the trembling bucking Rastaman, who sat with his legs spread wide above him. Gregory panted, his voice loud and high as the panting was interspersed with loud gasps, his arms flung up above his head as he tossed his locks ecstatically. Thom kept the dildo sliding rapidly in and out of Gregory's utterly open asshole as Gregory jerked and writhed above him.

'That feel good, man?' the tanned blond Australian called up to the helplessly excited and out-of-control black man, butt up in the air, feet up in the stirrups.

'Oh yes, man! Yes!' Gregory cried out throatily. 'Keep that fucker moving in my ass, man! Oh, fuck me, yeah!' Thom now had both hands on the greasy shaft of the dildo, and was sliding it in and out of Gregory's anal passage, marvelling at Gregory's total slackness, his capacity to accommodate the enormous dildo up his ass now with apparent ease and openness, and with such pleasure too.

Gregory's insides felt in thrilling electric chaos as Thom moved the dildo back and forth inside him, and an uncontrollable weight of excitement was building in his dripping, untouched and agonisingly rigid cock. Gregory started playing with his own stiff nipples to add to the complete feeling of chaotic sensual abandon, biting into them with his short nails to get himself off even more fully. It felt to Gregory as if each vigorous thrust of the dildo inside him was now pushing right up through his asshole, through his guts and into his pulsingly-erect cock, literally pushing the building pressure of spunk forcibly along its length with each thrust until finally, writhing and shuddering and yelling loudly in ecstasy, his arms thrown back behind his head, Gregory shot his load as Thom rammed the whole of the solid black rubber up him hard and to the very base. Gregory's boiling spunk spattered his stomach, his chest, his mouth, his nose; globs of his hot creamy load landed on his tightly closed eyelids and even sprayed into his hair as the solid black rubber balls were pressed firmly into the stretched shiny satin-brown skin between his buttocks.

Gregory let out a racking sob of relief and exhaustion as his cock stopped spasming and pumping jism, and, bringing his arched, straining body back under some sort of control, lowered himself slowly back down onto the stirrup-seat. As he did so, he let out a breathless groan. Now that he had climaxed, Gregory was desperate to have the dildo out of his over-stretched over-stuffed asshole as soon as possible.

'But slowly, man,' he emphasised to Thom, as Thom started to let the rubber length slide out of Gregory's body. 'Take it real slow or you *will* do me some damage, seen?'

'Take it easy, man,' Thom replied gently. 'I'll be careful.' He kept a firm grip on the slick greasy shaft of the dildo, supporting its heavy weight with a hand under its flat base, and let it slip out of Gregory's hot, slack hole an inch at a time, marvelling at the length of thick rubber that Gregory had been able to swallow up into his butt during their sex-toy session. Finally, the smoothly curving dome of the head slithered out of Gregory's open gaping ass with a juicy sucking sound. Gregory moaned softly as the dildo left his body, immediately missing the intense fullness its presence in his asshole had brought him, but relieved at being released from its insistent, relentless penetration.

Thom put the heavy rubber length down carefully on its side on the coffee-table. It was shiny with lube and from the juices inside Gregory's body. Seeing it so thoroughly used made Thom's hard-on, which had not gone away for a second, all the time he had been dildo-fucking Gregory, throb with an even greater intensity. Cold thrills ran through Thom's heaving chest as he tried to drag in a deep breath. Then he got to his feet and stood between Gregory's open legs, looking down on the lean handsome spread-open Rastaman, whose brown, glistening asshole gaped open pinkly and invitingly.

'Can I get myself off by fucking you, man?' Thom asked Gregory softly but urgently, stroking the insides of Gregory's smooth, sinewy thighs. Thom's long, thick erection was painfully, achingly stiff now, and he badly needed some relief, and nothing would give him more pleasure than to plug Gregory's juicy hole with his rigid fleshy length. 'Give you a bit of real cock?'

'I can't deny you nothing, man,' Gregory whispered hoarsely. 'A load of come up there'll be some sexual healing, too. So yeah, give me that good dick, man.'

Relieved that Gregory was up for some butt-fucking, Thom moved forward and positioned his hips against Gregory's ass, then pushed his cock up into Gregory's hot slack rectum. Gregory grunted softly but was so open that Thom's erection slid all the way up him to the root without the slightest resistance. Thom, now totally overcome by horniness, began to fuck Gregory up the ass with quick deep thrusts of his blood-filled rigid pole. Gregory half-closed his eyes and moaned a little as Thom fucked him passionately. His long brown cock twitched and stiffened to half-mast as Thom's hips pounded relentlessly against his ass and Thom's stiff purple cock slid in and out of his asshole. Thom leaned forward and – without breaking his rhythm – kissed Gregory on the mouth as he fucked him. Gregory wrapped his arms around Thom's back and urged him on.

'Pound that ass, man,' Gregory said breathlessly, breaking off their kiss momentarily to encourage Thom to fuck him as hard as he could, to get off in his insatiable open asshole.

'Oh, Jesus,' Thom said throatily. His cock felt so good, sliding back and forth in Gregory's backside, so juicy and hot, his cock-head rubbing against the silky-smooth lining of the inside of Gregory's rectum with each thrust, and each insertion pressing his balls hard against Gregory's upturned ass, too, adding to his excitement. Thom felt the weight beginning to build in his aching dick, so he pumped his narrow muscular hips harder against Gregory's high round buttocks, desperate for release.

In response to Thom's increasingly urgent thrusting into his body, Gregory tightened his slack relaxed asshole around Thom's thick stiff dick, determined to add to Thom's pleasure in butt-fucking him. Thom threw his head back as he pumped his throbbing hard-on in and out of Gregory's bunghole, closing his eyes and concentrating on the building excitement at the base of his balls and along the rigid length of his thick heavy cock-shaft.

Gregory reached up to Thom's lightly freckled chest and gripped his small erect nipples between his thumbs and forefingers, teasing them as Thom rammed his cock in and out of Gregory's gaping and aching asshole. Thom's golden hair was tousled on his forehead and his face was flushed and shiny with sweat; drops of it ran down onto his nose and lips and dripped onto Gregory's chest and neck and upturned face. Veins stood out on Thom's thick muscular neck and in his forehead. The extra attention to his nipples pushed Thom irreversibly towards his peak; his cock pulsed and felt heavy as iron and charged up with electricity as it slithered rapidly in and out of Gregory's backside. Suddenly, Thom was shouting and completely losing control and, with a vigorous thrust of his hips, he was shooting his load all the way up into Gregory's juicy, greedy asshole.

'Oh, Jesus, oh, yeah, oh, Christ, oh –' Thom yelled throatily as he pumped hot jism into Gregory's receptive bottom. He kept his cock rammed all the way up Gregory's asshole until it had stopped kicking and discharging. For a long moment then Thom felt as if he and Gregory had melted into a single sexual creature, and didn't know where his cock ended and Gregory's rectum began. He bent forward and kissed Gregory's lips gently, then slowly withdrew his semi-erect cock from Gregory's backside. Thom stroked Gregory's cheek tenderly as he did this, then ran his hand down the side of Gregory's body. Gregory trembled. His eyes were dark and full.

With great carefulness, Thom lifted Gregory's feet out of the stirrups and set them on the floor. Every muscle in Gregory's body was spent and he couldn't stand up unaided. The Australian body-builder lifted him gently, his own aching muscles bulging as he helped the shapely Rastaman to get to his feet. The two men hugged and, somehow, a little of Thom's strength passed into Gregory's body, and Gregory found himself able to stand. The trembling passed from him and a great warmth coursed through his body. He kissed Thom on the mouth, probing gently with his tongue.

'That was something else, man,' Gregory said eventually, gazing deeply into Thom's bright blue eyes with his rich brown ones. '*You're* something else.'

'So are you,' Thom said softly, his voice catching in his throat as he replied. Then they kissed again, hugging each other tightly as if each were greeting an old friend long missed and now met with unexpectedly.

Six

The techno pounded deafeningly as, switching his hips and shaking his big booty in skin-tight denim short-shorts, Bobbi worked his way across the packed dance-floor of Trash, the first club on his search-list. Trash was one of the cruisiest and most heavily sexually-orientated gay clubs in the West End, where bare sweaty rippling torsos of every colour, shade and shape glistened with sweat as narrow hips and curving thighs pumped in time to the rapid disorientating rhythm of the deafening music, lean chests bumping up against bulging pees, skin-tight lycra-covered crotches moving provocatively against denim-clad bubble-butts in eager pelvic grinds and swivels.

Bobbi threw his smooth hairless arms up in the air as he wiggled his way across the dance-floor, rotating his hips against tight muscular asses as he moved past them, or pushing his big butt out and against the bulging crotches of the horny and intoxicated heavily muscled guys gyrating behind him. Bobbi felt high just from being in this sea of men, a fluid part of the scene of men on men, men in men, cocks on asses, mouths on cocks, mouths on mouths, skin against skin, licking, drinking sweat and come; abstract, present, orgiastic.

As the crowd pressed tighter around Bobbi in the middle of the heaving dance-floor, and the heat of the muscular male half-naked bodies around him increased to a hot-house intensity that totally defeated the serpentine air-conditioning ducts whose openings gaped above the packed, strobe-lit space, Bobbi found himself longing to surrender to the overwhelmingly sexual and hedonistic atmosphere of the club. He was aching to get his shorts and his tight skimpy briefs down round his ankles, and give free access to his good hard dick and his willing hungry asshole; aching to plug the first receptive bunghole that offered itself to him with his stiff long cock, while at the same time getting fucked all the way himself by the first outsize hard-on that any well-hung horny stud wanted to push up his asshole from behind – the only way Bobbi could really get off on topping another guy. And then they could move in rhythm to the music, cock-in-asshole to cock-in-asshole until, eventually, the whole crowd would be fucking and getting fucked up the ass at the same time and moving like a single muscular butt-fucking machine.

I'm supposed to be looking for Don, Bobbi reminded himself as his hips were caught between the crotch and ass of two shaven-headed and tough-looking tattooed white guys in spray-on-tight white jeans, and Bobbi was sandwiched crotch-to-ass-to-crotch between them in a pumping pelvic congo-line. Excitement filled Bobbi's chest and he started to fall in with the two skinheads' rhythms as they swivelled their hips in time to something more primal than the thundering music, the rhythm of fucking, of coming, of wildness and release. The guy behind Bobbi – the taller and more pumped of the two – was definitely hard and well-hung, and Bobbi's own cock was rigid as he pushed it up and down in his skimpy shorts between the white denim-clad and muscular buttocks of the skinhead bottom in front of him. *I'm allowing myself to be distracted*, Bobbi chided himself after a titillating few minutes of pumping, and, not without regret, wriggled his hips out from between the thrusting butts and crotches of the two burly skinheads. *Oh well, I can always catch up with them later, if I find Don in here*, he consoled himself as he made his way over to the bar, which was up a low flight of steps, so he could order a drink and survey the scene from a raised position.

When Bobbi looked back across the dance-floor, the two

skins were now moving crotch-to-butt with each other. The shorter and more boyish one in front was bent forward and, tossing his totally-shaven head ecstatically, was pushing his buttocks against the other guy's out-thrust crotch in a horny simulation of taking a cock up his ass, rotating his butt as if he were desperate to take the man's long hard dick all the way up him to the root. The taller and larger skinhead gripped the shorter one's bare blue-tattooed shoulders and simulated fucking the shaven white boy bent over in front of him vigorously. At the same time as he pumped his hips against the ass of the boy in front of him, the crop-haired top-man looked around the club with burning eyes until his gaze located Bobbi, who was now leaning with one elbow on the bar and looking out over the dance-floor. Their eyes locked and, as he pumped his hips against the bent-over guy in the tight white jeans in front of him, the tall burly skinhead mouthed words to Bobbi: *I want you like this* – indicating with an inclination of his head the guy he was now mock-fucking from behind. As he moved his mouth, silver flashed in his pierced tongue. Bobbi smiled, embarrassed and turned on, flushed and looked down. He was sorely tempted. One of Bobbi's life-long fantasies was to take it up the ass in the middle of a crowded dance-floor, and the tough-seeming macho skinhead looked like he would respond well to Bobbi pushing his shorts down right there in front of everyone, and deliver the good public ass-fucking that Bobbi would clearly be asking for –

Find Don first!

Bobbi ordered a Budweiser from Trash's lean-hipped and petite nineteen-year-old Latino barman, Felipe. They exchanged small smiles as Felipe handed Bobbi his change. Bobbi glanced at Felipe's fingernails as he took his money: electric-blue and glittery. Felipe, who was otherwise wearing only black rubber shorts behind the bar, and had slicked-back hair and a pimp's pencil-moustache, was the only friend Bobbi had who was trampier than he was, and who inspired him to new heights of trashy behaviour. Like the time the two of them had been flat broke, and Felipe had come up with the idea of them putting on a live sex-show with an extremely large, extremely long double-headed dildo for a group of very tall, very tanned, very pumped, and very blond and buzz-cut American athletes who had come into the bar one evening in search of a good time, and something out of the ordinary. They were supposed to be in training for some international event, but they felt their dicks were in need of a demanding workout session, too – one that their coach was unprepared to give them. After the young black man and the Latino boy had put on their sex-show – ass-up and facing away from each other, both swallowing as much dildo up their buttholes as quickly as they could, competing greedily to see who could get the most length of solid rubber up his backside first (Bobbi won by a couple of inches that time, his hole being the more capacious) – the heavily turned-on American athletes had offered Bobbi and Felipe extra money to take real cocks up their assholes as well as just rubber. The two horny bottoms had been happy to oblige, turning round on their hands and knees on the small stage they had improvised in the athletes' hotel-room, and getting their greedy butts up in the air and ready for servicing. Side-by-side, their heads resting on their folded arms as their upturned asses got pounded, Bobbi and Felipe were in sexual heaven. The black boy and the Latino youth even started to kiss and tongue each other as one well-hung athlete after another gave their assholes a good, hard fucking, each seeing his own pleasure mirrored in the other's excited face as hot rigid cocks slid in and out of their bottoms and shot one hot load of come after another into their quivering, well-stretched rectums.

Afterwards, though, they had had trouble getting their

money off the athletes, who didn't see why they should pay when Bobbi and Felipe had so clearly enjoyed taking three large stiff cocks right up the ass to the hilt each.

'Hey,' Felipe had said, 'just because we enjoy our work, it doesn't mean we don't deserve to get paid for it. It's why we gave you an especially good time.' The young Latino had pouted angrily. 'You want someone who doesn't enjoy what they're doing?' he had continued. 'Then go find a hooker on crack down King's Cross.'

The athletes then said they would pay if Bobbi and Felipe ate each other's assholes out and licked out all the spunk that had been shot up their backsides. Bobbi and Felipe agreed to do this, providing the Americans gave them the money up front. The six horny athletes, who hadn't expected Bobbi and Felipe to agree to eat each other out, handed over the dollars eagerly and started to jerk off all over again as Bobbi and Felipe put on a felching show for them, each taking it in turns to lie back on the stage and wank while the other would squat over his face and get his slack ass tongued. Bobbi and Felipe were perfectly happy to throw in a felching show, but the incident had made Bobbi see that that kind of entertainment work could have a lot of drawbacks, and he had concentrated on his musicianship after that as his road to fortune and fame. Felipe had gone more fully into sex-shows, and it was rumoured that he had a Mercedes Sport that his neat butt and all-too-accommodating asshole had paid for. He and Bobbi were still friends, if not especially close, and, Mercedes Sport or no, Felipe still worked in the bar at Trash on a Saturday night.

'It's not the money, it's the contacts, darlin',' he would say, when Bobbi asked him why. 'And all the hot dudes,' Felipe would add, with a knowing smile. If he couldn't sell it, he gladly gave his butt away – especially if the guy was hot and hung.

Bobbi sipped his beer from the bottle and looked around the busy club, hoping to catch sight of Don. The tall skinhead had disappeared back into the heaving crowd on the dance-floor with his fuck-buddy and Don was nowhere to be seen. This was the upper floor of the club. Bobbi had already made his way through the dance-floor on the lower level, which favoured camp disco classics, in his search for Don, and had had a few offers on the way down there too. The most tempting of these had come from a handsome, lean and goateed Mediterranean guy wearing leather trousers and studded leather wristbands, who had said, 'Come to the toilets with me now. I have a twelve-inch cock and I want to stick it up your ass right now,' as he gripped Bobbi's beefy butt with a large and confident hand, pressing two long fingers against the seam of Bobbi's shorts where it ran tightly over his quivering and eager asshole. Bobbi had let the Spaniard have a good feel of his ass before disengaging himself with a smile and a 'maybe later,' and carried on looking for Don.

What'll be typical now, Bobbi thought to himself, *is that I'm turning down all these offers from hot-looking guys to find Don. Then I won't get to find him and so I'll have missed out on all that for nothing. And then I'll go to Prince Fela's party and they'll all be spuds or they'll all be bottoms and I won't get no satisfaction.*

Perhaps Don was in the upper floor toilets. Bobbi picked up his beer-bottle and sashayed over to them. No luck in there and he'd have to give it up and try another club. He ran through his mind all the clubs he was on the list for, and could get into free, and that Don might hang out in, and decided he would try Tropical next, which was popular with the faggamuffins. At the bottom of the list, for many reasons, from Bobbi's personal tastes to basic physical wear and tear, was 'Fist-To-The-Wrist' night at The Basket, a leather and denim joint that was too hard-core even for Bobbi's broadminded tastes. But he would even dip in there in his search for Don, if all else failed.

The large black-and-chrome toilet was busy: hair was being re-gelled at the wall-size and slightly smoky mirror above the four enamel sinks, hands were being dried under driers, and there were the soft sounds of sex coming from behind the row of closed cubicle-doors, half-audible above the muffled music leaking through from the dance-floor outside. Perhaps Don was in one of those cubicles, Bobbi thought. He would have to wait and see. He took up a position leaning against the sweaty wall, where he would catch sight of anyone emerging from them, and rested his beer-bottle on the formica surface next to him.

Next to Bobbi a pair of eye-catchingly large hard-bodied body-builders in striped shorts and mountain boots bent over a piece of foil on one of the sinks, snorting cocaine, while a good-looking Chinese guy with a goatee and a Bruce Lee haircut looked on, nodding approvingly as they snorted up the stuff he was selling them. One of the muscle-men had soft brown hair, moussed up in a neat quiff; the other had shiny blond hair, gelled flat. Bobbi gazed idly at the rockhard asses of the two men as they bent to inhale the coke, imagined spanking them and how the buttocks were so firm that the palm of his hand would probably smart as it made contact with their smooth blocks of tanned ass-muscle. Or perhaps deliciously untanned, a buttery contrast to the even cinnamon-brown of the rest of their skins. Bobbi's dick twitched as he speculated idly, knowing there was only one way to find out.

The two body-builders straightened up, sniffed and shook their heads. Pecs and torsos rippled and striated with sinew as the cocaine took effect. Bobbi watched as, under the guise of shaking hands, one of the tanned, lycra-trunked musclemen pressed several notes into the Chinese guy's hand. He remained leaning against the wall while the two men turned and headed back to the dance-floor. Bobbi checked their baskets out of the corner of his eye as they passed him – appealingly full – and found himself thinking back to the skinheads he had flirted with earlier. *They're coming in pairs tonight*, he thought. He realised that he was really in the mood for a threesome that evening. But right now, even more than instant sex, he really fancied a line of coke. *Just a toot, to keep me in the party mood*, he thought to himself. He didn't use any drug regularly, just once in a while to spice up an evening out.

Bobbi glanced back at the Chinese guy, who was looking at him with half-closed, speculative eyes, as if scenting that Bobbi might be on the lookout for drugs. Now that the distractingly obvious muscle-men were gone, Bobbi became aware of how handsome the oriental guy was, with wide feline glittering eyes and full sensual lips that were wrapped around a lighted joint from which he was inhaling, and framed by a neatly-clipped black goatee. He was five foot ten, just a little taller than Bobbi, broad-shouldered, narrow-hipped and lean, and he looked young but knowing. His buttery-peachy skin was flawless and smooth, and his loosely cut chin-length hair was blue-black. He wore an open leather waistcoat. A silver chain ran between unseen pierced nipples that Bobbi immediately wanted to take hold of and tug on, and there were elaborate tattoos of dragons and Chinese characters all down his arms. He had silver in his ears and plain silver and leather bangles round his wrists. He was wearing hipster black leather trousers pushed down low on his hips, above the fly of which the top of his black briefs and a tuft of dyed-blond pubic hair was visible. The leather hugged the Chinese guy's tiny neat butt shinily tight. He wore cuban-heeled bike-boots, around one of which a red handkerchief was knotted. His name was Raymond.

'Can I do you something, man?' Raymond asked Bobbi in a creaky dope-constricted voice, as he exhaled a sensual cloud of smoke, slouching back, affecting cool with seeming naturalness.

'You got a line to spare, man?' Bobbi asked, head inclined slightly, feigning indifference. He checked his appearance in the mirror Raymond was standing next to, suddenly wishing he'd put on just a hint of lip-gloss to make his cock-sucking lips more striking.

'I got everything your heart could desire, man,' Raymond replied easily. He had a strong Cockney accent. 'Coke, speed, uppers, downers, you name it, I got it . . .'

Bobbi nodded. 'But don't you get busted all the time in here?' he asked in a low voice, suddenly uneasy and glancing around for surveillance cameras. No need for the evening to end *that* way. A short stretch was *not* one of Bobbi's fantasies, and he knew that, as a black man, however fey, the chances of a custodial sentence for a minor offence were three times higher than if he had been of the Caucasian persuasion. He couldn't see any cameras so he relaxed slightly.

'Nah, man,' Raymond said, dropping the roach of his joint and treading it out with a swivel of a stacked heel. 'I got an arrangement with the management, yeah. A percentage cut for a blind eye.' He shrugged. 'So what can I do you for? Coke yeah?'

Bobbi nodded. 'How much?'

'Twenty-five.'

'That's just that bit too rich for this bitch,' Bobbi said, keeping his eyes on Raymond's, smiling and trying to look as cute and appealing as possible, even though Raymond might possibly be straight. Raymond's face was unreadable.

'Yeah, well, that's the entrepreneurial system for you, man,' Raymond said after a moment, shrugging. 'The price the market'll bear, yeah. Sorry, man.'

'Wait, man,' Bobbi said. 'Isn't there something else you'll take? Or I can give you?'

'So make me an offer,' Raymond said, slouching back with slanted hips against the glitter-sprayed black wall of the toilet, a curling, arrogant smile playing around his lips. He tugged on the belt-loops of his leather jeans, suggestively pulling the fabric tight around his bulging crotch.

Without a word, Bobbi sank to his knees and kissed the front of Raymond's bulge. The leather was soft and yielding, flesh-like, sensual, and smelt strong as Bobbi pressed his nose against Raymond's fly. Behind Bobbi, a cubicle door swung open, and the two skinheads he had been grinding with on the dance-floor earlier tipped out of the small space, awkwardly buttoning the flies of their tight white jeans over their spent cocks, their faces flushed and their bodies pumped and sweaty from their exertions, still naked to the waist. The taller one gripped the shorter one's ass and squeezed it possessively.

'You take cock like a pro,' he said to the shaven-headed young man he was feeling up. Then he looked round and saw Bobbi on his knees in front of Raymond. 'I bet you do, too,' he added, flashing a smile at Bobbi as he threw a lanky muscular arm around the shorter skin's shoulders and the two men made their way to the door back out to the noisy dance-floor beyond.

'I bet he's right,' Raymond said huskily, looking down on Bobbi's orange-dyed crop as Bobbi kissed the soft warm leather front of Raymond's trousers, sticking his ass out invitingly as he knelt there before the muscular young oriental man.

Bobbi glanced up at Raymond. 'There's a cubicle free,' he said with a boyish and inviting smile.

'Oh no, man,' Raymond said, waggling a finger in Bobbi's face. 'No, no, no. The deal is, you suck me off right here in front of everyone who comes in. So everyone knows what you'll do for a bit of coke. Everyone'll get a good look at you sucking my cock.'

Raymond's voice thickened as he spoke, and Bobbi realised that the Chinese guy had an exhibitionist streak in him too. Bobbi responded wordlessly to Raymond by pressing his lips hard against Raymond's full crotch and gripping Raymond's small firm ass in both hands so he could bury his face between Raymond's strong thighs. Raymond exhaled softly and grunted. 'That's it, man,' he said, flicking his dark glossy hair back. 'Be a good cock-sucker for me, man. Earn that line. What's your name, cock-sucker?'

'Bobbi, man,' Bobbi said throatily. Feeling the rigidity of Raymond's cock behind the soft leather had got him hard in his short-shorts, and the idea of giving a blow-job in public excited him, too. There was also the anticipation of another mouthful of hot spunk, Bobbi's favourite treat — way back from when he had had a crush on a guy at college, Ashton.

Ashton had been the college's best sprinter: mixed-race, shaven-headed, smoothly muscular, popular with the boys *and* the girls, and well-known as the college stud. Ashton had guessed that Bobbi fancied him and had found the idea cute and flattering. He had enjoyed having Bobbi hang out with him, although he claimed that he couldn't reciprocate. 'I can't swing that way, man,' he always used to say. But what Ashton *could* do was give Bobbi his used rubbers. Obsessively fearful of getting a girl pregnant, Ashton always used a condom whenever he fucked. He would keep the condoms once he had shot his full milky load inside them, knot the well-stretched latex tubes and give them to Bobbi the next day. Bobbi would take the spunk-heavy rubbers home, lock himself in the bathroom and lick them out thoroughly, beating himself off vigorously as he did so. The spunk wasn't fresh and hot like he wished it was, but it had been shot out of Ashton's beautiful big cock, and he savoured the salty flavour keenly.

For all his claims of straightness, Ashton would sometimes give Bobbi come-filled rubbers even when he wasn't seeing a girl. 'I just sheathed up to jerk off 'cause I knew you'd appreciate my jism, man,' he would say as he slipped Bobbi the used condom at the back of class or in the college toilets.

One time, Ashton had said, 'I'd like to see you lick out that rubber right in front of me, man. I'd get off on it. Would you do that for me, man?' Exhibitionistically excited, Bobbi had obliged, sliding his long, eager tongue all the way up the stretchy latex prophylactic, his cock stiff and obvious in his tight trousers as he licked Ashton's spunk out of the condom until it was clean and shiny. Ashton had got a hard-on, too, which had made Bobbi hopeful that he was getting more broad-minded, as did his remark, 'I bet you give better head than Melissa, man.' But then term had ended and Ashton had moved away that summer before Bobbi had had a chance to try and push things any further. Apart from the impulse to seize the day at the earliest possible opportunity, his experience with Ashton had left Bobbi with a compelling and lasting appetite for other men's come, and that had led to the eagerness with which he had dropped to his knees in front of Raymond in the Trash club's toilets.

Bobbi slid his hands round from Raymond's ass to the front of his black leather trousers and started to hungrily unbutton the fly. Raymond lounged back, leaning on the sink, enjoying the fact that the cute brown boy kneeling in front of him was happy to do all the work. Already eyes were wandering in the mirror as guys fixing their hair or washing their hands were starting to wonder if they were going to be treated to a free sex-show, and a few heads were turning towards where Bobbi knelt on the tiled floor as he deftly unsnapped the Oriental man's fly-buttons.

Bobbi opened Raymond's fly and slid his trousers down to his knees, revealing black bikini-briefs through which Raymond's large thick cock jutted stiffly, the darkness of the fabric contrasting sharply with the light buttery tan of his hairless skin. Bobbi leant forward and kissed the head of Raymond's heavy erection through the soft cotton fabric of his briefs. Raymond moaned and pre-come immediately wetted the front of his underwear where his cock-head was pressing heavily against it.

The watching eyes became more intent and hands began to be pushed into trouser-pockets and down the fronts of shorts as Bobbi ran his hands up the backs of Raymond's thighs and slid them up inside Raymond's briefs, massaging Raymond's smooth buttocks as he kissed and nibbled on Raymond's swollen dick through the soft black cotton. Raymond sighed and arched his head back, gazing up at the matt-black ceiling and enjoying the good feeling of Bobbi's deft hands on his ass, and Bobbi's attentive lips and teeth on his cock. Usually when he'd allowed himself to be convinced to trade drugs for sex, it had been a bad deal for Raymond. He often jerked off several times before dressing to go out clubbing, just so he couldn't really be tempted. But this time, he felt like he was going to come out ahead: Bobbi really knew how to put on a show, and how to give a guy a good time. If he sucked cock half as well as he looked like he was going to, Raymond would come out well ahead on the bargain they'd struck. He'd even give Bobbi top-drawer gear for his trouble, not the heavily cut shit he usually palmed off on club-goers already too wrecked to notice the difference. *He's taking it in the mouth so he can take it up the nose*, Raymond thought to himself, his cock now achingly stiff and painfully constrained by the waist-band of his bikini-briefs. The young orange-cropped black man kneeling before him was somehow so provocative to Raymond that even the idea of just seeing Bobbi snort, the nostrils in his small slightly tip-tilted nose dilating and quivering, was in a strange way a turn-on. But still –

'Get to the real deal, man,' Raymond ordered Bobbi, his manner playfully arrogant, looking down on the curvy young man in the skin-tight short-shorts kissing his rigid cock-shaft through the fabric of his bikini-briefs. 'I want to get my dick blown, and you're the cock-sucker to do it.'

The three or four guys who had been half-watching Raymond and Bobbi reflected in the mirror above the washroom's sinks now turned, with flushed faces, to watch the unfolding scenario properly, no longer making any pretence that they were fixing their cropped or gelled hair or checking their skins for imperfections.

Bobbi gripped the elasticated waist-band of Raymond's black cotton briefs and pulled them down slowly and firmly. Raymond gasped as his thick hard prick sprang up, heavy and bobbing, and shivered at the feeling of the elastic being slid over his smooth thighs.

'Mm, you've got a tasty-looking cock,' Bobbi said, smiling and licking his lips theatrically, before kissing the oriental guy's large, swollen, purple crown reverently. The skin of Raymond's cock-head was matt and smooth and hot, and pulsing with hidden life. Raymond sighed at the feeling of Bobbi's full lips on his slit, as did the skimpily dressed men who had started watching the dick-sucking scene with feverish intensity at the first sight of some real action.

'Tongue it, man,' Raymond ordered, his voice a little hoarse. Bobbi obeyed, teasing the dark and now gaping slit in Raymond's blood-hardened glans with the bright pink tip of his long tongue. Raymond could feel excitement coursing along the length of his cock-shaft, making it twitch and buck. Bobbi pulled his head back from Raymond's cock-head, drawing out a clear sticky strand of pre-come that hung in a falling curve between his quivering tongue and Raymond's shiny slit, enjoying knowing that he was being watched as he did so.

'Man, you're into it,' Raymond said breathlessly, looking down at Bobbi; the youth's boyish features were all eagerness as he gripped Raymond's stiff shaft firmly in one hand and went back to licking Raymond's slit some more. Then Bobbi took Raymond's smooth cock-head into his mouth and moved his lips down on his hot thick pole, taking it in all the way to the base, at the same time moving his hand to Raymond's balls and squeezing them firmly. The wet and warmth and tightness of the inside of Bobbi's greedily sucking mouth made Raymond's cock stiffen even more. He could feel the raised veins pulsing heavily against the inner linings of Bobbi's cheeks and the tightly pursed circle of Bobbi's well-practised lips.

'Wow, man, you're *good*,' Raymond said to the kneeling Bobbi. 'I bet your old lady didn't need no vacuum-cleaner when you were around the house. I bet you could suck the cork right out of the bottle, man – oh!' Bobbi had moved so far down on Raymond's throbbing manhood that its head was pressed against the back of his throat; the sudden rigidity at the top of Bobbi's oesophagus against his crown as Bobbi opened his throat to swallow Raymond's thick hard-on all the way down made Raymond gasp loudly. Thrill after thrill of pleasure shuddered the length of his cock and clenched balls and up through his body to his hairless chest, almost, but not quite, bringing him to orgasm.

The toilet door banged open as a couple more guys, slim and clean-cut eighteen-year-old boys with cropped gelled hair and tight black rubber shorts, DM boots and skin-tight white vests came in with glowing eyes to watch Bobbi blowing Raymond in the middle of the toilet floor.

Raymond's throat was cotton-dry as Bobbi moved his

eager mouth repeatedly backwards and forwards on the Oriental man's thick stiff prick, gripping his tight ass with one hand and cupping his big ball-sack with the other. Raymond moaned as Bobbi began to probe between his tightly clenched buttocks with an impeccably manicured index finger for Raymond's puckered asshole while carrying on sucking him off. Normally, Raymond would have been pissed off at a cocksucker being so presumptuous as to try and finger-fuck him while giving a blow-job, but Bobbi's rapidly moving mouth felt so good on his heavily ridged and veined erection that, before Raymond realised it, Bobbi's finger was sliding easily up his asshole and questing for his prostate with practised expertise. Surprising himself, Raymond impulsively pushed his hips down slightly to get Bobbi's finger all the way up him to the knuckle. It felt good in there.

Raymond twisted his taut toned torso, the flaps of his open waistcoat brushing Bobbi's head as the kneeling Bobbi pumped his mouth on Raymond's rigid cock and worked his index finger in Raymond's asshole, and reached for the half-empty bottle of beer Bobbi had been drinking. He toasted the watching guys, then tilted his head back and drained the bottle, flicking his glossy black hair back, relieving the dryness of his mouth, and somehow enjoying the now-warm fluid pouring down his own open throat. He was enjoying receiving pleasure simultaneously from all his orifices: his seeping slit, finger-fucked asshole and beer-swallowing mouth. He put the empty bottle down on the glitter-sprayed surface next to the sinks with a thump and looked down on the eager cock-sucker who was pleasuring him so thoroughly, with a face bloated with excitement.

Bobbi's public performance had attracted quite a crowd into the toilet by now, and they were now standing around watching his exquisite oral techniques, turned on and perhaps a little envious of the young brown-skinned boy with the orange hair in the butt-hugging short-shorts who had the nerve to be so brazenly trampy and do what they all wanted to do, or of the 23-year-old Chinese guy having his big stiff dick so expertly sucked. Obviously word had been passed around the club because, as well as the various guys who had been using the toilet for more mundane purposes when Bobbi had first sunk to his knees, and the two fey eighteen-year-olds in the black rubber shorts, the skinhead couple had come back in, as had the two stripey-shorts tanned bodybuilders who had bought coke from Raymond a little earlier. In amongst them various other lean and muscular men, stripped to the waist, some with pierced nipples, noses and lips, some preppy and clean-cut looking, stood watching in voyeuristic excitement, shifting their postures every so often to accommodate their stiffening pricks in their tight jeans or crotch-hugging lycra shorts.

It was the blonder, more boyish and clean-cut looking of the two body-builders who got his cock out first, not looking at the guys around him, only at where Bobbi knelt moving his head rapidly in front of Raymond's crotch. The bodybuilder's dick was long and hard; it curved pale above golden-brown neatly trimmed pubic hair, the rectangle of his hips untanned and creamy pink. He gripped his thick circumcised erection and began to move his fist slowly on it, all the time watching Bobbi sucking Raymond's big stiff dick, burying his full lips in Raymond's surprising dyed-blond curling pubic hair each time he swallowed Raymond's shaft all the way down his open throat, taking the Chinese guy's pole to the root.

Once the handsome blond body-builder had got his cock out, all the other voyeurs eagerly followed suit, pushing shorts down and unzipping or unbuttoning flies, relieved now that they had been given permission to enjoy the spectacle unconstrained by decorum. Some wanked faster, some slower. Some were cut, some were uncut; some dicks were thicker and more veiny, others longer, smoother and more aerodynamic. Free hands casually explored erect neighbouring nipples and accepting butt-holes, but all eyes remained on Bobbi, kneeling in front of Raymond.

Bobbi pumped his mouth greedily up and down on Raymond's rigid dong, lubricating its shaft with his saliva, and feeling his mouth overflowing with Raymond's now freely flowing pre-come, his own cock achingly stiff and painfully constrained in his ball-crushingly tight shorts.

'Hey, Bobbi,' Raymond said hoarsely, picking up the almost-empty beer-bottle and downing the dregs in a quick swallow. 'We're giving these fuckers a good show, ain't we, man? Me and my big cock, you and your big cock-sucking lips . . .'

Bobbi seemed to nod as he carried on pumping his mouth on Raymond's thick throbbing erection, swallowing the Chinese boy's pre-come as he did so.

'We could give them something freakier yet, man,' Raymond continued, looking down on Bobbi's rapidly-moving head, hoping that Bobbi would go for the idea that was now filling his mind. 'Could you go for something freakier than just horny cock-sucking, Bobbi, man?'

Bobbi broke off blowing Raymond for a moment, sliding his hot wet mouth slowly up the stiff length of Raymond's cock and allowing Raymond's erection to pop up out of his open mouth. Then Bobbi looked up at Raymond over Raymond's throbbing manhood, his upturned face glossy with excitement and sweat, his lips wet and glittering with saliva and pre-come. He gazed up at Raymond with soft brown eyes.

'I could go for any freaky thing, man,' he answered Raymond in an intense, low voice, and Raymond believed him. Then Bobbi gripped Raymond's balls firmly and pulled them down hard, yanking Raymond's rigid heavy dick down to an accessible angle of only forty-five degrees, and slid his wet eager mouth back down over Raymond's thick shaft. Raymond groaned in pleasure as Bobbi swallowed his cock-head down the back of his throat before beginning to pump his mouth up and down again on Raymond's hot pole with fast deep strokes.

'Why don't you unbutton those tight, tight shorts and push 'em down, man?' Raymond began in a rough, breathless voice, as Bobbi carried on sucking him off fast. 'Push 'em down and give your cock and ass an airing. 'Cause you got a good ass, Bobbi, man. And then maybe you could –' Raymond picked up the empty beer-bottle, wrapped his well-shaped lips around its neck for a second to wet the smoothly-curved green rim – 'maybe you could sit that hot brown ass down on this beer-bottle while you blow me, man. I sure would get off on seeing that, Bobbi. I'd give you the biggest load you ever swallowed for that, man.'

While still pumping his mouth rapidly on Raymond's erect and dripping manhood, and enjoying the buzz of near-pain on the insides of his cheeks all this cock-sucking had given him, Bobbi slid his index finger abruptly out of Raymond's now slightly open asshole.

Ah, shit, Raymond thought, regretting the sudden absence of Bobbi's attentive digit from his rectum, *I've pissed him off now, with my freaky ideas. I'll be lucky to even get a decent blow-job off him, now. Shit.* Raymond got ready to take hold of Bobbi's head and fuck Bobbi's face quick and hard if Bobbi began to show signs of losing interest in sucking Raymond to a full climax.

But then, to Raymond's delight, and to the delight of the turned-on wanking onlookers around him, the kneeling Bobbi started to fumblingly unbutton his denim short-shorts as he sucked on Raymond's big stiff whanger even more hungrily. In a moment, the fly was open and Bobbi was hooking his fingers in the waist-band of his shorts and the briefs inside them, and pushing them both down to his slightly bruised knees, where they made a comfortable kneeling-pad for him as he continued pleasuring Raymond orally. Bobbi's balls hung down full and heavy between his legs and his cock arched dark and thick up towards his firm curving belly as Bobbi stuck his smooth butt out for the admiration of the masturbating voyeurs around them.

'Sit on that bottle, man,' a throaty voice came from behind Bobbi: one of the two tanned body-builders, the chiselled blond guy with the immaculately slicked hair, who had been the first to get his cock out. There were breathless calls of assent from the other horny masturbating men. 'Go on, man,' 'You can do it,' 'Sit on it, like the bottom you are,' 'Suck that bottle up your ass –'

Raymond picked up the bottle and bent forward over Bobbi to place it just behind him on the floor beneath his ass; the Oriental guy's lean belly pressed hard against Bobbi's forehead as he did so, and the gold chain that hung between his pierced nipples brushed Bobbi's cropped orange hair. *Don't forget to take hold of that*, Bobbi reminded himself as he felt it brush against him. Then, still sucking Raymond deeply and wetly, he reached back and held his buttocks open so that the watching men could get a good look at his greedy chocolate star before he got into the anal action. Then he slowly began to lower his ass onto the glittering green bottle, careful not to break his dick-sucking rhythm as he did so.

It took Bobbi a couple of squats before he had positioned his receptive hole right on top of the cool curving lip of the bottle-neck. A shiver of anticipation at the thought of such a smooth anal penetration ran up through Bobbi's body, making him gasp around Raymond's thick, hard cock. Bobbi gripped Raymond's thighs to help him balance as he squatted down onto the glistening beer-bottle beneath him.

Bobbi's asshole opened easily and he sat down on the bottle to the base of its neck in a single, relaxed movement, bringing murmurs of approval and calls of, 'You're doing it, man, you're sitting on that bottle, it's up your ass –'

'Go for more,' Raymond ordered hoarsely, feeling an irrevocable heaviness starting to build in his dick in Bobbi's firm, eager mouth, and wanting to come with Bobbi sitting right the way down in front of him.

Eager to please, Bobbi pushed his body down onto the beer-bottle beneath him, his own dick twitching as he did so. Bobbi's accommodating asshole opened to accommodate the bottle's shoulders, dilating to the necessary width to swallow the whole bottle into his ass. Shifting slightly in his heavy boots to keep the bottle at a comfortable angle, Bobbi slid his anus down over the bottle's length, feeling its smooth shape filling up his rectum gratifyingly. Pre-come beaded Bobbi's cock as he squatted down as far as he dared – any further and he knew the bottle would get sucked right up his ass, and that wouldn't be convenient or wise. He tried to get a pumping rhythm going, gripping the bottle between his heels and moving his ass up and down on its smooth length in short quick strokes, while still enthusiastically working his mouth on the pulsing hard-on of the Oriental man standing in front of him.

Bracing himself using just one hand to grip one of Raymond's thighs as he moved his mouth faster and faster on Raymond's prick, and bouncing his ass up and down on the bottle beneath him in a horny pumping rhythm, Bobbi reached up with his free hand for the golden chain hanging glittering between the Chinese youth's pierced nipples. In a moment, Bobbi had found it. He curled his fingers around the fine metal cord and began to tug on it, playfully at first, then harder. Raymond grunted loudly.

'Oh, man, my tit-chain,' Raymond gasped. 'Yeah, man, *yank* on that fucker! Suck my cock and yank that fucker like it's a emergency on the Tube, man! Like it's a fucking bomb alert!'

Sweat poured from Bobbi's skin, and every muscle ached as he worked hard to keep up the three rhythms simultaneously – his ass pumping up and down on the shiny beer-bottle beneath him, his hungry mouth pumping backwards and forwards on Raymond's throbbing erection before him, and now his right hand tugging hard on Raymond's tit-chain above him – and all the time Bobbi's own large, swinging erection bobbed, unattended, between his smooth brown thighs.

Raymond's breaths came fast and hoarse and high now, as his heavily veined and pulsing hard-on gained uncontrollably in weight in Bobbi's hot wet mouth, and spasms of unbelievable pleasure lanced through Raymond's chest each time Bobbi tugged enthusiastically on the gold chain between Raymond's nipples. Raymond's heart hammered against his rib-cage as he was uncontrollably lifted towards an explosive climax by Bobbi's rapidly-moving mouth.

'Oh man, you suck cock so good, man,' Raymond shouted hoarsely, his face flushed, raven hair tousled on his forehead, his breath rasping and short. 'Oh, man, you suck cock so good, I'm coming. I can't stop it, man, oh, man, I'm coming, oh, fuck, oh, Christ, oh –' Raymond slammed his hips up against Bobbi's face hard in short, passionate thrusts, bruising Bobbi's swollen lips, pumping his jism into Bobbi's eager mouth, knocking Bobbi back so he almost *did* sit right the way down on the beer-bottle. But Bobbi managed to get a hand back down on the floor behind him quickly enough to brace himself and keep his sweaty ass off the tiles and his well-filled rectum out of the emergency room. Bobbi also kept right on sucking on Raymond's discharging hard-on as he pushed himself back upright in front of Raymond's crotch, determined not to miss a single drop of Raymond's hot sour load as it pumped into his bruised, aching and open throat. The Oriental youth's thick creamy load tasted of dope and nicotine, and its particularity excited Bobbi as he eagerly – and exhaustedly – swallowed it down, his lips tight around Raymond's swollen pole of muscle.

Then Bobbi – with the beer-bottle still jammed three-quarters of the way up his ass – slipped his tired wet mouth off Raymond's still-hard and glistening dick, wrapped his fist around its pulsing shaft, and started to squeeze the last few drops of Raymond's come onto his quivering tongue.

Around this time, knowing the show was almost over, the movement of fists on dicks in the watching crowd got faster, more urgent. First to explode, with a loud grunt and exclamation, was the chiselled blond body-builder, whose stripy trunks were now pushed halfway down his waxed thighs. His load shot violently from his cock in a white spattering line onto the freshly polished tiles of the toilet floor in front of him, as his hips jerked forward and his fist pumped rapidly on his large and throbbing hard-on.

To the delight of the masturbating onlookers, Bobbi, who had heard the blond muscle-man climaxing behind him as he tongued the last drops of spunk from the head of Raymond's now-softening cock, turned and moved quickly across the room on all fours – and with the beer-bottle still up his butt, his shorts now slid down to his ankles – to where the body-builder was still standing looking down at him, his come-spattered fist still moving slowly on his long firm cock. Bobbi darted his head forward and down, and began to greedily lick the well-built blond man's jism up off the clean white tiles. It had a different taste: no nicotine, less salty, a slight taint of something sour – poppers, maybe. Bobbi sat up on his haunches, clenching his sphincter to keep the beer-bottle in place, and began to attentively lick the come off the body-builder's smooth warm fist.

'Wow, you like the taste of jizz,' the body-builder said a little breathlessly, enjoying the feeling of the come-hungry youth's warm wet tongue on his fingers and knuckles. 'I bet a lot of these other guys would shoot in your mouth, if you wanted,' he continued, looking down at Bobbi kneeling before him. 'I bet all you'd have to do is just keep right on kneeling there, with your mouth wide open, and they'd all just line up to beat off in your mouth –' The muscle-man looked around. The men around him, their fists now moving mid-tempo on their stiff dicks, nodded yes. The few who had already shot their loads during Bobbi's cocksucking show felt cheated but were still eager to watch on till the end.

So Bobbi found himself in a delirium of pleasure, kneeling with a beer-bottle stretching his ass in the middle of the Trash club toilet as one man after another lined up to jerk off into his open mouth. And all Bobbi had to do was swallow the creamy load as it came! His eyes began to glaze over in ecstasy as one big cock after another bobbed in front of his face, had a fist move rapidly up and down on its rigid swollen length and finally – after a torture of anticipation as to when the next hot load would be delivered, and how much it would be, and whether it would be delivered with a grunt or a gasp or a growl – squirted hot white jism in pearly gobbets straight into Bobbi's waiting mouth.

Before he lost count, Bobbi knew for certain that he had had a mouthful of hot, fresh come from both of the well-groomed body-builders, the skinhead couple, the two trampy eighteen-year-olds in the black rubber shorts, a lean guy with a bolt through his ball-sack and a shaven crotch, and a pumped black go-go dancer called Leo, who wore glittery gold trunks and gold eyeshadow. There had been at least three or four others apart from Raymond. Last of all, a pair of slim brown hips encased in shiny latex positioned themselves in front of him. Bobbi recognised Felipe's circumcised brown hard-on as Felipe pushed the shorts down in front of him to allow it to spring up stiffly in Bobbi's face. Flushed with a sudden nostalgia for their old sex-show days,

Bobbi stuck his tongue forward and opened his mouth wide to make sure he didn't miss any of the Latino barman's hot jism as Felipe beat off rapidly into Bobbi's mouth.

After Felipe had shot his load onto Bobbi's tongue, and let Bobbi lick the rest out of his slit, Bobbi had finally managed to stumble to his feet, the beer-bottle slipping out of his butt-hole with an audible pop. Felipe had turned to the guy behind him, a muscular and freckly red-head with a remarkably ripped physique and a very large and very stiff cock, and said, 'Sorry mate, this bitch is *full*.'

The guy had looked over hopefully at Bobbi then, who was wiping his shiny lips with the back of his hand and looked exhausted. To the red-head's delight, Bobbi, glistening with sweat, smiled back at the freckled, muscular, well-hung white guy and sank back to his knees in front of the man's purple-headed, circumcised cock.

'Girl, you are such a *tramp*,' Felipe said as Bobbi opened his mouth wide, extending his long pink tongue over his lips for one more hot load as the ripped young white guy moved his fist quickly on his long hard dick.

'Shit, girl, I just don't know how to say no, that's all,' Bobbi replied, after the red-head had come in his mouth with a grunt, gratifyingly giving him the largest and saltiest load of the evening so far. Bobbi wished he could beat himself off, wishing that he didn't have to save himself for Prince Fela's sex-party. 'And anyway, it didn't stop you from giving me a load, did it?' he added.

'Yeah, well, I thought you came to find Don,' Felipe replied, ignoring the second part of Bobbi's statement as Bobbi got back to his feet and awkwardly buttoned up his sluttishly tight and ball-crushing shorts. His stiff cock pushed out of one of the leg-holes but Bobbi didn't seem to notice, much less care. 'Not just to satisfy your own base carnal pleasures.'

'Have you seen him around at all?' Bobbi asked, belching softly from all the come he'd swallowed.

'This guy who just bought me a drink –' Felipe began.

'What, you, bitch? What was he, blind?' Bobbi interrupted cattily.

'No. Classy,' Felipe replied snippily. 'Do you want to hear this or not? You do? Well, keep that all-too-open mouth of yours shut for five seconds, and I'll tell you, OK? Anyway, this guy told me he saw someone who sounds like he looks a lot like Don getting blown on the dance-floor of Tropical, about half an hour ago.'

'Yeah, but Don isn't exactly unique,' Bobbi objected.

Felipe shrugged. 'If you've got any better pointers then go follow them,' he said, turning down the corners of his mouth in indifference. 'Just try to keep your eyes above waist-level, yeah?'

As it turned out, Don wasn't at the very-cruisey Tropical, though Bobbi did exchange friendly greetings with quite a few former tricks of both his and Don's there. Nor was Don at the mostly-black Hot Spot, although a hot young white boy with a slept-in-looking indie haircut and a pierced tongue had begged Bobbi to let him rim him in the back room there, and Bobbi had been unable to refuse the horny youth's request. The extra sensation caused by the rounded steel stud thrust through the boy's eager tongue had certainly added to Bobbi's pleasure, and it had been all he could do not to beat off and shoot his load, despite wanting to save it for Fela's party, as the boy rimmed him deeply and thoroughly for over a quarter of an hour. At Jizz, Bobbi had felt obliged to felch a very smooth and pretty Indian youth with waist-length hair and a lean body, after the androgynous man had been serially fucked by three horny Asian skinheads in quick succession. And, at Strap, Bobbi had found himself bending over a pommel-horse while looking out for Don, and having his shorts pulled down, then being spanked and vigorously dildo-fucked by a Germanic buzzcut blond body-builder in chaps and a leather jock, to the general entertainment of other club-goers; some of them had taken turns in swivelling the hard rubber length in Bobbi's rectum, stretching it extensively in every direction.

It was gone one a.m. by the time Bobbi finally made his way down the steps of Booty, a small, dark club known only to the night-life *cognoscenti*, and the last place he could think of to look for Don. Bobbi's thighs ached, his lips ached, his butthole ached – but in a good way. He hadn't seen any sign of Don anywhere in Booty, either, and had started to get annoyed because Prince Fela's party was meant to have started around midnight, and he didn't want to miss any of the notoriously outrageous action that was supposed to be happening there that night.

At Booty, Bobbi had got flirting with a hard-bodied white guy called Nate, short and broad and heavily muscled, very pale and with a dark mohican and dark eyes. Nate had a steel rod through one nipple and a blue tattoo of a carp on one shoulder, and was wearing nothing except heavy army boots and a camouflage jockstrap which failed to conceal a large, thick erection that had begun to appear the moment Nate set eyes on Bobbi.

'I'm Nate and I want to fuck you up the butt,' Nate had said in an intense voice, by way of introduction.

'What makes you think I'm that cheap and easy?' Bobbi had asked playfully, turned on by Nate's top-man directness.

Nate had looked down at Bobbi's big stiff cock, thrust sideways in his tight constricting shorts, and the way Bobbi's balls were splayed bulgingly either side of the wrenched-up seam that also cut up between his buttocks, and shrugged. 'I dunno, mate,' he had said. 'Something subliminal, I guess.'

Then he had laughed: a sexy and provocative laugh. 'Maybe I'm just projecting.' He kept his eyes on Bobbi's. 'Maybe not,' he continued, bringing his face closer and kissing Bobbi hotly on the mouth. Bobbi wrapped his arms around the punk's shoulders and sucked greedily on Nate's penetrating tongue.

Soon Nate had got Bobbi turned around and with his shorts round his ankles, in a corner of the club away from the bouncers and bar-staff, and was fondling Bobbi's stiff nipples deftly from behind, while fucking Bobbi hard up the ass with his long thick pole. Bobbi gasped heavily with each thrust of Nate's large, circumcised manhood. Again Bobbi had to avoid touching his own dick, which was now dripping with pre-come; and he might come anyway, without touching it, if Nate carried on pounding his ass hard and long enough the way he was currently doing. Nate moved his hands to Bobbi's shoulders and, gripping them firmly, began to ram his thick hard dick up Bobbi's asshole as hard as he possibly could.

'Oh, yeah, do me, baby,' Bobbi moaned, tossing his head in excitement as Nate's gasps came faster and louder behind him and the pumping of his hips against Bobbi's ass became more rapid and more violent. 'Fuck my ass! Fuck my slack ass!'

'Oh, oh, oh, oh, fuck, oh, shit, oh, fuck!' Nate yelled, slamming his cock right the way up Bobbi's asshole and holding it there as his rigid pole bucked and shot its load into the depths of Bobbi's rectum, pushing Bobbi forward hard so his head was pressed against the sweat-slickened wall in front of them. 'Oh, yeah, oh, *yeah* . . .' Nate growled thickly, swivelling his hips and pushing his cock around inside Bobbi's body, stretching his rectum in a way that made Bobbi moan, 'Oh, yeah,' too.

A moment later Nate withdrew his firm but softening cock from Bobbi's slack backside with a soft slurp. Then, before Bobbi could even straighten up, much less turn round, something curious happened. At first, Bobbi thought Nate had just moved his hands slightly on Bobbi's shoulders. But then Bobbi realised that he could smell a different brand of cologne, and that the hands now gripping his shoulders had rings on them – he could feel the slight coolness of the metal against his skin – so they definitely belonged to someone else. Them Bobbi felt a thick, smooth cock-head being guided towards the entrance to his already well-fucked asshole. Before Bobbi thought to protest, a large cock was firmly pushed all the way up his ass to the root. And the protest died in his throat anyway, as the good feeling of being butt-fucked flooded through Bobbi's ass and groin and chest. The man behind him began to pump his large erect dick in Bobbi's asshole with deep strokes, eliciting groans of pleasure from Bobbi as he fucked him. Bobbi glanced round out of the corners of his eyes, but all he could see was dark hands with chunky gold rings on them, and all that told him was that a brother was fucking him.

The big stiff new dick in Bobbi's ass moved backwards and forwards, faster and faster, slamming in and out, harder and harder, making Bobbi grunt and gasp loudly and breathlessly.

'Oh, baby, that cock's so *big*!' Bobbi gasped as the thick rigid pole slid in and out of his open asshole with relentless repetitiveness.

'Man, your hole's well open,' the well-built black man behind him grunted. 'Tighten that slack bitch-hole on my hard chocolate pole,' he continued. He slapped Bobbi's ass. 'Tighten up, bitch!'

As the well-hung top-man behind him ground his crotch against Bobbi's upturned butt, Bobbi became aware that the muscular black guy bum-fucking him had no pubic hair, in fact, had a totally shaven body. No pubic hair . . . But his long, hard cock felt so good in Bobbi's butt that Bobbi couldn't think straight. All he could think of was the pleasure the thrusting erection in his rectum was sending juddering through his body. He tightened his anal ring around the black top-man's cock, eliciting a groan from the horny guy butt-fucking him.

'Fuck me, man,' Bobbi gasped to the well-hung black man behind him. 'Fuck me hard!'

'Man, you're such a whore, Bobbi, man!' Don said hoarsely behind him, pounding his dick up the trampy bass-player's anal passage as hard and fast as he could.

'I knew it was you all the time, man,' Bobbi lied breathlessly as Don rammed his long rigid hard-on all the way up into Bobbi's now achingly stretched rectum.

'No way you did, man,' Don replied, his voice catching in his throat as his heart began to pound against the walls of his well-pumped chest; heaviness began to build in his achingly stiff dick as he poled Bobbi hard. 'You just knew another geezer with a big dick wanted to fuck you and you just gave it up like the tramp you are, Bobbi, man.'

Normally Bobbi would have protested at being called a tramp by Don, just on the principle that Don liked fucking even more than Bobbi did, but the feeling of Don's thick erection sliding greasily in and out of his hot open asshole pushed all complaints out of his mind. 'Fuck me harder, Don,' was all Bobbi could think to say by way of a reply. 'I need it, Don. Fuck my ass harder with that good stiff prick.'

Bobbi braced himself against the wall, resting his head on his folded arms, and stuck his ass out and back, making it as available as possible to Don. Don pounded Bobbi's asshole like a jackhammer, his long thick hard-on sending spasms of pleasure the length of Bobbi's body. Bobbi gasped and moaned and tossed his head as his bobbing cock dripped long shining threads of pre-come onto the club's glittery-black linoleum floor. Bobbi had never had Don's cock up him before, although he had always been curious because Don had the reputation of being an exceptionally hard, rough top-man, and the idea of being topped by Don had always turned Bobbi on. Just, the situation had never arisen. Until now.

'Fuck me like a slut,' Bobbi gasped, his thighs trembling and his asshole stretched and aching as Don slammed his rigid manhood in and out. 'Fuck me like the tramp I am – oh, Jesus!'

Don gripped Bobbi around the waist and forced his stiff cock right the way up Bobbi's ass, as hard as he could, his balls bouncing against the balls of the panting pretty boy bent over ass-upwards in front of him. Then Don started to fuck Bobbi with short rapid strokes, slapping Bobbi's butt as he did so, making Bobbi cry out sharply with each combined slap and thrust. Don's cock throbbed and gained in weight and rigidity as he pounded it in Bobbi's rectum, slamming his smooth cockhead firmly up Bobbi again and again and again, until finally he lost control of his surging dick inside Bobbi's hot wet anal cavity.

'Oh, Jesus, Bobbi, man!' Don cried out in a loud, throaty voice. 'I'm gonna come in your ass, man! I'm gonna shoot my load all the way up your trampy ass!'

'Shaft me good, Don, man! Shoot that load up my ass!' Bobbi gasped loudly, playing with his own nipples to add to his pleasure as Don rammed his rigid hairless pole in and out of Bobbi's slack butthole, his gold-ringed fingers digging into Bobbi's hips as he held Bobbi in position and butt-fucked him as hard as he possibly could.

And then, with a sharp exclamation, Don came, with his cock deep in Bobbi's asshole – 'Oh, man, I'm coming, man; I'm losing it. Oh, take it up the ass, man, take my hot load up your horny ass, man, like you're taking my hot dick right up your battyhole, right up to the root, man –'

Grunting hoarsely, Don pumped his hot load up Bobbi's slack back-passage and thrust hard against Bobbi's buttocks;

he exploded inside Bobbi's well-stretched rectum so vigorously that Bobbi's head was banged hard against the wall.

Now he had come, Don pulled his still-hard cock straight out of Bobbi's slippery asshole, making Bobbi gasp sharply at the abruptness of its removal. Bobbi's own cock stood out from his closely clipped pubic hair, long and brown and hard, and shiny at its crown, and his face was flushed with sexual excitement. He could feel Don's heavy load of come starting to slip slowly out of his still-open asshole.

'Aren't you going to toss yourself off, man?' Don asked, slightly surprised at the way Bobbi was keeping his hand off his cock, as he pulled up his white Calvins and ass-hugging black jeans, and began to button his fly.

'I'm saving it for Prince Fela's party,' Bobbi said, admiring Don's heavily-muscled arms and tattooed chest as he said this.

'Oh, yeah, the party,' Don said, feigning disinterest, looking down at his booted feet and glowering.

'Hey, man, why don't you come?' Bobbi said, trying to make it sound as if he had just suddenly come up with the idea. 'I've got an invite, and I'm allowed to bring a guest.'

Don looked up at him sceptically. 'Yeah?' he said. Then the shaven-headed black man's brow wrinkled and he gave the boyishly grinning Bobbi a shrewd look. 'You ain't invited Malcolm to this thing, have you?'

Bobbi shook his head. 'No, man. It's not his scene,' he said. 'It's for hard-core sex-freaks, the open-minded and the *très très* horny. But maybe now you've shot your bolt, you'll be worn out for the night and you're not interested.'

Don bridled at this critique of his sexual stamina. 'Fuck that, man. We leave right now; by the time we get there, I'll be ready to get it on, believe me, yeah. I'll be horny to freak with the freaks.' He grinned a broad, gold-toothed grin. 'Oh yeah, man. 'Cause I'm *super* freaky, you know what I'm saying? Or does your asshole tell you different, man?' he asked cheekily, stretching his grin a little wider.

Just then the stocky mohawked Nate, who had fucked Bobbi earlier, passed by with a beer. Don caught him by the arm. 'I just shot my load up this guy's tasty brown butt, man. Why don't you get round behind him and get on your knees and eat the brother's asshole out, man? You know you want to . . .

To Bobbi's surprise – and delight – Don's assertive manner worked on Nate, and the stocky young white man knelt down behind Bobbi and buried his face in Bobbi's ass. Bobbi reached back and held his buttocks open so that Nate could get his mouth right up against Bobbi's open butthole, and squatted down onto Nate's upturned face. Nate pressed his hot lips firmly against Bobbi and began to tongue him hungrily, breaking off every so often for a drag on the lighted cigarette he was holding, but always eagerly returning to rimming Bobbi's butthole afterwards. Bobbi enjoyed the feeling of Nate's long tongue licking out his asshole, of Nate even blowing smoke up there, and again played with his own stiff nipples to heighten his sensual enjoyment at being so eagerly and unexpectedly felched by the handsome white punk squatting behind him.

After a couple of minutes Nate struggled to his feet. His lips were shiny and his handsome face was flushed purple-red. He placed a proprietorial hand on Bobbi's smooth ass and turned to Don. 'That ass is now thoroughly cleaned out, sir,' he said to Don, then kissed him full on the mouth. Don responded hotly, and gave Nate's crotch a brief, firm massage as the two men sucked face for a long moment. Then Don broke off the kiss and turned to Bobbi, while still feeling Nate up. Nate opened his thighs to accommodate Don's hand, and Don could feel the mohawked white guy stiffening inside his snugly-fitted camouflage jock against his fingers.

'Get your pants up, Bobbi, man,' Don ordered Bobbi, wiping Nate's saliva and traces of his own come from his mouth. 'If we're gonna go to this party, let's get going, yeah. We probably already missed the *hors d'oeuvres*, you know what I'm saying?'

Nodding, Bobbi pulled up his denim shorts, yanking the seam up between his buttocks and bisecting his ball-sack with thrilling painfulness, and struggled to button the fly across his long thick erection. 'Did you hear about the Prince Fela guarantee?' Bobbi asked Don as he forced the copper studs through the frayed denim buttonholes of the shorts.

Don shook his head. 'No, man,' he said, giving Nate's upthrust crotch a final squeeze before releasing it and pushing Nate away. 'What is it: you can sue if it's boring or you don't fancy no one or you don't get no satisfaction or shit?'

Bobbi shook his head, then met Don's eyes with an unexpectedly intense gaze. 'Not exactly, Don,' Bobbi said. 'Just, he guarantees that nobody ever leaves one of his parties without doing something they never thought they would do.'

'Yeah?' Don replied sceptically, half-intrigued, hooding his smoky eyes. 'Zat true?'

'I've only been to one other of his parties, man,' Bobbi said. 'But from that I can give you the *Bobbi* guarantee that it's absolutely true.'

'Yeah?'

'Yeah.'

'So what we waiting for, man, the Second Coming?' Don asked, turning to go, adjusting his stiffening cock in his pants as he turned and thinking, *Something I've never done before* . . .

'Oh, fuck!' Bobbi said abruptly, cutting across Don's line of thought.

'What, man?' Don asked, puzzled.

'I forgot to get my line of coke off Raymond! Shit, after all that!'

'Ah, you loved it, man.'

'You don't know what I had to *do*, Don, man,' Bobbi complained.

'Yeah, but whatever it was, man, you loved it, I bet,' Don replied.

Bobbi shrugged, then laughed. 'Yeah, but I *still* want my line, man.'

Seven

The night was cloudless but still and warm, and the moon shone bright above the city as Malcolm roared up Ladbroke Grove, towards Notting Hill Gate, on his powerful motor-bike. The buildings he passed shifted from tower-blocks and multiple-occupancy dwellings to large Georgian terraces and detached near-mansions with wrought-iron porticoes and walled secluded gardens, the preserves of the rich and super-rich. It was a whole other world to Malcolm, and he was both intrigued by it and – although he would have denied it – afraid of it. He felt like a burglar sizing up a job as he slowed his bike outside a large four-square white-washed and pilastered building, set back a little from the quiet streetlit road by the curve of a half-moon gravel drive, behind tall black wrought-iron railings. He glanced down at the invitation he was holding tightly in one hand. Yeah, this was the place, all right. Prince Fela's yard. The windows were all tall, ten feet or more, but tightly curtained and, disconcertingly, no sound seemed to be coming from within.

Still feeling like an interloper, Malcolm turned his bike and rolled into the drive. Underneath a spreading cedar tree were parked a silver Mercedes sports and a black Cherokee jeep, and two or three other flash motors gleamed half-hidden in the shadows. Malcolm kicked out his bike-stand and parked the bike alongside the Mercedes. Then he swung off it, his heart beginning to pound in his chest. He had always been shy at parties, and this wasn't going to be no ordinary spliff-and-Thunderbird affair, he knew.

He had ridden to Prince Fela's house wearing a tight black zip-fronted leather jacket with nothing under it, heavy bike-boots, and – for the first time outside his own home – his tight black leather shorts. He had also – another first, perhaps inspired by Don, despite their blow-up that morning – shaved his long *café-au-lait* legs. He pulled off his crash-helmet and ran a large hand over his tightly plaited hair, to make sure nothing had come loose on the journey. He unzipped his jacket to reveal his large pumped chest and ripped stomach and, cradling his helmet under his arm, walked slowly over to the glass-roofed portico which extended down from the large four-panelled front door to the gravel curve of the drive. Malcolm climbed the black-and-white tiled steps to the large heavy door, hesitated a moment, then rang on the bell.

There was no sound from within, and no immediate answer. Malcolm glanced down at his watch. It had gone one. Surely the party would only just be getting going, he thought; it couldn't already be over, could it?

The door swung open noiselessly. From beyond came the reassuring faint pulse of heavy, mesmerising trip-hop. In front of Malcolm stood a tall willowy African man with a shaven head and smoky eyes. A joint trailed from his large lips. His skin was incredibly dark and flawless and his physique was lean and shapely. He wore a black and gold sarong around his waist, cowries around his neck and gold hoops in his ears. Around one of his upper arms was a bronze band. He looked down on Malcolm wordlessly, his expression blank. Malcolm handed him the rather creased and soiled invitation. The African man scrutinised the gold-inscribed card minutely, as if he suspected it was a forgery. Then he looked Malcolm up and down again; it seemed to Malcolm that, this time, the willowy man was checking out Malcolm's smooth muscular legs and the provocative tight-ness of his ass- and basket-huggingly tight black leather shorts. Then the African guy's face split into a broad toothy grin.

'Come this way, brother,' he said, turning and gesturing for Malcolm to follow. Malcolm stepped inside the hall hesitantly, closing the front door carefully behind him, then had to hurry to keep up with the tall African. The horns of antelope and wildebeest adorned the walls of the half-lit corridor. The African guy stopped in front of a second door and turned back with glowing eyes.

'I am Camara,' he said, a strong lilt to his accent: from where exactly, Malcolm couldn't tell. With long fingers, he extended the roach of the joint towards Malcolm's soft brown lips. Malcolm pushed his head forward and toked on the joint, drawing down sweet relaxing smoke. The African man withdrew the spliff from Malcolm's lips and drew on it himself. 'I am also called "Miss Camara", because of the role I prefer to play when I am with a man,' he continued in a creaky voice. 'And beyond this door –' he gestured languidly '– is paradise.'

Malcolm's heart began to pound loudly again in his chest as Camara turned the gleaming brass knob and swung the inner door open. 'Enter,' Camara said with a theatrical flourish and another broad smile, standing aside to let Malcolm pass.

As he passed the tall African, Malcolm turned and looked deep into his sculptured face. 'Where are you from, man?' he asked, partly genuinely curious and partly because he was suddenly afraid of passing through that door.

'Guinea,' Camara said, still smiling. 'I was a sergeant in the army for nine years there. I saw many things. Good and bad. Bad and worse. And then I left the army to look for something new. And I came here. And I found it. Something for me.'

'Did you ever shoot anyone?' Malcolm found himself asking.

Camara shrugged ambiguously. 'Now I make love, not war,' he replied.

Behind them, the doorbell sounded. New guests were arriving. 'I must leave you now,' Camara said, stroking Malcolm's arm. 'But perhaps we will – talk – more later.' Malcolm nodded, and Camara turned and sashayed back down the hall towards the front door. Malcolm watched his high shapely ass, outlined clearly through the tightly wrapped material of the sarong, as he went. Then Malcolm took a deep breath and stepped on through into the house's interior.

Malcolm found himself standing on a brass-railed internal balcony, looking out on a large high-ceilinged and lamp-lit room which was scattered with oriental rugs, animal skins and cushions. Above him, vast skeins of bright richly patterned fabric had been gathered into a canopy to create the feeling of being inside a vast tent. Food of all sorts, caviar, dried fruits, bottles of wine, bottles of beer and spirits, cigarettes, cigars, spliffs, pottery bowls of glittering lubricants, sex aids and sex-toys of every size, shape and function were scattered on low lacquered tables. A vast window took up the whole of the facing wall, a full twenty feet high, and looked out on a lush garden, dense with shrubs and ornamental trees, also tented in and lit with lanterns. Folding screens were set up to partition off many areas within the main room, suggestions of privacy that also put the inhabitants within on display as if on many small stages.

Bass-heavy, saturating trip-hop played from large speakers set up around the room, and a larger stage had been set up against one wall and draped with brightly-printed African fabrics. On it sat an elaborately-carved African stool. Beside the stage, on one side, was a pink-and-blue neon-lit bar at which pretty, smooth-skinned and muscular black and blond youths, wearing nothing but white and black jockstraps and elasticated gold bow-ties around their necks, shook silver cocktail-shakers and served drinks. On the other side, a blond dreadlocked and Raybanned rangy mixed-race guy, with a bull-ring through his nose, a pierced navel and pierced nipples, and wearing only skin-tight silver shorts through which his large, semi-erect dick and bulging balls were clearly visible, was DJing behind a state-of-the-art mixing desk, moving languidly to the trip-hop beats.

But what had rammed Malcolm's heart up into his throat, taking his breath away, and made his dick grow from softness to painful, throbbing rigidity inside his tight leather shorts in under a second, was what was going on in the centre of the dimly-lit room.

In the exact middle, a lean white punky boy with a low green Mohawk, wearing DM boots and a studded leather belt around his narrow hips, knelt on all fours, and was being fucked vigorously from behind by an Asian muscle-man whose head was shaven round the sides, the top pulled tightly back into a short ponytail, and whose huge tits were pierced with gold rings. The Asian guy's hands were covered with gold and he slapped the punky boy's ass smartly as he fucked him hard up the asshole. Then he would slide his ringed hands down and grip the white boy's narrow hips and pound the youth up the butt for a few strokes. Then the Asian guy would pull his large and heavily-veined hard-on right out of the punk's asshole and plunge it right the way back in to its Number One shaven root in long vigorous thrusts.

Malcolm caught the glint of a large gold Prince Albert rammed through the smooth slickly lubricated brown head of the muscular Asian man's dick before he slid its whole length back into the juicy asshole of the turned-on punk in front of him; the punk wiggled his increasingly reddened ass from side to side to add to the pleasure of the man fucking him and get that stiff brown cock as deep inside his bunghole as possible, bulging solid metal piercing and all.

In front of the white punk, a short, muscular punky

black man was kneeling. He too had a low mohawk, and he was wearing nothing but ripped-up denim shorts, DM boots and no underwear. He had thrust his long erection and balls out through one of the leg-holes of the revealing shorts and was fucking the punky boy's open mouth with his thick dark pole in long strokes, keeping time with the Asian guy fucking the white boy up the ass from behind. He gripped the slim, muscular submissive youth's short, green-dyed mohawk with strong, dark fingers and pushed the youth's mouth down onto his long hard cock, even as he fucked the boy's face. As the black punk and the Asian muscle-man moved their hips against the heavily turned-on white boy's face and butt – he was tossing himself off excitedly as he got pounded from both ends – the two top-men passed a joint between them, taking deep tokes as they pumped their rigid cocks in and out of the mouth and anus of the sexy punk sandwiched between them, their chests swelling.

The Asian guy looked up and saw Malcolm watching them from the balcony. Without breaking the rhythm of his ass-fucking, he called up to him, 'You like what you see, man?'

Malcolm nodded, his mouth dry.

'Come down and fuck him then, man,' the body-built and gold-ringed Asian man shouted, pulling the whole length of his cock out of the white boy's ass and then sliding it right the way back in again, without encountering the least resistance. 'Look how slack he is. He loves taking it up both ends, man. Whichever you prefer.' Then he smiled wickedly at Malcolm. 'Or maybe you want to be where he is, man . . . It's cool . . . Just get down here . . . On your hands and knees, whatever, man . . .'

Malcolm blushed and looked away slightly as the muscular Asian guy and the black mohawked man continued pounding the smooth-skinned young punk on all fours between them.

Next to that threesome, a very hard-looking raggamuffin youth with mid-brown skin, gold teeth, sovereign rings on his fingers, a flat-top fade and a lean hard physique was moving his tight shaven asshole up and down on the exceptionally large and thick cock of a muscular Mediterranean-looking guy who lay sprawled on a rug beneath him. The raggamuffin youth's hands roamed over the curves of the Italian guy's chest, finding his nipples and twisting them dextrously, continuing to pound his pert butt up and down on the shining and rigid pole that stood up from the Italian guy's cropped crotch. The black youth tossed his head ecstatically as he pumped his buttocks up and down on the Mediterranean man's thick hard cock, and his lips were parted in sensual abandon as his rectum was filled to capacity with another man's large and well-lubricated erection.

Beyond this couple, two slender Rastamen, with shoulder-length dreads, were standing entwined, arms around each other, tonguing each other's mouths. As Malcolm watched, one of them turned the other sideways and bent him over. Malcolm got a good view of the bent-over Rasta's rounded ass, and saw the stem of a butt-plug protruding from his butthole. His partner reached over and pulled the butt-plug out, surprising the watching Malcolm with the size of the rubber object that came slipping out of the bent-over man's asshole: it wasn't much smaller than a balled-up fist. The Rasta's asshole opened smoothly and easily as he stuck his ass back and up to allow the butt-plug to slide out from inside his rectum. The dominant Rasta placed the shiny outsize plug on the floor and beckoned to a lean, shaven-headed black guy with an incredibly ridged stomach who was wearing black-and-white silk boxer shorts and lace-up boxer's boots. Intricate patterns had been shaved into the guy's close-cropped scalp.

He reached between the bent-over Rasta's legs and

squeezed his balls, then gripped the submissive Rastaman's cock and began to move his fist on it in slow firm strokes. While he was doing this, the shaven-headed black guy pushed all four fingers and the thumb of his free hand up the Rastaman's asshole. It opened easily and, after a moment's resistance around the knuckles, the shaven-headed young black man's hand disappeared straight up into the Rasta's round ass. The lean boxer – or that was what he looked like, to Malcolm – began to move his fist back and forth easily in the Rastaman's rectum, his bicep and tricep standing out rhythmically as he did so, and sinew cording in his forearm.

The other Rasta, whose large cock jutted up from his crotch and wagged heavily as he watched his friend being fisted, bent forward to hold his bredren's buttocks open and allow deeper manual penetration. Sweat ran down the boxer's boyish features – he looked to be in his mid-twenties – as he concentrated on the hand-balling session, his own cockhead jutting up thick and hard against the front of his silk boxer shorts as he did so. Then the boxer began to slide his hand right the way out of the Rastaman's slack and capacious bunghole, which stayed gaping open when the boxer's fist was removed from it, then slid his balled fist all the way back in, punch-fucking him; the Rasta tossed his locks and played with his own nipples as the bunched fist was rammed in and out of his gaping fully dilated rectum.

Glancing over at the bar, Malcolm saw that the pretty blond barman was now on his knees, sucking off a tall, well-built African guy with smooth dark skin, and a shaven head. He had a gold chain round one ankle but was otherwise naked, and was actually talking on his mobile phone as the shapely and milk-smooth white youth kneeling before him moved his candy pink lips up and down on the African guy's cock. The shaven-headed black man cradled the phone under his chin so he could carry on talking while gripping the tousled golden hair of the young man kneeling before him, enabling him to hold the boy's head in place and fuck his face with deep regular thrusts of his hips.

In another corner a masculine-looking moustachioed black man with *café-au-lait* skin and a defined body, who wore a studded leather jockstrap, was kneeling on one of the low lacquered tables, while two fey boys in skimpy gold bikini briefs and army boots – one Asian, the other white, both with spikily gelled quiffs and ankle-chains – pushed a variety of dildoes up his upturned ass. They shoved the rigid rubber lengths up there as hard as they could, challenging the butch black bottom to refuse to take them right the way up him. As Malcolm watched this scenario, a crew-cut blond body-builder with a heavy erection bobbing in front of his shaven crotch and wearing only bike-boots, who had been cruising around the room all this time, touched the Asian boy on his bare shoulder. The boy turned and the flush-faced body-builder pushed his purple-headed cock into the pretty boy's mouth. The Asian youth immediately gripped the body-builder's heavy-hanging balls and got down to some serious cock-sucking, leaving his young blond friend to start pushing an exceptionally thick – four-inch width – black rubber dildo up the glistening open asshole of the black muscle-man kneeling ass-up before him on the table in his leather jock. The Asian youth stuffed a hand down the front of his gold lamé bikini briefs and began to move his fist vigorously on his cock as he knelt sucking greedily on the blond body-builder's pulsing dick, swallowing its head to the back of his throat.

Beside them, another muscular blond man, green-eyed with a goatee, was lying back on a zebra-skin rug, his surfer dreads spread out around his head on a silk cushion. He sprawled back as a crop-headed and dark-skinned African guy, who wore green ass-hugging combat trousers and army boots but was otherwise stripped to the waist, lay spread-

eagled between his legs and sucked his stiff cock enthusiastically. As Malcolm watched, another – totally naked –
black guy stumbled out from one of the partitioned-off
areas. He was shiny with sweat and had a toned body and
one pierced nipple, in which a small gold ring glinted. This
smooth-skinned black guy immediately straddled the blond
surfer's face then slowly sat down on it. The surfer opened
his mouth wide and extended a long tongue in anticipation
as the brown ass was lowered onto his waiting face,
smothering him. The surfer reached up and gripped the
black guy sitting on his face around the waist, pulling him
down as hard as he could onto his mouth, clearly felching
the guy's juicy asshole with a passion, while the African
man in the army trousers sprawled between the surfer's
thighs, working his mouth hard on the goateed white guy's
stiff red-purple cock.

Behind them, men of various colours and types, wearing
little or nothing except boots and sometimes shorts or
thongs, leant against the walls with hard-one, swigging on
beers and watching the scene, taking a brief break from the
action and deciding what hole to exercise or penetrate next.
Every so often, other guys would come and kneel in front
of them and start sucking them off, or exchange a few words
and one would lead the other off to one of the partitioned
areas for more hot fucking.

As Malcolm watched, one of the standing men not being
blown – a hard-bodied white skinhead with a pretty and
sullen pouting mouth, wearing red DM boots and a studded
wristband – was turned to face the wall by a lean black guy
with a large afro, light-brown skin and a very large cock,
and fucked summarily. The skinhead put up no resistance:
in fact, reached back and pulled his pale buttocks open to
make it easier for the afroed guy to get his big dick straight
up into the accommodating skin's anus in a single deep
thrust.

While the skin was being firmly butt-fucked, one of the other guys waiting about – a lean, petite Asian youth with a goatee, flawless skin, and ragga patterns cut into the sides of his jet-black hair, who wore black wet-look trunks through which a big hard-on was clearly visible – slid round behind the afroed guy. The Asian youth went down quickly onto his knees, and began rimming the black man while he fucked the skinhead's ass. The light-skinned black guy reached back behind himself, without breaking the rhythm of his buttfucking, and pulled his own large buttocks open with both hands, so that the Asian youth could rim him more deeply.

As the young Asian man tongued ass eagerly, an older black guy with a peroxide crop, who was sprawling on a cushion being blown by the slim and pretty black bartender, reached over in a leisurely way and pulled the Asian boy's trunks down at the back, exposing a shapely shaven brown butt. Then – still being sucked off vigorously by the enthusiastic bartender – the blond black man reached over to one of the low tables beside him and stuck his fingers into a bowl of glittering gel. Then he reached over and stuck two shining fingers straight up the kneeling Asian youth's asshole. The lean young man wriggled his butt so that the fingers would go further up him, and carried on rimming the hot brown asshole in front of him without a second's pause.

Malcolm took in all this feverish, orgiastic activity in a matter of seconds. The seams of his skimpy leather shorts cut painfully into his cock-head, constricting his throbbing shaft and his bulging balls, and even rubbed thrillingly against his puckered asshole. Without being aware of having moved, he realised he was at the bottom of the wrought-iron spiral staircase that went down from the balcony he had been standing on to the room below. His mouth was watering. He wanted sex and, at the same time, he was curious about the action he couldn't see, the things going on in the partitioned areas and in the garden, and, no doubt, in other rooms. And curious too about his host, Prince Fela, King Bitch. Was *he* one of these guys? Malcolm wished Camara was there to ask, but he wasn't anywhere to be seen.

Malcolm made his way among fucking and sucking, writhing and gasping couples and threesomes and four-somes and crossed to the bar. He asked the bar-boy who wasn't engaged in cock-sucking – a brown-haired and cute white youth with lightly-tanned skin and tight silver hot-pants – for a beer, then turned to look around a little more, and to decide which way his first pleasure lay. Did he want to fuck ass first, get his dick sucked, go down on a stiff, dripping cock of whichever hue, or even experiment with something a little freakier? Dildoes, maybe . . .

A very pretty black youth, who Malcolm had noticed peripherally wandering around the room because he was actually dressed – and in white tennis shorts and a V-neck T-shirt, with a stripy jumper tossed casually over his shoulders – touched Malcolm on the arm flirtily.

'Hi,' the young man said, smiling boyishly. 'I'm Winston.'

'Malcolm,' Malcolm said awkwardly, extending a hand and shaking Winston's finely manicured one with feigned masculine ease. 'So,' he carried on, groping for conversation, 'where's our host? Prince Fela?'

'The Anal Cave?' Winston said, stroking Malcolm's mus-cular upper arm through the soft material of his open leather jacket playfully. 'Entertaining in her private room upstairs. She'll be showing off her capacity any minute now, I expect.'

'The Anal Cave?' Malcolm echoed, curious. Winston nodded. 'So what gets you off, man? I mean, if it ain't personal,' Malcolm asked him. 'Just, 'cause you're the only guy here with his clothes mostly on. You a voyeur or something?'

Winston fingered the rim of the glass of champagne he was holding. 'Who doesn't like to look?' he said softly, looking down at the half-empty glass. 'But when you want to take a leak, come to me,' he carried on, looking up again with a bright smile. 'Wearing nice clothes encourages me to make sure I swallow every last drop. More golden stream than golden shower.' Seeing the ambivalent expression on Malcolm's face, Winston added, 'Or I can drop my shorts and you can fuck me up the ass and then piss inside me that way. I mean, if that would get you off more . . .' Winston shifted his posture to make his obvious hard-on more comfortable in his tight white tennis-shorts. 'I don't really like sex regular,' he added, shrugging.

Malcolm was trying to think of a suitable reply that wouldn't make him sound starchy and repressed – and fighting the niggling latent curiosity that Winston's brazenness about his enthusiasm for piss-drinking had aroused in him. *I mean, if it's what he wants, man, why not? You came here to try something different. To see it might be kind of wild, hot piss cascading down this hot black youth's open throat. But still . . .* 'There's always Wade, anyway,' Winston continued, indicating the skinhead whose tight, muscular ass was being pounded by the tall, lean light-skinned black guy with the afro to their right. 'He's the other toilet for the evening. Whatever works for you.'

'I prefer porcelain, man,' Malcolm finally managed to say, hoping that sounded sufficiently easy-going, looking at Winston's bulging crotch in his shorts, and thinking how much he would like to fuck Winston's big butt. 'No offence, yeah,' Malcolm added.

'None taken,' Winston said lightly, sipping delicately from his glass, looking out around the room speculatively. 'Oh, here's Leo.'

At that moment the muscular older black guy with the peroxide crop ambled up to the two of them, stroking his semi-erect cock idly. He ran his free hand down the side of Winston's smooth, flawless cheek. 'Man, I need to take a piss,' he said in a deep, sexy voice to the pretty young guy, whose full lips were parted and shiny with anticipation. 'Are you thirsty, man?' For a moment, Malcolm imagined himself on his knees, drinking the handsome dark-skinned older man's hot piss, and it seemed suddenly unspeakably exciting to him. His cock unexpectedly became even harder in his tight black leather shorts, his piss-slit pulled wide open.

'Later, guy,' Winston said to Malcolm as he took the blond black man's arm and was led away towards a doorway Malcolm hadn't noticed beneath the balcony. 'I've got some serious drinking to do.'

Malcolm almost asked if he could watch, but decided against it. *Well*, he had to admit, *this party's every bit as freaky as Bobbi said it would be. And it ain't really got going yet, you know what I'm saying?* He shifted to adjust what was beginning to feel like a permanently stiff cock inside his butt- and crotch-hugging leather shorts, on the one hand feeling uncomfortably constrained by them, on the other finding that sexy, and that the black leather of the shorts – and the jacket – made him look provocative and a little freaky himself.

He took a swig of his beer and looked up at the balcony, where he had noticed some new arrivals standing while he had been talking to Winston. To his annoyance and pain, he recognised Kam standing there between two well-built crop-haired guys in camouflage-trousers and army boots, one black, one white: Joe and Bertil, though of course Malcolm didn't know who they were. Kam himself was wearing nothing but a glittering gold pouch that contrasted with the soft cinnamon smoothness of his skin, and gold patent monkey-boots. Malcolm could see his small stiff dick jutting erect, stretching the shiny gold material tight. Kam had his head tilted back and the two men fondled his ass uninhibitedly as they looked out over the room.

Malcolm turned to the boyish barman with the tousled brown hair and the smooth body, who was wearing only ball-crushingly tight silver hot-pants. 'Suck my cock, man,' he ordered the barman urgently, not knowing if he would be obeyed. The young white man immediately put down the cocktail he was shaking and squeezed around the end of the bar, and sank to his knees in front of Malcolm. *Fuck Kam*, Malcolm thought, staring up at the Japanese boy. *When he looks down here, he's going to see a pretty boy's mouth on the big stiff cock he used to love me ramming up his ass, seven nights a week.*

Malcolm let the black leather jacket slip off his shoulders and reveal his powerful chest with its erect nipples, his pumped upper arms, and the all-over smoothness of his creamy brown torso. The barman slid down the zip of Malcolm's shorts, tugging it awkwardly over the rigid oblique bulge of Malcolm's long thick erection. Then the tousle-haired white youth pulled the front of Malcolm's shorts open, as if he was peeling a banana, folding back the soft black leather and allowing Malcolm's large and throbbing hard-on to spring out and bob heavily in front of his boyish face, which was now flushed with excitement and anticipation.

Malcolm gasped excitedly as his painfully-stiff cock finally sprang free, and looked away from Kam and down on the pretty young man kneeling subserviency before him. The youth had smooth peaches-and-cream skin and a small but well-formed butt, hugged with indecently-revealing closeness by the skin-tight silver hot-pants, and he thrust it out invitingly behind him in a 'fuck-me' way as he wriggled Malcolm's shorts down to the bulky tops of his bike-boots. Malcolm bent forward and slapped the kneeling young white man on the butt, then gripped him between the buttocks, pressing four fingers firmly against the boy's sphincter through the tight silver fabric. The young man wiggled his ass appreciatively and gasped softly.

'You like that, yeah?' Malcolm said throatily, probing assertively through the fabric with strong fingers.

'Yes, I like it a lot,' the boy said, his accent strongly Parisienne. A dance student, Pierre had come to London a couple of years ago to study and gain 'experience in living'. He had finished his studies and was now concentrating on gaining all the life-experience he could. He had learnt most, and most enjoyably, from serving at Prince Fela's parties. He also enjoyed the bonuses he received from Fela for the enthusiastic 'say yes to anything' attitude that Fela valued in all his staff. As a rule, Prince Fela only employed bar staff who would have done it all for free anyway, but he found Pierre particularly and gratifyingly open to possibilities and made sure he always got work when any was going. Though it had to be conceded that Pierre was not as open as his best friend Marlon, whom Pierre had got an audition to be one of Fela's bar-boys, too. Marlon, the petite black eighteen-year-old in the white jock, currently giving the blond-dreadlocked black DJ a blow-job behind the mixing-desk, turned out to have such an appetite for fists being shoved up between his buttocks that he actually couldn't shoot his load without a hand being rammed back and forth inside his rectum.

At the end of the evening, if he hadn't received thorough anal satisfaction from the horny guests, Marlon would often go-go dance on the bar, naked except for tractor-boots, yelling desperately, 'Fist me! Fist-fuck me! I'll take on all comers!' And he would, too. But that was all Marlon really enjoyed, being thoroughly hand-balled, so he was a less valued member of Fela's entourage than the exceedingly flexible Pierre.

Pierre only liked to take a hand occasionally, so he would always direct any guys who wanted to fist-fuck to Marlon first. Marlon would lie back on the bar with his ass exposed and his long shapely legs flung up in the air at the slightest suggestion of the firm manual action he needed to obtain release.

'I used to feel like a pervert, until I come to Fela's, man,' Marlon confided in Pierre at the end of one long rough evening, a few months earlier. 'Now I know I'm just a specialist who gives a special service. 'Cause I got capacity, and I like to make the most of it.' Certainly, Marlon was in regular demand at every party, and took the pressure off the other bar-boys, who were generally less slack and internally roomy.

Marlon regarded being fisted as the real thing; everything else, like cock-sucking, was just work to him – though he did always make sure he always brought professional lips, tongue and throat to the job, and always strove to give satisfaction.

By contrast Pierre loved cock-sucking as much as fucking or being fucked. He gazed at the light-brown curve of Malcolm's rigid cock. It was so thick, he knew it would fill his mouth completely. He gripped Malcolm's shaft and slid back the foreskin. Above the kneeling Pierre, Malcolm groaned throatily. Pierre kissed Malcolm's cock-head and lightly tongued his glistening slit, tasting a drop of his pre-come, then started to swallow Malcolm's glans. It tasted sweet and a little salty. Pierre opened his soft pink lips wide and stretched them around Malcolm's large cock-head, then slowly began to move his mouth down on Malcolm's throbbing erection, swallowing it to the back of his throat.

Malcolm sighed in pleasure as the pretty French boy kneeling before him began to move his hot wet mouth on Malcolm's hard-on; at first slowly, as if its thickness was stretching his cheeks and then his throat, and the boy had to relax his oral cavity to accommodate such a big cock, and then faster. With each bob of his head, the kneeling Pierre swallowed more of Malcolm's thick brown cock, and his lips got nearer and nearer to the clipped pubic hair at the base of Malcolm's long prick-shaft.

'Fondle my balls,' Malcolm ordered, and the French boy reached up and massaged Malcolm's ball-sack firmly while continuing to pump his mouth on Malcolm's hot cock. Then Pierre let Malcolm's now-glistening erection spring out of his mouth for a moment. The air on his slick whanger felt cool to Malcolm, and he was about to order Pierre to carry on sucking his aching prick, when the eager French boy began to nibble his way up and down the length of its sinewy underside, sending shivers of pleasure up through Malcolm's body as he moved up to tease Malcolm's frenum. Then the white youth's mouth was hot and wet on Malcolm's pulsing hard-on again, sucking enthusiastically, moving quickly.

And all I have to do is just stand here and let myself be sucked off, Malcolm thought to himself, as he looked down on Pierre's sweat-tangled brown hair moving backwards and forwards in front of his crotch. And suddenly he realised that he didn't care about Kam any more: not really. Maybe he'd even fuck Kam again this evening, for old times' sake. Maybe he'd fuck him at one end while another guy filled Kam from the other, just like Don had suggested, and maybe he'd get off on it . . .

Don. Malcolm was still angry with Don. But that didn't seem to matter much, now that Malcolm's hot and throbbing hard-on was being so enthusiastically sucked by the eager cock-sucking French boy with the attentive mouth and hands.

Malcolm then felt cool fingers caress his solid buttocks gently, and soft lips kissing his large cheeks from behind. As he glanced back to see who was now kneeling behind him, Malcolm noticed that the blond-dreadlocked DJ was adjusting his cock inside his skimpy silver shorts, having clearly just shot a load, and so Malcolm wasn't surprised to find that it was the other bar-boy who was now kissing his ass with large, soft, warm lips.

'Rim me, man,' Malcolm instructed Marlon. Marlon immediately held Malcolm's ass-cheeks open and began to lick between them. Then he began to tongue Malcolm's trembling asshole, teasing it, relaxing it with gentle attention. Fresh shivers of pleasure coursed up his well-shaped torso and made Malcolm's heart pound at the sensation of a hot eager mouth moving on his cock, and at having soft full lips pressed firmly against his spit-wetted asshole at the same time. The excitement made Malcolm's butthole dilate and open, allowing Marlon's tongue to penetrate him, and Malcolm felt himself enjoying the pretty black boy's attentive tongue. He reached back and pushed a hand through the young man's short hair, gripped it, and held Marlon's face firmly against his ass. With his other hand, Malcolm reached forward and gripped Pierre's tousled hair, pulling the French boy's head all the way down onto his cock.

As Malcolm was being doubly pleasured, fore and aft, the blond dreadlocked DJ turned off the music, leant into his microphone and announced, 'Gentlemen, cock-suckers, ass-fuckers, butt-munchers, bottoms, tops, versatiles, come-eaters and dick-beaters, voyeurs, exhibitionists and down-and-dirty freaks, your host, Prince Fela . . .'

Malcolm looked round to see if this announcement would bring a halt to the sucking and fucking around him. The reaction was mixed: all those not actively involved looked over at the waiting stage. Some of the cock-sucking stopped, but most of the fucking continued. Malcolm was relieved that the two horny bar-boys, Pierre and Marlon, continued attending to his wet and shiny cock and asshole, moving their heads backwards and forwards in a regular rhythm that seemed intended to give him the most pleasure for the longest possible time. He realised that his situation was ideal. He was being very professionally sucked off and very professionally rimmed, and he had a clear view of the freaky show his enigmatic host looked like he was going to put on. What more could Malcolm ask for?

But love, Malcolm realised. Right now, however, he was too turned on, too curious, to care. A light played on the low rug-strewn stage.

And finally Prince Fela, King Bitch, the Anal Cave, stepped up onto the stage. He was a tall African man in his mid-thirties, with very dark smooth skin and a heavily worked-out body. He had large smooth slabs of pectoral muscles and protuberant upright nipples, a ridged stomach, an extremely tiny waist and a large, very muscular ass, a masculine outline so extreme it acquired a feminine aspect in its wasp-waistedness and big-chestedness. One nipple was pierced, and had a large gold hoop in it. Fela's handsome head was shaven and his clean-shaven face had large features, most especially large and well-defined lips. There were tribal scars slashed across his high cheek-bones; he wore gold hoops in his ears and a gold sarong wrapped around his waist. He wore gold eye-shadow, and hints of gold on his lips. His legs were long and strong and shapely. He had an alienating and compelling quality that drew all eyes to him, that fascinated all onlookers, that stiffened even the most well-used dicks. Even the fucking ceased.

Without a word, Prince Fela moved a hand across his waist theatrically, and began to unwind his sarong, flicking the shimmering golden fabric around his waist to the ground in falling curves. With a sharp snap of his wrist, he flung the material aside and stood before the crowd with arms outstretched; his dark flawless body was entirely shaved and smooth, naked except for the gold in his ears and nipple, and the thick and shining gold cock-ring that gleamed around the base of his semi-erect cock and bulging ball-sack. Fela turned this way and that on the small stage, his arms raised, clearly soaking up the attention of his guests – exhibitionistically turned on by it too, judging from the gradual hardening of his shaven cock.

Fela turned so his back was to the audience, and the watching, horny men gazed at the beauty of its sinuous 'V' and the concave curves of Fela's big buttocks, the length of his athletic legs. Then Malcolm, mesmerised by Fela's start-ling physique, and feeling strangely confused as his impression of it was blurred by the movement of Pierre's mouth on his cock, and the feeling of Marlon's tongue exploring his asshole, noticed that a golden cord was hanging down between Fela's buttocks, ending in a neat fingerwidth loop. Malcolm looked on, puzzled, as the bar-boys continued blowing and rimming him.

Camara joined Fela on the stage. He, too, was wearing a cock-ring, stainless steel this time, but he came on stage fully erect, his large dick wagging heavily above his heavy balls. A link chain hung from the metal ring and looped down between Camara's thighs, parting his balls. As the willowy African turned, Malcolm saw that the chain looped up between Camara's shapely high buttocks was attached to the handle of the stainless-steel butt-plug that Camara had inserted before going on stage.

Camara bent forward slightly and began to rub Fela's big buttocks firmly, massaging them. Then he gave one of them a light slap. Then the other. Then Camara cracked the palm of his hand against Fela's ass-cheeks, hard. A shiver ran up Fela's body as Camara spanked him, and he wiggled his ass theatrically. Camara slapped it again. Fela shivered again, and gasped softly. Camara reached round in front of Fela and took hold of his now totally erect cock, and began to move one hand on it, at the same time whacking Fela hard on the ass with the flat of his other hand. Fela moaned as

Camara spanked him repeatedly. Even through the darkness of his skin, Fela's smooth ass-cheeks began to redden. Then Camara went back to massaging Fela's buttocks firmly with both hands, leaving the Prince's stiff cock to bob unattended. Finally, Camara's hand slid down to the gold cord hanging down out of Fela's bottom. Camara slid his forefinger through the loop at the end of the cord and began to pull on it.

The shining cord tightened and Fela groaned audibly as Camara started to flex his sinewy arm to draw its glittering length out of Fela's asshole. Fela bent over and braced himself, gripping the sides of the royal ceremonial stool in the centre of the stage, sticking his ass out towards the audience; his butt was magnificent on top of long, beautiful legs, his shaven hole tightly puckered, the cord glinting gold against brown.

The Prince grunted as something inside his rectum began to work its way out towards the watching, turned-on crowd. His asshole bulged outwards and began to open, revealing something red and smooth and shiny and round inside his ass. Fela's anal ring dilated wider and wider, getting thinner, smoother, shinier and more flawless as it spread and opened. Malcolm watched, mesmerised – obviously Fela had some sort of ball on a cord up his ass, but how big was it? As big as a cricket ball? No, it would have popped out by now: it was bigger than that. The good feeling of Pierre's mouth on his stiff and dripping dick, and of Marlon's tongue inside his own asshole, made Malcolm wish he was up on stage in Camara's place, pulling on Fela's golden string, opening the African prince up in front of everyone.

'Ah! Oh! Yes!' Fela gasped as the smooth red ball popped abruptly out of his asshole with a slurping, disgorging suddenness. It was a little bigger than a cricket-ball: about the size of a large, perfectly spherical grapefruit. To Malcolm's surprise, the ball didn't drop to the ground with a thump, but hung between Fela's muscular thighs, suspended in the air by the golden cord from above and below: below, being pulled on by Camara; above, stretching tightly out of Fela's puckering, juicy asshole. Malcolm realised this meant that there was another sphere up Fela's ass. He watched as Camara tightened his grip on the golden cord and began to pull it again.

Grunting more loudly this time, Fela thrust his ass back and up again. His shaven hole opened much more easily this time, and a second grapefruit-sized red sphere slid out of it and hung down weightily on the golden cord. All around him, Malcolm realised, guys were starting to jerk off at the spectacle of Fela's public ass-opening, his freaky, beautiful exhibitionism. Camara began to draw the string out of Fela's butthole a third time, his arm tensing as he pulled on it. Fela's slack anal opening spread and opened; a third large red sphere bulged, then popped out of his princely backside. Now three big balls hung on the string hanging down from Fela's asshole. And Camara kept on pulling on the golden cord . . .

A mesmerised crowd watched as, one after the other, six large red spheres were drawn out of Prince Fela's gaping back passage. Put end to end, they would have made a compact, unyielding solid six-inch diameter, two-foot length in total. Malcolm realised that the spheres must have filled Fela's rectum, been forced up into his bowels, and the rigid twenty-four inches must have pushed up against his diaphragm and pressed it up against his stomach – and the golden string was still hanging out of the gleaming African prince's asshole! Every muscle in Fela's body was tense except the ones inside his bowels. There was now total silence, except for the dry rustling sound of hands moving backwards and forwards on cocks, the slap of swinging balls, and the soft slurp of Pierre and Marlon's mouths on Malcolm's asshole and hard-on as they knelt before and behind the mesmerised man.

Finally, and with a loud, sucking slurp, the seventh sphere emerged; all seven connected red balls fell to the floor of the stage, with a heavy thump. Fela turned to face the crowd. His long dark cock was stiff and shiny with pre-come. He raised his well-proportioned muscular arms for applause, and he got it. Fela's gold-lidded eyes were wild and a little crazy. *Now I know why Winston called him the Anal Cave*, Malcolm thought to himself. *To fuck Prince Fela's hole, man. That would be something freaky, something new, to experience such utter slackness . . .*

Camara stepped forward as Fela sat on the ornately-carved stool, his thighs spread open, his dick jutting out from his shaven crotch and the gold cock-ring shining around its base; his expression was pouty, horny and defiant. Camara raised an elegant hand.

'His Highness instructs me to say that he will personally indulge the pleasure of any guest. Any pleasure whatsoever.' Camara glanced back at Fela, who nodded seriously. 'Fearing your inhibition, His Highness will demonstrate his sincerity,' Camara continued. He then gestured to a figure standing at the back of the room – a figure Malcolm hadn't noticed before because he was shadowed under the balcony.

A tall lean black man with gold studs in his ears and cropped silver hair came forward, his massive twelve-inch cock wagging stiffly above his pendulous ball-sack as he moved. It was Oba, the taxi-driver who had fucked Kam in the back of his cab earlier that day, while being fucked himself by the soldier Joe, avoiding family commitments once again by coming to perform at Prince Fela's wild and freaky sex-party.

'I have to work night-shift tonight,' Oba had told his long-suffering wife, before heading off for a night of orgiastic man-on-man fucking and sucking. Oba had always enjoyed anal sex – both ways – and had known a woman could never really satisfy him, both because he enjoyed being fucked anally himself, and because vaginal sex left Oba cold. Only ass-fucking could get his twelve-inch shaft really hard, and even when he did occasionally get it up adequately for her, his wife complained that his cock was just too big for comfort, while at the same time refusing to gratify him anally. He had married to please his family, and for no other reason. By contrast, the horny battyboys who longed to have Oba's twelve-inch whanger up their eagerly-offered buttholes *never* said it was too big for them or, if they did, what they always really meant was, 'ram it all the way up me anyway, fuck me harder.'

Oba stepped up onto the stage. Prince Fela stood, his own dick wagging. Oba put his hands on the Prince's wasp-waist and turned him so he was sideways on to the spectators. Then, as the whole room watched, wanking slowly, Oba guided his large cock-head towards Fela's anal opening, found it, and began to push it in. Fela moaned and then gasped as, with a grunt, Oba slid the entire foot of his dick up Fela's gaping backside.

As Oba began to pump his shaft in and out of Fela's asshole, Camara slid to his knees in front of Fela and took Fela's uncut cock-head into his mouth and began to slide his big lips up and down its substantial length, jerking himself off as he swallowed Fela's cock to the back of his throat. Fela was now shining with sweat and moaning loudly as he was fucked up the ass and blown at the same time. The body-built African prince began to toy with his own nipples to add to his pleasure, rolling his tilted-back head in ecstasy as he was vigorously anally penetrated by Oba's massive manhood and simultaneously orally pleasured by Camara's eager mouth and full, firm lips on his hot, stiff erection.

As he watched Fela being sucked and butt-fucked, at the same time enjoying being sucked off by Pierre himself, Malcolm became aware that Marlon had removed his tongue from Malcolm's now slippery butthole. Malcolm was about to turn round and ask him why he had stopped rimming, when he became aware of Marlon sliding something small and smooth into his sphincter. Before Malcolm could say anything, he felt the cool trickle of warm fluid being pumped into his rectum.

'What's going on, man?' Malcolm said, slightly alarmed and looking round; his concern mostly dissipated by the good feeling of Pierre's firm lips on his stiff cock. Marlon was kneeling behind him, grinning boyishly and squeezing on a large rubber bulb, which was attached to a blunt-ended tube that he had pushed into Malcolm's asshole.

'Red wine, sir,' Marlon said, looking up and smiling. 'The alcohol soaks through the lining of the rectum and makes you feel good, real quick. It makes you loosen up and throw away your inhibitions.' Marlon squeezed the ball flat firmly, then slipped the tube out of Malcolm's asshole. Then the pretty black boy bent forward and pushed his face between Malcolm's big buttocks and kissed Malcolm's tight, muscular star.

Intoxication spread up through Malcolm's smooth, bulky, pumped-up body quickly, and he felt dizzy and exultant as Pierre carried on blowing him. His ass full of red wine and Pierre's mouth full of his throbbing cock: really what more could he ask for? He began to feel so good, so fast, that he found himself regretting his fight with Don that morning. Don *had* been right about Kam, and Malcolm had wanted not to believe it, which had made him be especially hard on Don. OK, so they'd fucked, Don and Kam, but then here Kam was, only fourteen hours later, and he hadn't wasted any time finding more studs to give it to him in the mouth and up the ass. Hardly a long period of melancholy reflection, Malcolm reckoned. And he realised that he really didn't care about Kam any more. If only Don was here, they could make up and the band could make its gig tomorrow; it wouldn't be a problem.

'Suck me, man,' Malcolm groaned. 'Swallow that love-muscle all the way down, yeah.' Pierre opened his throat obligingly, going all the way down on Malcolm's aching hard-on to the root.

On stage Oba was ramming a grunting Prince Fela hard and roughly up the asshole, and Camara was pumping his mouth on the Nigerian's shiny cock as Fela took the foot of cock willingly up the ass while being enthusiastically blown. At a signal from the butt-fucked prince, the DJ put on another record, a fast Jungle track with a coarse, lewd ragga vocal by a Jamaican artist, Stixie, beginning the music again. The voyeuristic crowd began to turn away from the stage on which the Prince was being so thoroughly pleasured and returned to their own sucking and fucking, inspired by his exhibitionistic performance.

While he was being sucked by Pierre, his own cock now heavy and throbbing, Malcolm turned to the bar to ask the other bartender for another beer. The pretty black boy nodded, reached into the fridge for a can of Bud, popped it, and handed it to Malcolm.

'You know this track they're playing now, man?' the bar-boy asked, leaning forward confidentially as Malcolm took a swig from the can. Malcolm nodded. He had wondered slightly why this track, a big hit earlier in the year, was being played at Fela's party, as Stixie was reputedly a notorious womaniser back in Jamaica. 'You see that parti-tioned-off bit over there?' Marlon said, pointing to a corner of the large room that Malcolm hadn't had the chance to peer into yet.

'Yeah, I see it,' Malcolm replied, gasping as the kneeling Pierre started to massage his balls with great firmness while sucking hard on Malcolm's cock-head.

'The guy singing on this track's in there,' Marlon said. 'Taking two big, stiff dicks up the ass at the same time, and sucking off a third guy while he sits right the way down on the other two.'

'Shit, man,' Malcolm said. 'You're kidding me, right?'

Marlon smiled. 'See for yourself, man. He likes spectators. You can probably plug him yourself, if you want to go star-fucking. Just come on real dominant: he likes to pretend he's being forced. His Highness always trying to persuade him to do a stage-show in front of everyone but he says he won't, on account of he don't want to look too willing about it.'

In a bit, Malcolm decided, intrigued at seeing a macho male ragga star being willingly multi-fucked, but not wanting Pierre to stop blowing him. The tousle-haired French boy really knew how to use his lips, his tongue and his teeth to tease Malcolm's throbbing cock. It now seemed to buzz heavily in Pierre's hot wet mouth, and the firm massaging Malcolm's balls were receiving from Pierre's dextrous hands was sending waves of pleasure rolling up his body and through his chest. His heart was pounding against his rib-cage and his mouth was dry. He knew he was going to come really soon in the young Frenchman's mouth.

Suddenly, Malcolm felt a hand fondle his muscular ass. Looking round he saw the white guy in combat trousers with close-cropped hair, who had been feeling Kam up on the balcony, earlier. Malcolm looked at him dazedly; the mouth on his cock and the red wine up his ass made any focused thoughts of anger or confrontation difficult.

'I just wanted to say we're sorry,' the soldier – Joe – said, caressing Malcolm's shapely butt with practised confidence.'Me and Bertil.' Malcolm realised the crop-headed black guy who had also been feeling up Kam was standing just behind Joe.

'And we just both wanted to say –' the combat-fatigued black guy chimed in. 'Well, just, we'll do anything to make it up to you, man. And so will Kam.'

On stage, Oba was ramming Fela hard, his fingers biting into Fela's hips; Fela was gasping in a high voice with each hard thrust, jerking his hips against the kneeling Camara's face in small spasms and biting into his own protuberant nipples with his fingernails, to turn himself on as much as possible, while being roughly serviced anally. Suddenly, Oba was groaning heavily and holding Fela's hips in place while he shoved his cock right the way up Fela's asshole; he held it there as he shot his load deep into Fela's anal canal.

'I gotta go,' Bertil said at the sight of this, and stepped quickly over towards the stage. 'Catch you later, yeah. And I do mean I'm up for anything, yeah,' he said over his shoulder as he hurried away.

'I've never seen a guy turn so hot for felching,' Joe said to Malcolm, continuing to caress Malcolm's smooth butt as he and Malcolm looked back over at the stage to watch Oba withdraw his shiny manhood from Fela's slack bunghole and stand back. Then, to the delight of the many still-wanking onlookers, Oba gripped his thick cock in both hands, bent over his own crotch, squeezed the last pearly-white drops of spunk out onto the smooth brown head of his still semi-rigid member, and licked the thick drops of jism off the head of his own cock with his tongue. Then, straining to bend his lean torso even further forward, Oba bobbed his head down another few inches and took the head and the first two inches of his own cock into his mouth, sucking it clean.

Meanwhile, Bertil beat any other potential asshole-eaters to the stage and got on his knees behind Fela and began to lick between his muscular buttocks while Camara carried on sucking the Prince's juicy cock. Bertil pressed his lips firmly against Fela's now permanently open hole and began to work his tongue up into Fela's slack back passage, licking Oba's heavy load out of the Prince's hot, wet, extremely well-fucked and thoroughly dilated rectum. Bertil pushed his combat trousers down to his knees and began to beat off his own decent-sized cock rapidly as he ate out Fela's spunk-filled asshole.

'I guess Bertil's going to be busy for a while, man,' Joe said, reaching for one of Malcolm's erect nipples and toying with it. 'But anything I can do, just say.'

Malcolm groaned at the additional pleasure that having his tit toyed with gave him. He was beginning to have trouble controlling his anal sphincter, and he could feel a trickle of wine escape it and run gleaming down the insides of his thighs. 'Find a guy called Winston for me,' Malcolm asked Joe hoarsely. 'Tell him I've got something for him right now, if he likes. But it's got to be right now, tell him. Uh,' he grunted, clenching his shiny sphincter as hard as he could.

'Sure, guy,' Joe said, continuing to nip Malcolm's stiff nipple dextrously with his short nails, making Malcolm arch his pumped chest excitedly. 'Anything else?'

'Yeah,' Malcolm gasped. 'Get Kam fucked by as many stiff dicks as you can, man. And if he still ain't satisfied, tell him I'll fuck him last of all. Oh –' Malcolm gasped again as Pierre slid his tongue-tip a surprising way up Malcolm's oozing slit, while keeping Malcolm's throbbing cock-head in his mouth, making Malcolm groan. 'But find Winston for me right now, man. Tell him I've got a surprise for him, yeah.'

The soldier nodded, letting go of Malcolm's nipple, which made Malcolm sigh in relief and disappointment and relax his chest. Joe turned and headed off into the crowd. Malcolm looked down at the sexy young white lad kneeling before him. 'Suck that dick, man,' Malcolm said throatily. 'Tease that piss-slit then get that cock-head right down your throat, like the greedy little cock-sucker you are. Oh, yeah, use that tongue, man. Use those lips, oh yeah –'

Bobbi and Don had arrived on the balcony just as Oba was starting to pump his dick up Fela's asshole really hard and fast. As Camara was also on stage, giving the Prince a thorough blow-job, they had been let in by Artie, a tall blond body-builder with a razor-sharp flat-top who wore a black patent-rubber leotard and heavy boots. Bobbi had checked his top with the beefy blond, but kept on his trashy short-shorts and boots. Don had checked his T-shirt and black jeans, and was now wearing only Cat boots and soft black trunks, which his hard-on was stretching and wetting at the front as he looked out over the roomful of horny men of every colour and type, all of them self-proclaimedly up for anything.

Bobbi's stiff dick was sticking out at an angle from one of the legs of his tight denim shorts, his heavy ball-sack hanging conspicuously out of the other. Bobbi had actually left the club like that, cock and balls out for everyone in the club and then the street to see, and had wandered up the road waving for a cab. Two had whizzed straight by in the usual way, but then a third had pulled abruptly with such a sharp screech of tyres on asphalt that the driver was obviously more than eager to give a ride to such a trampy piece of trade. Don had fondled Bobbi's cock and balls conspicuously in the back of the cab, putting on a free show for the handsome and broken-nosed white cab-driver in his mid-twenties. Bobbi had got into the sluttish performance, moaning loudly in pleasure and throwing his head back as Don tossed him off casually.

When they had arrived at Fela's, and Don had asked how much the fare was, as Don had hoped and intended, the cabbie had smiled and squeezed his own stiffly-bulging crotch in his tight faded jeans, and said, 'I should be paying you, mate. That was some show you guys were putting on for me. Either of you ever need your cocks sucked or a butthole to come in, I'm your man.'

'Thanks, man,' Don had said. 'I'll keep your greedy mouth and slack bitch-hole in mind, yeah.' The cabbie had grinned, handed Don a fistful of blank receipts, pulled up his window, and driven away.

At first, Don and Bobbi had been too engrossed in the stage show to look around the room with any care; they had watched Prince Fela being butt-fucked and sucked off at the same time, then been drawn into Bertil's enthusiastic ass-eating. Bertil's trousers were round his knees and his tongue up Fela's asshole; the way he was passionately eating Oba's hot fresh come out of Fela's slack butt, as he beat himself off, kept their eyes glued to the stage. Bobbi licked his lips hungrily, envying Bertil for getting a tongueful of that good thick jism – and in front of a crowd. But with a roomful of open-minded, big-dicked men, Bobbi didn't have too many worries about getting his share of creamy man-load.

Bobbi was mesmerised by the felching, but Don's eyes started to wander when the butt-fucking was over. Soon he saw Malcolm standing at the bar having his cock sucked by a pretty white boy with tousled brown hair; the young man knelt before Malcolm, wearing only a black jock and tractor-boots and a silver bow-tie around his neck, moving his mouth on Malcolm's hard-on. Don was about to be angry with Bobbi, because he realised that he had been set up; that Bobbi must have known Malcolm was going to be here, in fact had probably persuaded Malcolm to come. But then he was struck by the extreme beauty of Malcolm's body: his broad shoulders, his narrow waist, his muscular ass, the smooth curve of his thighs, the sculpturesque aspect of his profile, his flawless light-brown skin, his immaculately-braided hair, the size of his cock as the young white lad slid his mouth eagerly back and forth on its rigid length . . .

As Don watched Malcolm being sucked off, a young and pretty-looking black guy in his early twenties came up and touched Malcolm on one shoulder. He was wearing tight white tennis shorts and a V-necked white T-shirt. Don watched, intrigued, as the two men exchanged a few words.

The pretty young black man was Winston and, as Malcolm had hoped, he had turned out to be more than happy to drink warm red wine as it flowed from Malcolm's tightly clenched asshole, and slid to his knees round behind Malcolm eager for the flow to begin. While making sure Pierre kept his mouth moving up and down on his cock, Malcolm squatted down slightly on Winston's upturned face.

'Just make sure I've got time to get my lips pressed tight over your sphincter, man,' Winston said from where he knelt before Malcolm's ass. 'Then let it come gushing out.' Winston licked his tongue up between Malcolm's buttocks. 'Mmm,' he said. 'That juice tastes *good*, man. Sit on my face and let go.'

Malcolm squatted down lower, holding his buttocks open so that Winston could get his eager mouth into place.

'You ready, man?' Malcolm asked. Winston nodded behind him. For a long moment, Malcolm couldn't release his sphincter; the good wet feeling of Pierre's mouth on the top-man's throbbing dick made him clench instinctively. But then, toying with his own nipples to relax himself, Malcolm felt his straining asshole open, and his whole body warmed and shuddered with ecstasy and relief as the red wine flushed out of his rectum and down Winston's waiting throat.

'Oh, Jesus, oh, God,' Malcolm groaned, as he emptied out into Winston's mouth, feeling unbelievably turned-on and freaky and outrageous. The excitement of opening up like that, combined with the rapid movement of Pierre's tight mouth on his swollen cock, started to shove Malcolm towards a delirious climax. His dick grew uncontrollably heavier and heavier, and his balls started to tingle and clench. Spasms ran along the length of his thick shaft and, with a loud cry, and struggling to keep his flexing ass firmly on Winston's upturned face, Malcolm shot his creamy load straight into the kneeling Pierre's open mouth; jism jerked in pearly globs from the gleaming brown head of Malcolm's bucking erection and landed in pumping squirts on Pierre's extended tongue.

Malcolm arched on his calves, his whole body knotting with sinews, then sank down onto the flats of his feet again as the last few drops pumped out of his dick. He felt suddenly, exhiliratingly evacuated. His cock was empty, his balls were empty, and his rectum was empty. He bent forward and helped Pierre to his feet. The pretty French lad's lips were swollen with excitement and bruising and Malcolm found himself thinking, *Give me ten minutes to recharge and I'm going to fuck you up the ass too, boy, and every bit as hard and long.* Sex without fucking was never the complete act for Malcolm. Behind Malcolm, a well-filled Winston staggered to his feet.

'Thanks for the drink, man,' Winston belched, wiping a hand over his shiny lips. 'It's like it's me who needs to take a leak now. I'm gonna find Wade . . .'

As Winston turned away, Malcolm felt a hand touch his shoulder softly. Malcolm looked round and saw Bobbi smiling at him boyishly, looking spectacularly horny and fuckable, with his heavily erect cock and large balls hanging out of his trashy denim short-shorts.

'Oh, hi, man,' Malcolm said hoarsely, still out of breath from his violent orgasm. He guessed Bobbi must have been watching him, and was surprised to find that he really didn't care.

Bobbi pecked him on the cheek, then turned to Pierre and, without a moment's hesitation, kissed the pouting French cock-sucker full on the mouth. Pierre gasped as Bobbi probed the white youth's mouth with his tongue, licking out any spunk that Pierre hadn't yet swallowed down. Malcolm fondled Bobbi's (barely) denim-clad ass as Bobbi sucked face with Pierre, once again marvelling at Bobbi's total lack of inhibition when it came to getting what he wanted sexually. Bobbi ground his crotch against the front of Pierre's jock as he tongued the French boy's mouth, his thick cock sticking up between Pierre's thighs, and gripped Pierre's buttocks tightly, holding them open and casually probing Pierre's accommodating sphincter through the tight silver fabric of his hotpants with an inquisitive index finger. Then Bobbi took his spunk-smeared lips off Pierre's and turned to Malcolm.

'I'm going to get fucked by as many guys as I can, tonight,' Bobbi said. 'I'll catch up with you, after I've got myself rammed a couple of times.'

'Sure, man,' Malcolm said easily, reaching for his beer. 'I'm gonna circulate and get me some ass to fuck, yeah. Then maybe I'll watch you getting yours.'

'Sure,' Bobbi said, letting go of Pierre's ass-cheeks, then fingering his bunghole again, harder, with a probing digit. 'This horny bottom needs to be fucked real badly,' he added, indicating Pierre. 'Don't you, man? You'd like a stiff brown cock rammed up there, wouldn't you?'

'One or – more than one,' Pierre agreed breathlessly.

Meanwhile, the music pounded and the sex got hotter and wilder. Don slipped behind Malcolm, not wanting a confrontation until he was ready for it, and disappeared into one of the partitioned-off parts of the room. As it happened, he found himself in the one where a line of thick-cocked guys were linked up, stroking their hard-ons casually, all waiting to fuck the ragga star up the ass. The handsome and rough-looking star, who had short aerial dreads, had been bent forwards over a pommel-horse, and then his wrists and ankles had been tied to metal loops on the feet of the horse. His muscular butt was up and in position and as each man, one after the other, plugged the ragga star's well-used asshole with a thick hard prick, he growled, 'Oh, yeah, *fuck* my battyhole, man! Fuck it! Plug me like a bitch!' Turned on by the singer's dedication to anal ecstasy – there was no way he could touch his own long, stiff and dripping cock; all his pleasure was being taken anally – Don joined the line of determined butt-fuckers.

When Don got to the head of the line – Stixie having taken six stiff dicks up his juicy battyhole while Don was waiting – he wanted to give the randy Jamaican something more. Reaching between the brown-skinned guy's spread thighs, Don gripped his cock and roughly twisted it round and back between his legs. The ragga star moaned and inhaled sharply at the rough attention suddenly being paid to his pulsing tool.

'What you doing, man?' he called out hoarsely, trying to look round at Don from where he was tied, face-down, over the pommel-horse.

'I'm gonna stick your own cock up your ass and stick mine in alongside it,' Don informed him brutally. 'Then I'm gonna fuck you and you're going to be fucking yourself at the same time, man. Maybe you're even going to shoot your load up your own asshole. That get you off, man?'

'Shit, bredren,' the star said breathlessly, 'Me couldn't stop you now, could I? Me strapped down, man. Me can't stop you a go do anything you want to. If you a want force my own dick up me battyhole then me must take it and like it.'

'Yeah, man,' Don said, getting the measure of how the ragga star wanted to be treated. 'And if I just wanna fuck you up the ass so rough and hard your bunghole bursts, you just have to take it like a bitch, yeah.'

'Yeah,' Stixie said. 'So what you waiting for, man? Make me your bitch! Oh, Jesus –' he gasped sharply as Don brutally twisted his stiffly curving cock back and yanked it up hard between his beefy buttocks, before pushing its slick head into the ragga star's slack, slippery asshole. The singer's balls hung down heavily either side of his inverted shaft and he groaned as Don kept firm hold of his twisted dick and roughly and rapidly rammed its head and the first inch or two in and out of Stixie's already well-fucked battyhole.

'Oh, yeah!' he shouted out as Don started to push his own thick hard-on into the ragga man's upturned asshole alongside his own bent-round cock. The two cocks filled the star's asshole, stretching it, and Don's long, thick erection held the ragga man's twisted one in place up his own ass. As Don began to pump his dick in and out of the ragga star's anal sphincter, the singer groaned and gasped and tossed his head, his short dreads flicking back as he did so, ecstatic at receiving the ultimate pleasure from Don. A long, hard cock poling his ass and filling it with deep, muscular strokes and, at the same time, the extra stretching he was getting from his own dick being up there too, *and* the slippery, juicy excitement he was getting from the feeling of Don's rigid manhood sliding slickly back and forth along his own swollen cock, the pre-come from the two men's dicks providing the lubricant for a smooth wet ride.

Don fucked Stixie until he came up the muscular black man's upturned ass with violent thrusts of his hips; the ragga star gasped high and shrill as he was butt-fucked poundingly hard with two cocks at the same time. When Don pulled out, he carefully held the star's dick in place up his own asshole. Turning to the next guy in the line, Joe, Don said, 'Keep this cock up his ass when you fuck him or he's too slack to satisfy you. He won't be complaining. You won't need lube; the load I shot up there'll keep his passage slick.'

Then, his dick at half-mast, Don slipped out of the partitioned-off area and went in search of a beer. *Maybe I'll get myself rimmed*, he thought idly; he stepped over Kam, who was lying spreadeagled and face-down on a rug, having a shiny black dildo slithered rapidly in and out of his dilated asshole by a squatting Asian boy. *I could do with an eager tongue up my butt and a pair of hot lips on my asshole.* Glancing back, Don noticed that the brown-skinned boy was sitting his own shapely butt down on another dildo, a rubber cone that was a near-impossible seven inches across at the base. Don stroked his semi-erect dick idly, and watched for a while as the young man lowered his narrow hips further and further down onto the black rubber cone, dilating his elastic anal ring wider and wider until, finally, his buttocks were brushing the rug and his asshole had been stretched open to such a width, Don was surprised that his pelvic bone hadn't cracked. As he opened himself up, the handsome Asian youth made sure he kept the thick rubber dildo moving rapidly in and out of Kam's slack asshole. Kam wriggled his hips, grinding his slickened cock-head excitedly into the rug beneath him.

Up on stage, Prince Fela was casually fisting Marlon the bartender; the pretty black youth bent over his lap as Fela sat on his ornately carved stool. Marlon lay there limply, with his legs open and his ass up, enjoying the back-and-forth movement of Fela's impeccably manicured hand inside his anal passage. Camara stood alongside Fela, watching the spectacle engrossedly, the butt-plug was still up his ass, and the steel cock-ring round his hard-on and heavy ball-sack. Catching sight of Camara's swollen, bobbing cock-head out of the corner of his eye, Fela turned his head and started to suck on Camara's throbbing dick. As Fela moved his mouth back and forth on the now softly moaning Camara's rigid erection, the African prince also moved his hand inside Marlon's asshole in time with it.

While all this was going on, Bertil clambered up onto the stage to join them, and slid round in front of Marlon on all fours, then pushed his muscular brown ass up into Marlon's face for the young man to rim and eat out. Fela's fist was still thrusting back and forth in his asshole; Marlon struggled to focus enough to get his soft tongue between Bertil's buttocks and push it past the black soldier's sphincter and into his rectum. Bertil opened with the easiness of a guy who's just taken it up the ass – which he had, from two well-hung guys, in quick succession – and Marlon could taste the hot fresh spunk in the soldier's open asshole.

Meanwhile, Bobbi had dropped his shorts and was eagerly taking on all comers. Oba had recognised him from the taxi-ride earlier that evening, and had demanded a fuck, and Bobbi had been delighted to oblige him. Oba lay back on the floor and kept his foot-long pole held upright with both hands. Bobbi squatted down on it and, after an initial moan of how Oba's massive dick was just too big for him, had given Oba a thrill by sitting right the way down on it all at once, sucking all twelve stiff inches straight up into his back passage with only a soft gasp as he pushed his buttocks firmly into Oba's crotch, eager to make sure he had got every last inch of Oba's monster cock up inside his ass. Bobbi bounced his asshole up and down on Oba's love-muscle, sliding his anal ring up and down its shaft, and finally – now he was here at Fela's party – free to work a hand on his own cock as he rode Oba's rigid muscle like a pro.

At the same time as he was taking it so enthusiastically up the ass, Bobbi licked his pouty lips and gestured for any hard-on that bobbed past him to come over for a complimentary blow-job. While he rammed his asshole up and down on Oba's throbbing pole, Bobbi quickly sucked off the young white punk with the green mohican and the Asian muscle-man with the gold Prince Albert, around which pre-come flooded as he pushed it into Bobbi's willing mouth. Bobbi gripped the men's muscular buttocks to brace himself so that while he eagerly gave head he could slam his juicy butthole up and down on Oba's massive cock as hard as possible; the African man groaned beneath him and stretched his arms out above his head as Bobbi's anal love-muscle gripped his cock-shaft and slid rapidly and firmly up and down its rigid length. Bobbi pumped both his holes hard, moving like a pro, eager to taste hot spunk being shot into his mouth, and feeling that nothing would satisfy him except a flood of hot jism up his well-fucked ass.

By this time, Malcolm had the tousle-headed Pierre bent over the bar, had pulled his hot-pants down to his ankles, and was fucking him hard while he watched Bobbi squatting on Oba's outsize weapon. As Malcolm fucked Pierre's accommodating asshole, the lean black boxer with the exceptionally-ridged stomach and the elaborate patterns shaven into his scalp, now naked except for his boxer-boots, came over to him. To Malcolm's surprise, the boxer sprang up onto the bar and stood up on it, straddling Pierre. The boxer's rigid dick bobbed temptingly in front of Malcolm's mouth. While he continued fucking the horny barboy bent over in front of him, Malcolm kissed the pulsing brown head of the boxer's smooth dick. The glistening pre-come tasted good on Malcolm's soft lips. He slid his mouth further down the boxer's shaft; the boxer moaned in pleasure and let his head fall back as Malcolm began to suck him off.

'Man, you know how to suck a cock,' the boxer said

throatily, as Malcolm started to move his mouth hungrily backwards and forwards on the bobbing hard-on, swallowing its sweet length to the back of his throat and pressing his lips firmly against the cropped stubble at the base of the boxer's shaft. His balls hung smooth and heavy against Malcolm's chin as Malcolm swallowed the boxer's cock-head right down his throat, gagging excitedly as he did so; he was gratified to force a groan out of the young black man standing above him, looking so hard and so fine and sweaty and wild, while still sliding his dick rapidly in and out of the asshole of the white boy bent over before him.

Behind Malcolm, and as yet unseen by him, Don had sprawled back on a pile of cushions, getting his ass up in the air. He moved a gold-ringed fist on his long dick as a succession of guys came over to rim him, licking and tonguing his immaculately hairless chocolate star. The cute would-be tough skinhead, who had been fucked by the afroed guy earlier, had licked Don's ass with hungry thoroughness, as had the moustachioed black muscle-man who liked having dildoes rammed up his ass. But the best rimmer was Camara, who had come down off stage after shooting his load into Prince Fela's greedy mouth. His long, muscular tongue opened up Don's wet hole more than Don ever thought possible; his compulsive top-man assertiveness normally prevented him from getting his ass up in the air, in any circumstances, even to be rimmed.

Don's star was so wet and slippery with saliva and anal juice that he wasn't aware of Camara slipping the head of the enema-tube into his asshole until the strong red wine began to flow into his rectum. Like Malcolm, Don had been powerless to resist it, the attentive rimming relaxing him and making him open to possibilities. The alcohol soaked straight through the lining of his ass and intoxicated him; the exciting stretching of his rectum as a bottle and a half of strong red wine was pumped into his upturned asshole was irresistible. Don shivered and shuddered and gasped as the wine poured in; he threw his quivering legs wide open.

'Jesus, man –'

Camara stopped his mouth with a full, passionate kiss. He pulled the tube out of Don's puckered asshole, put down the enema bulb and, still tonguing Don's now wide-open mouth, Camara reached between Don's legs and folded his long cool fingers around Don's thick, throbbing cock and began to move his fist slowly up and down on Don's hot, rigid pole.

'Oh, Jesus, that's good, man,' Don moaned. 'Oh, man, keep that hand moving on my hot hard love-muscle. Oh, yeah . . .'

On stage Prince Fela, gleaming like a muscular ebony god, was fucking the muscular black punk with the low mohican while Kam knelt behind Fela in tight golden briefs, his skin glowing, his shining black hair tumbled over his face, and buried his hand up to the wrist between Fela's dark smooth buttocks, his fist well up the Prince's accommodating asshole. Kam rammed his closed hand backwards and forwards in Fela vigorously as Fela slammed his cock in and out of the juicy asshole of the horny black punk who was sticking his ass back and out for Fela to fuck it hard. And Bertil was kneeling on one side of the stage, waiting for the Prince to shoot his load up the black punk's juicy bunghole, so that Bertil would have another asshole to eat come from. As he knelt there, waiting hungrily, combat trousers around his ankles, Bertil allowed the blond-dread-locked black DJ to fondle his ass possessively, and eventually stick two fingers up it and work them in Bertil's butthole vigorously, in between changing records.

Meanwhile, the boxer's chest began to tighten as he pumped his saliva-slickened prick in and out of Malcolm's eager mouth, while Malcolm continued to fuck Pierre up the ass.

'Oh, man, I'm gonna come,' the boxer called out throatily, gripping Malcolm's head with steely fingers as he held Malcolm's mouth in place on his throbbing cock, making sure that Malcolm would swallow his load when he climaxed. 'I'm gonna come, I'm gonna come, oh –' Jerking his hips upwards, the boxer pushed his dick to the back of Malcolm's throat and ejaculated violently; the hot jism filled Malcolm's mouth and spilt down his throat. Malcolm swallowed the boxer's come, keeping his hips pumping against Pierre's upturned and now bright-pink ass as he did so.

Now that Oba had come up his ass, Bobbi had lured Bertil down from off the stage to felch him, and was squatting over the black squaddie's face, pressing against Bertil's lips, letting Bertil eat him out; he enjoyed the sensation of Bertil's eager tongue in his well-fucked asshole.

'Eat me out, man,' Bobbi instructed Bertil throatily as he sat down more fully on the soldier's flushed face. 'Eat the good African spunk that twelve-inch cock shot up my open butthole.'

After Camara had given him the red wine enema, Don had become so hot and turned on and dizzy he thought that there was nothing he wouldn't try, but in the meantime he had quickly had to go and find a toilet. Coming out of the cubicle, after emptying out, he had found himself sucking face with the bleach-blond, dreadlocked white surfer-guy, leaning against the sink to steady himself. Now Don was fucking the passive surfer-guy in the middle of the main room on a vast Persian rug, the surfer was spreadeagled face-down on the floor. Don held the horny blond down and poled his juicy, stretched pink asshole; the surfer grunted excitedly into the pillows his goateed face was half-buried in, with each thrust of Don's cock up his eagerly-offered backside. The blond man's willingness to be fucked turned Don on heavily, and yet – most unexpectedly – Don found himself feeling that his own asshole needed filling, that he needed to be satisfied as he was satisfying the dreadlocked white guy.

Don reached back and began to finger-fuck his own asshole with the index finger of one hand as he fucked the surfer beneath him. Malcolm, still thoroughly poling Pierre, had first noticed Don's presence when Don came out of the toilet with his hand on his ass of the blond-dreadlocked guy. By this time, Malcolm had guessed that Bobbi had managed to trick Don into coming to Prince Fela's party, too, to get him and Don to sort out their differences; Malcolm was happy, because he wanted to make it up with Don. And now here was Don, Mister Top Man, fingering his own asshole like he wanted something good and hot and stiff up it. It was just too tempting; Malcolm couldn't resist . . .

Malcolm slid his dick out of Pierre's asshole. Pierre gasped loudly, in mingled relief and disappointment that Malcolm wasn't going to give Pierre his load. Malcolm slapped Pierre on the ass, to signify the fucking was over, and turned away; his thick cock bobbed and glistened above his heavy ball-sack. Then he went over to Don and touched him on the shoulder.

'Peace, man,' Malcolm said as Don looked round at him, his narrow hips grinding against the blond surfer's upturned butt as he swivelled his cock around inside the slack rectum, his forefinger stuck up his own ass now to the knuckle.

'Peace and love, man,' Don replied hoarsely. Malcolm knelt, bent forward and kissed him on the cheek. Don squeezed his eyes shut. 'Fuck me, man,' Don whispered unexpectedly. 'Go up in me.'

'What, man?' Malcolm said, surprised, but immediately intensely turned on at the idea of fucking Don's unploughed top-man bunghole.

'Please, man,' Don begged him. 'Do me. Do me good. Fuck me wicked. I need it, man. And only you can do it.

Only you can be my man. I couldn't give it up for no one else, man. So please fuck me, yeah?'

'Get your cock out of this bitch and I will,' Malcolm said breathlessly, indicating the surfer with a nod of his head. 'I want all the concentration going on in your ass.'

'Yes, man,' Don said, pulling his dick out of the handsome surfer's asshole. 'Sorry, guy,' he mumbled to the dreadlocked blond as he struggled to his feet. 'I just got to go and get fucked myself, yeah.'

The white guy shrugged. 'Whatever, man,' he said, leaning over and picking up a shiny black dildo, then reaching back and starting to work its thick rubber head in his slack hole, pleasuring himself thoroughly with the sex-toy until the next top-man wanted to give him a real dick up there, keeping himself loose and ready for action.

Don and Malcolm slowly got to their feet. Malcolm gripped Don's hand and led him like a virgin bride to one of the partitioned-off parts of the room, his dick harder and heavier than it had ever been at the prospect of fucking Don's shaven hole.

As they disappeared behind an embroidered screen, Kam lay sprawled on his back with his legs up in the air and held open by the Asian body-builder with the pierced tit and the gold Prince Albert. He was enthusiastically pumping his lean hips against Kam's upturned butt, sliding his pierced erection in and out of Kam's exceptionally slack and well-fucked asshole. Kam grunted with excitement as the Asian guy rammed his throbbing cock deep into Kam's stretched rectum, his breathing impaired by the fact that another man – a good-looking white body-builder with slicked-back dark blond hair – was now straddling the pretty Japanese youth's face and fucking his throat with his dick, making Kam feel totally and utterly used. He lay back, surrendering deliriously to the hard ramming he was receiving in both orifices. He suddenly realised that the feeling of fullness and surrender as both hard cocks pushed into his body, down his throat and up his asshole, was what he had always needed. Kam could never be satisfied by a single man, he could never have been happy with Malcolm or anyone else. He needed a cock in his mouth and one in his ass at the same time, to really shoot a truly satisfactory load, to really be satisfied. Liberated by this awareness, he reached back and pulled his ass-cheeks open as wide as he could, to ensure that the Asian man's gold-pierced cock would be slammed up him as far as humanly possible, and tilted his head back as far as he could, so that the blond body-builder could get his cock-head in as deeply as possible.

Meanwhile Bobbi's attention had been caught by a handsome, mixed-race guy with a tight physique and boyish features; his circumcised cock stood out from his crotch like a projectile. It was must-suck dick for Bobbi. He went over to the guy, who looked to be in his early twenties, and was about to sink to his knees in front of him, when the clean-cut young man said, 'It's Bobbi, ain't it?'

'Yeah,' Bobbi said, looking at the handsome black guy intently; he was puzzled, sensing some familiarity but not quite making the connection. 'I never forget a cock,' Bobbi continued. 'If I'd sucked you off, I know I'd remember your smooth chocolate pole. And why wouldn't I have got my lips round such a tasty looking weapon, man? It looks like a perfect fit for my mouth and throat.' Bobbi stared at the good-looking black man's flawless face and wrinkled his brow.

'I'm Ashton,' the black guy said.

'Oh, my God!' Bobbi squealed, remembering his adolescent crush on the college's top sprinter, remembering licking out the used condoms that Ashton regularly presented to him to give him a taste of his load. He remembered the time he had licked one out in front of Ashton, trying to drop to his knees and nuzzle Ashton's bulging crotch, get Ashton's beautiful cock out of his pants and give him the thorough oral pleasuring that only one man can give another. Bobbi's stiff dick bucked and he almost came just from the memory – and from being confronted with Ashton's beautiful big dick so unexpectedly, right now, long and thick and stiff and inviting.

'All these years, I've wished I'd asked you to suck me off, back then,' Ashton said, nervous and excited, his dick rigid and throbbing, pre-come beading his slit. 'I've fantasised about your pretty lips on my cock, your eager mouth moving up and down on my rock-hard shaft. And now here you are, man, like a dream, like a fantasy. Would you still like to suck me off, man? 'Cause I sure could use a killer blow-job.'

Wordlessly, Bobbi sank to his knees in front of Ashton's beautiful hard-on and kissed its head. The taste of Ashton's pre-come sent shivers of pleasure running through Bobbi's chest and his own heavy erection twitched and bobbed painfully, excitedly, in response. Bobbi slid his lips firmly over the smooth hard-on he had fantasised having in his mouth for the last few years. As it filled his mouth, Bobbi became so excited that he realised he was about to come without touching his cock, just from the total, utter turn-on of having Ashton's cock finally where it belonged, filling his mouth and sliding down his throat. Bobbi's pulsing dick bucked between his legs and his hot load exploded in thick, violent spurts, spattering onto Ashton's feet and ankles and the rug Bobbi was kneeling on. But Bobbi gripped Ashton's buttocks in both hands and kept right on sucking. This was the load he'd waited years to taste.

Behind one of the many folding screens in the large rug and cushion-strewn living-room, Don and Malcolm were kissing passionately; Don's well-defined lips were hot and soft and yielding, electrically charged against Malcolm's larger *café-au-lait* ones. Malcolm ran his hands over the shorter, aubergine-dark-skinned man before him, while Don explored Malcolm's light brown body gently, running his hands over the fan-like spread of Malcolm's back as they ground their stiff dicks together, their heavy ball-sacks fusing softly beneath their throbbing erections. Don's hands ran down to Malcolm's newly depilated buttocks; a current crackled up through the palms of his hands at feeling such extreme and utter smoothness.

'Man, you shaved your ass,' Don whispered breathlessly, choking on his words. 'And your legs,' he added, working his hands down Malcolm's curving thighs. 'Man, your skin's just so fucking – smooth, man. So beautiful.'

'I did it for you,' Malcolm replied, his light hazel-green eyes on Don's dark-brown ones. 'Because when you're like that, you look so cool, all shaven and waxed smooth. So hot. And I wanted a bit of that, like on me, 'cause I never thought I'd ever be able to get any of the real thing. Any of your real thing.'

Now Malcolm breathlessly explored Don's totally smooth ass, moaning softly as they ground their crotches together.

'I want to give you the real thing, Malcolm, man,' Don groaned, before kissing Malcolm hotly. Malcolm slid his tongue into Don's receptive mouth, exploring it, feeling Don's heart hammering through his pumped chest as he did so. Don and Malcolm's built-up chests pushed together, tingling mocha nipples brushing against electrically charged mid-brown ones; the thrill of excitement from their contact almost tipped over into pain, it was so extreme. Both felt as if their skins had suddenly come totally alive, as if they had stepped from a sauna into the snow and every nerve in every square inch of their skin were crackling with static. Passion was pulling their breath away. Don reached for Malcolm's hand, brought it to his lips and kissed it, then sucked on Malcolm's fingers.

'I need you inside me, man,' Don said hoarsely to

Malcolm. 'I need you to make me feel complete. Shit, man, it looks like that's what I always needed. Maybe that's why I did Kam. To make you jealous. To make you see the sex in me and push him out. 'Cause I wanted you, man. Only you.'

Malcolm lifted Don's gold-ringed hands to his lips, kissed Don's gold-covered knuckles reverently; he was so moved he was unable to reply. All Malcolm knew was that he had to plug this beautiful black brother, had to give him what he needed. And more than that, Malcolm *wanted* to be inside Don: not to punish him by topping him, but to give him the utter ecstasy and relief that he was begging for, that he could only accept from Malcolm.

'C'mon, man,' Malcolm said gently after hugging Don close for a long minute, leading Don to a low couch spread with a soft zebra-patterned rug at the back of the partitioned-off area. As if by some psychic awareness, the other revellers sensed that Don and Malcolm didn't want an audience, and did no more than peep inside the shadowy space before passing on in search of more ready exhibitionists.

Don lay back on the couch and sprawled out on his back, arching to display his magnificent physique. Malcolm slid on top of him and they kissed hotly on the mouth, sucking on each other's tongues, probing each other for what felt like hours as they writhed their bodies sensually together: bodies that felt molten, that felt as if they were fusing, muscle into muscle, hot throbbing cock into hot throbbing cock, vein and sinew meshing together in pulsing heat. Eventually Don looked up at Malcolm with intense and needing eyes.

'Make love to me, man,' he begged hoarsely. 'I ain't never taken a cock before. But I want to take yours. I want it bad, man. But don't be rough with me, yeah? 'Cause I never done this before.'

Don's eyes were frightened. Malcolm, moved, nodded. 'I'll be gentle, man. I'd never do anything to hurt you. I just wanna make you feel good. 'Cause you're a gentleman, Don. And a beautiful black man.'

And Don opened his firm, muscular legs for Malcolm, spreading them wide and raising them to offer up his chocolate star to the handsome black man standing before him with bright hazel-green eyes, full lips and tightly coiled plaits. Don's cock arched stiffly above his totally-shaven crotch and pressed its shining head against his belly, dripping and throbbing. His tingling balls hung down heavily above his gleaming asshole. Malcolm's rigid pole extended heavily from his trimmed crotch towards Don's waiting hole, bobbing and pulsing as he looked down on Don opening himself beneath him, and his heart hammered in his chest.

Don yielding to him so unexpectedly turned Malcolm on more than anything he could have ever imagined, and he almost came, just looking down at him lying there and spreading himself open so eagerly. Malcolm took hold of Don's ankles lightly and opened Don's thighs, until Don could grip his own ankles and hold his legs totally spread and get his ass up and available. Then Malcolm reached for one of the nearby bowls of lube and smeared the thick length of his dick until it was slick and shiny and, pulling his own foreskin back, positioned his smooth cock-head against Don's unfucked sphincter. Then Malcolm pushed his cock slowly and smoothly into Don's virgin asshole. Don gave a moan of pure pleasure at being finally taken up the bunghole, and by a man as handsome and as loving as Malcolm, and taken by a cock as thick and satisfying as Malcolm's. In his sudden ecstasy, Don opened more easily and more smoothly than either of them had expected, and sucked the whole length of Malcolm's rigid pole right the way up his asshole, to the root.

'Ah, shit, you're up me, Malcolm, man,' Don groaned loudly. 'You're right the way up me and it feels so fuckin' good, man.'

Malcolm began to pump his dick in and out of Don's asshole: a tighter, more exciting and more satisfying asshole than any Malcolm had ever fucked before. His movements were slow and easy at first, as he slid in and out of Don's butthole, then built in rhythm, in depth and intensity as Don – now gasping and writhing as Malcolm impaled him on his sweet hard-on – showed he could take a serious butt-fucking.

'Use my ass, man,' Don ordered throatily as he lay back, heart hammering, ass up, legs thrown wide open, now totally into it; the cock filling his rectum filled his chest with a soaring ecstasy that he could never have imagined, and that made him have to shout out, 'Fuck my hot, tight ass with your hot brown pole! Make that asshole yours, man! My butthole is yours! Fill me with dick! Pound me! Fill me with your come, man! Fuck me! 'Cause I'm yours, man! I'm totally, utterly yours! Give it to me, man! Fuck me up the ass!'

Malcolm leaned forward as he poled Don's tight smooth hole and kissed Don so hard on the mouth it hurt; he swallowed Don's panting breaths as he bruised his lips with his passionate hunger for Don's kisses, Don's tongue, Don's glittering saliva.

Don wrapped his arms around Malcolm's broad shoulders as he felt Malcolm's hot erection slither in and out of his open backside – the first cock he'd ever had up him, in his rectum, inside his body – gasping and groaning from being so fully and passionately anally filled. They kept their mouths pressed hotly together for the whole time they fucked, all their anger with each other understood now, and transmuted as Don finally gave it up for Malcolm, surrendered to Malcolm utterly and completely. And found an ecstasy Don had never believed was possible as he yielded to the beautiful, thick and rigid brown cock sliding in and out of his juicy, dilated asshole with increasing weight and speed, pushing Don uncontrollably up to his own climax as it rammed against his pulsing prostate with greater and greater firmness.

'Oh, Jesus, man!' Don yelled. 'Fuck me, man! Fuck my motherfucking brains out! I love you, man! Give me that big brown love-muscle till I can't take no more! Oh, Malcolm, oh, God –!'

And later, with a load of Malcolm's hot come up his thoroughly-fucked asshole, Don called Gregory up on his mobile and told him to get his slack ass over to Prince Fela's, along with their gear. Gregory drove over with Thom, and the Boot Sex Massive performed their first ever live gig for the freaky revellers at Prince Fela's place in Notting Hill Gate.

Afterwards, as dawn was crawling up above the skyline, Don turned to Bobbi. 'You were right, man,' he said, rubbing his bleary eyes.

'Course I was, man,' Bobbi said, yawning sleepily. 'Uh, what about?' he asked.

'The party, man,' Don said. 'No one leaves without they've done something they never did before.'

'In so many ways, man,' Bobbi said thoughtfully. His lips ached, his throat ached, his stomach was queasy from swallowing so much spunk, his thighs and arms ached, his still semi-stiff dick ached, and his asshole ached so much it was pulsing warmly.

It had been one of the best nights Bobbi could remember.

Coming Up from Idol

MAN ON!
Turner Kane
ISBN 0 352 33730 3
5 September 2002
£6.99

Greg Williams of Middleton United is young, talented and handsome, a favourite with both fans and players alike. But when he signs his new football contract with Weston City, and when he starts sleeping with his soon-to-be-wed best friend Matt, things start hotting up, both on and off the pitch.

SUREFORCE
Phil Votel
ISBN 0 352 33736 2
10 October 2002
£6.99

Working-class Manchester. A seedy underworld populated by rough, butch security guards and club owners. Amongst its denizens is Matt, recently discharged from Her Majesty's armed forces and now employed by the security firm Sureforce – a company ruled by an iron-fisted, well-muscled boss. It's good money and there are plenty of perks – including hanging with the beefiest, meanest, hardest lads in town.

STREET LIFE
Rupert Thomas
ISBN 0 352 33741 9
7 November 2002
£6.99

Ben is eighteen and tired of living in the suburbs. As there's little sexual adventure to be found there, he runs away from both his A-levels and his comfortable home to a new life in London. When the friend he'd hoped to stay with is away, Ben is forced to spend the night on the street, cold and afraid. He's befriended by Lee, a homeless Scottish lad who offers him the comfort of his sleeping bag. Both become involved in a web of prostitution and sexual conspiracies, but when Ben is taken hostage by a mysterious client, Lee takes it upon himself to help Ben escape.